PRAISE FOR KELLY ROMO

"*I Am the River* is a profoundly terrifying novel, make no mistake, with an evil character at the heart of the story that you will never – NEVER – forget. But this is a remarkably hopeful novel, too. Kelly Romo does a pitch-perfect, astonishingly empathetic job of writing about real people."

MIKE MAGNUSON, AUTHOR OF *LUMMOX*

"In this compelling sequel to DEAD DRIFT, Kelly Romo proves she is the undisputed Queen of Whitewater Thrillers. Her feisty heroine, Emmy Jenkins, is as brave and clever as she is in DD."

CRAIG LESLEY, AUTHOR OF WINTERKILL

I AM THE RIVER

A WHITEWATER THRILLER
BOOK 2

KELLY ROMO

PAPERMOON
PRESS

"At any given moment you have the power to say this is not how
the story is going to end."
    —Christine Mason Miller

PROLOGUE

HIM

THEY CANNOT BIND OR CONTAIN ME, FOR I AM THE RIVER, AND the river is free. My flesh bleeds, but there is no pain. I am transforming. I climb onto our rock, just above Steelhead Rapids, where grandpa took his last breath—where he taught me to fish and to revere the river that springs from the earth. Where I will finally join him.

I step out of my shorts, and my bloody feet stain the rock with the last of my footsteps upon the earth. The flesh is weak. The river is eternal. Water gives life and takes life. It is the fluid, and I *was* the flesh.

"Skid!" Brian stands there like my savior. He always plays the righteous role.

"You are not better than me."

"Come back, and let's talk this out."

"There is no talking it out. They took all my nymphs from me, and you think you have released my last one. But you are wrong. Once I am the river, I will take all the nymphs I want. I will hold them in me until they shudder and breathe me into their lungs."

"You are not thinking straight. This is not you."

"No. This is me. You never knew me. You and Jake and Erin always thought you were the powerful ones. Now everyone will know it was me."

Brian starts toward me. He thinks he can stop me and that he can save me. "Stop, or I'll jump in."

He stops. Brian thinks he is a god on the river with his raft, his oar, and the girls all over him, but he is nothing but muscle and bone. He is a creature of the land.

"You and Jake are no better than me. Just because you didn't take the girls' lives, you still took from them and left them empty and broken. At least I did not leave them to suffer and live in fear."

It is time to wash away the pain and release my soul. I slide off the rock and wade into the flow. Brian is nothing but a blur of flesh as I hold out my arms, fall back, and release my body to the river. It cradles me and I let it take me where it will rage and churn and slam my soul from my flesh. It is time to wash away the pain, for I am the river, and the river is me.

PART 1

1

EMMY

I STOP AT THE MOUTH OF THE TUNNEL. TOO BAD I CAN'T REEL IN all that has happened since Amber and I first went through. We thought that living in the same house with a pedophile was the worst that could happen to us. Boy, were we wrong! My entire future starts once I get to the other side—and it is a future without her.

I take a deep breath and lift my foot from the brake. I pass by the graffiti that says *DEATH*, *Jason loves Candie* and a giant red penis and balls right next to *Becky Sucks Dick*. . .and I come out on the other side.

Just over a year ago, Amber and I went to Lodell for a white-water rafting trip, and I never left. Amber did, but they took her out in a body bag. I have no idea where she is. I don't know if they buried or cremated her. What does the state of Oregon do with dead foster children?

My chest feels heavy, but I am finally free. Free for what? I don't know. I am not the same person I was a year ago when we drove into town, and I have no idea what will happen with Brian. They have taken him away in handcuffs. I run my tongue across my swollen lip, and the lump feels the size of a marble.

As I follow the cloud of dust Sheriff Briggs's truck kicks up, all I know is that we are going to the Canyon County Sheriff's department for me to give a statement. After that, I have no plans other than to wait for them to release Brian, and I have no idea where I will sleep tonight.

Otis, Brian's taxidermy bobcat, sits on my passenger seat and stares at me with his glassy black eyes. His fur is dusty, like everything else in this damned desert. My suitcase, with everything I own in this world, sits on the floorboards and bumps against the glovebox with every rut in the road.

We finally hit the asphalt, and the dust clears to a bright blue sky and billowy white clouds with dark underbellies. I follow behind the sheriff's white SUV with tinted windows. When he drove me to get my car and belongings, it smelled like Big Red gum, and the air conditioner blew fresh cool air, nothing like the nasty-smelling air coming from the vents of my car.

The sun dips low and casts the long shadows of juniper trees, tumbledown shacks, and barbed wire fence posts across the dry land. In the distance, the snow-tipped volcano peaks of the Cascades seem like a beautiful and teasing backdrop to the dirt, rock, and scrub brush. Even in all this dryness, my chest feels like it is filling with so much water that I cannot swallow.

Sheriff Briggs comes to a highway, and his right turn signal blinks red. He waits for an eighteen-wheeler and a faded blue pickup to pass, then he turns onto the highway toward Silverdale. If not for Brian and my shitty beater car that might conk out any moment, I would turn the opposite way and gun it. I would put the pedal to the metal and get the hell away from this mess.

We drive across a flat plateau for about twenty minutes with cars coming up on my tail, then dropping back when they realize a sheriff is in front of me. He finally slows at a green and white sign with Silverdale printed above a long arrow. He puts on his blinker and turns.

The road drops down and winds into a canyon that looks like some prehistoric river carved it out. Nothing is left but dry cliffs and a thin crooked line of blue water at the bottom. We pass miles of farmland with red or bare wood barns. In the fields, crop sprinklers that look like they were made with giant erector sets on wheels shoot massive streams of water. Black and brown cows graze behind white fences or barbed wire. They are not the spotted dairy cows in kindergarten coloring books. These are born and bred for the slaughterhouse. I wonder if they know it.

At the bottom of the canyon, we drive beneath a giant black metal archway with Silverdale, Est. 1882, centered in gold lettering. The four-lane highway goes straight through town with a double yellow line and old-time brick buildings mixed in with a Mcdonald's, a Burger King and a Taco Bell—all with drive-throughs. I have not seen a single chain restaurant in a year.

The sun sets behind us as Sheriff Briggs passes a big brick courthouse with a fountain and a white bell tower topped with an American flag. The wisp of a thin orange cloud in the shape of an angel drifts over the courthouse.

The sheriff pulls into a parking space in front of a huge wall with *Canyon County Sheriff's Office and Jail* in large black metal letters. I pull next to him. My engine sputters and dies when I turn the key. I look over and can only see the outline of his face and cowboy hat through the windows.

I absolutely, with every fiber of my being, hate government buildings. They are all part of the system that has controlled me my entire life in foster care—and even before that, with child protective services harassing my parents. I thought I would be done when I aged out, but here I am.

Sheriff Briggs comes around his SUV and stands on the sidewalk between our vehicles. He is thin and slightly bowlegged with a dark blond and gray goatee. He is what my eighth-grade foster dad would call *amiable*.

As I expected, the lobby is big, brick, and empty, with no tenderness or comfort. One wall is lined with portraits of Sheriffs past—important-looking men in uniforms—leading to one big photo of Sheriff Briggs, the current man in charge. A receptionist with long and curly blond hair sits behind a glass partition with the American flag on one side and the blue and yellow Oregon state flag on the other.

My heartbeat throbs in my swollen lip as Sheriff Briggs punches a code onto a keypad next to a glass door, and it clicks. He holds the door open for me to step into a long hallway lined with doors.

"Second one on the right." He sounds annoyed.

It took him forever to bring me in. He had to wait for me to pack, and I took him to the shoe tree and pointed out the shoes of the murdered girls. He had to call it in and wait for a deputy to come and rope it off with crime scene tape, take pictures, and collect the evidence.

I stand beside the closed door. "Is Brian here?"

He unlocks it and motions for me to enter. "Brian?"

"My boyfriend. The one who rescued. . . ." What do I say? The kidnapper? The serial killer? The one who saved the life of a killer?

"Have a seat."

"Is he here?"

"Yes, ma'am. He's here."

Brian must be locked behind one of the doors. I need him to wrap his arms around me and tell me everything will be okay.

"Can I see him?" The room is the size of a janitor's closet, with nothing but three padded chairs and a bare table pushed up against the wall.

"Not right now." He holds his hand out toward one of the

chairs like he has selected where I will sit. My high school attitude clicks in, and I sit in a different chair.

"Do you need any medical attention?"

"No."

"Can I see your driver's license?" He reminds me of my old high school principal with his blondish-gray goatee, and *I'm the man in charge* attitude.

"Am I a suspect?"

"No. We need to verify who you are."

I pat the empty pockets of my shorts and then put my hands in the air. "I don't have it on me."

He gives me a half-amused and half-exasperated look. "Yet, you drove here?"

I don't tell him it is in my car. He may search it and confiscate all my crap, thinking it could be evidence—especially if he finds Brian's box of cash in my trunk.

He stands with his back to the door in his cowboy hat and tan and green uniform. When he smiled at me earlier, it was friendly, but that is gone. He has to deal with a kidnapped girl, a serial killer at the hospital, and three people who need to be questioned. His night will be long.

He pulls a small notepad and pen from his pocket. "Can you give me your full name and date of birth?"

"Emmy Renee Jenkins. November 18th, 1988."

A deep and booming "Fuck you" comes from the hallway. Jake is here.

"So you're nineteen?"

"I want a lawyer," Jake yells.

"Yes," I say. "Does it matter?"

"It does if you're a juvenile."

A big thud, like a body, slams against the wall, followed by, "Get your fucking hands off me."

Sheriff Briggs turns his head toward the door, then back at me. "Do you know your driver's license number?"

I shake my head.

"Do you know your social security number?"

"Am I under arrest?"

"Like I said, we need to verify who we have here in the station." His voice is short and harsh. He has lost his patience with me. I have that effect on authority figures. "It's procedure. You are not under arrest, and you are not a suspect. We just need to get your formal statement. We will need your fingerprints if you can't give me any other form of identification."

A number pops into my head. I think it is my driver's license, so I give it to him. "After I give my statement, what will happen?"

"That depends. We already called a victim's advocate, and she will come to help you when we're done."

I cross my arms. I am the victim here, and the *system* is supposed to take care of me like it has my whole life. I know how this goes.

"Just sit tight. Someone will be right with you."

Once he steps out and closes the door, I count to thirty before trying the handle. It is locked, and my heart starts to race. I am not someone who should be locked anywhere. *Breathe.* When I take a deep breath, my ribs ache. I bet they are bruised.

Brian is here somewhere. I love him, and I owe him my life. I would be dead if Brian did not come home when he did. This is the second time he saved my life...or the second time he put me in danger of losing my life, depending on how you look at it.

2

———

EMMY

I can't stop thinking of Crystal strapped to the floor on that stained mattress, naked with a ring of pee around her hips. This is imprinted on my brain, and I will never get this image out of my head. Is that what happened to Amber? Was she still alive and being tortured the day I stood at the edge of the cliff to watch the rescue teams search for her?

I could not save Amber, but Brian and I saved Crystal—and now they show their appreciation by locking us up in separate rooms. My stomach feels queasy.

I should be in a room with a couch. I am a victim, not a suspect. I am not entirely innocent, but they do not know that yet unless Brian tells them. No, he won't do that. Now that they have my name and driver's license, they will run me through their database. What are the charges they will find? Aiding and abetting? Harboring a minor?

My head spins, and I need to lie down before I get sick. I slide off the chair and onto the carpet, the industrial kind that is one step up from cement. Damn, my ribs hurt. I curl into the fetal position and rest my cheek on my arm. I am braless and still wearing Brian's *Paddle Faster, I Hear Banjos* t-shirt that smells like his sweat and deodorant. I love Brian so much it hurts.

Someone knocks twice. Before I can say, *come in*, the door opens, and an older man in a blue dress shirt with a sheriff's badge clipped to his belt steps in. He holds a black leather portfolio, a water bottle, and a small black tape recorder. Once he closes the door, he steps up to me and looks down. "Hello, Emmy. I am detective Perry. Are you not feeling well?"

My attitude kicks in. "I'm great. I just like lying on a dirty carpet."

"I have some water for you."

"Why am I being treated like a criminal?"

"The doors are locked because we can't have people roaming around the halls. It is a secure area."

"Can I leave?"

"We are waiting for the victim's advocate to arrive. She will help you find a place to stay and...."

"Am I free to go now?"

"We would appreciate your cooperation. We need a formal statement." He has a long face, deep-set eyes, and a creeper mustache. "Please, have a seat."

I stand up and brush off. The side of my leg has bumpy indentations from the carpet, and my fingers are numb.

"Nice shirt." He smiles, trying to be friendly.

I look down and see *Paddle Faster, I Hear Banjos*.

"Please," he says and motions to the chair.

Once I sit, he lowers himself into a chair across from me. *Breathe, Emmy, breathe.* Pain spreads across my ribs when I inhale through my nose, so I keep it shallow and slowly blow it out of my mouth—just like my old school counselor taught me. I only need to tell him about Skid and what happened with Crystal. He can't force me to say anything that might incriminate Brian or me.

He hands me the water bottle and sets the tape recorder on

the table between us. When he pushes a button, the little black teeth of the cassette start to spin.

"Emmy Renee Jenkins interview at Canyon County Sheriff's Office at 7:15 pm by Detective Glen Perry." He opens his black leather portfolio that has a notepad inside. "Miss Jenkins was advised that Detective Perry is conducting an official criminal investigation for the Canyon County Sheriff in the state of Oregon."

Detective Perry has a rectangular head, like Herman Munster or Frankenstein.

"Miss Jenkins was further advised that we are requesting her voluntary cooperation and that any information obtained during this official criminal investigation may be referred to the Department of Justice or other appropriate agency."

The teeth of the recorder turn around and around.

"Miss Jenkins agreed to cooperate and provide the following recorded statement, which will then be transcribed for her approval and signature."

He pulls a pen from a holder inside the spine of the portfolio.

"Miss Jenkins, you must understand your rights before I ask any questions. You do not have to make any statements or answer any questions. Any statement you make or answers you give may be used against you in a court of law or other proceedings. You have the right to talk to a lawyer for advice before you answer any questions, and you have the right to have a lawyer present during the interview. If you decide to answer questions now without a lawyer present, you still have the right to stop the interview at any time. Do you understand your rights?"

I nod my head.

"Can you verbally consent so it is evident on the tape?"

"Yes, I understand."

"Please give me a little background information about where

you currently live, your telephone number, where you were born, your level of education, and where you currently work."

"As of today, I don't live anywhere. I lived with Brian in Lodell, but we can't return there. Neither of us will be welcome. Brian rented from Jake Unger of the Lodell Ungers, who own the whole damned town, and he has also been arrested—because of us." He keeps the pen hovering above the notepad but doesn't write anything down. "I don't have a phone number. We have a house phone, and that stays with the house. Cell phones don't get service in Lodell, so I inactivated mine."

When I stop talking, he nods and asks another question. "Where were you born?"

"Alder Creek, Oregon."

"Do you have an address there? Maybe your parents' house?"

"I have about fifteen addresses in Alder Creek and about as many families."

He cocks his head, and his eyebrows pinch together.

"I grew up in foster care but aged out of the system."

"What is your level of education?"

"High school." I didn't graduate, but I don't tell him that. I dropped out the moment I turned eighteen, so I could get out of foster care.

"Do you work?"

"I did until today. I was a housekeeper at the Whitehorse Inn, which is also owned by the Ungers."

"To the best of your knowledge, please tell me what led to your discovery of Crystal Rhodes."

"From the beginning?"

"That would be preferable."

I don't want to go back all the way to the beginning. I know my rights, and I don't need to incriminate myself by telling him how I helped Amber escape her group home. She was seventeen, and I was eighteen, which made me an adult harboring a minor.

"I was drugged in the middle of the night by Skid. I mean Dylan Unger. If Brian did not come home when he did, you would be searching for my body in the river."

He looks up in concern and tips his head to the side. "Were you sexually assaulted?"

"No."

"Are you sure?"

"I'm positive." His eyes narrow, so I add, "I would know if I was raped."

Detective Perry nods and writes something down. "You said his name is Dylan Unger?"

"Yes, Dylan Unger. The son of Russ Unger, the police chief. That is why we called the Sheriff's office instead of the local police."

He sighs and shakes his head slightly like he knows this case just got more complicated. He writes something on his notepad, then looks back to me. When I don't continue, he asks, "How did he drug you?"

My hand goes to my shoulder. "He injected me with something."

He leans forward and narrows his eyes at the tiny pinhole.

It's tender, and there's a tiny bruise.

He pulls a pair of glasses from his pocket, unfolds them, and slips them on. "Do you mind if I come around to look?"

I shake my head, and he stands up. He comes around and peers at my shoulder, right where I point.

"Do you mind if I photograph it?"

I shake my head again, and he pulls a compact camera from his shirt pocket. When he presses a button, the lens telescopes out, and he snaps several pictures.

"Skid also grabbed my mouth so I couldn't scream, and my lip is swollen."

He snaps photos of my lip from several angles and has me lift it up so he can get the inside.

"Anywhere else?"

"My ribs hurt like hell. I think they are bruised."

He looks at my torso beneath Brian's baggy shirt. "I'll need a female in here to photograph that." He presses the button on the camera, and the lens retracts.

He does not sit down. "We need to get a blood draw and a urine sample."

"Here?"

"No, I'll drive you to the hospital as soon as you're done giving your statement."

"I don't want to go to the hospital. I feel fine."

"If you have drugs in your system, it can be used as evidence."

This day just keeps getting shittier. I hate hospitals. They remind me of my mother, but I tell him I'll go. I'll do whatever it takes to keep Skid locked up.

"Who did this to you?" He goes back around to his chair.

"I already told you, Dylan Unger, but he goes by Skid."

"And you are sure it was him?"

"Yes, I saw him."

"He's the same man who you found with Crystal Rhodes?"

"Yes, he's a serial killer."

His eyebrows pinch together, and his eyes squint like the gears in his brain are cranking them tight. "What makes you think that?"

"He killed my friend, Amber. Do you remember her? They searched for her last summer. She was one of the girls pulled from the river. Remember all the drowned girls? Amber Ward, Shawna Hall, Kate Harris, and Mandy West? Do you remember when they closed the dam and lowered the river to recover them?"

"I remember." He shakes his head and writes on his notepad like he either does not believe me or knows this case will be a nightmare. The room is silent except for the sound of his pen and the scratchy spin of the tape recorder. When he is done, he looks up with his sunken eyes. "I do remember the girls. Weren't they ruled accidental drownings?"

"Technically, they were, but they did not get drunk and accidentally kill themselves in the river. Why would their shoes be in the shoe tree?"

His eyebrows pinch tighter and the scratch of the tape recorder fills the silence.

"Didn't Sheriff Briggs tell you? I showed him the shoe tree where Skid threw the shoes of the girls he killed. They are hanging there. No girl would throw her best shoes into a tree then drown herself…no matter how drunk she was."

"Can you describe any of the shoes?"

"Amber and I both had lime green Converse. Crystal had on some sparkly gold heels. Kate wore a pair of black cowboy boots. And Mandy had some sparkly turquoise tennis shoes."

"And all these shoes were thrown into a tree?"

"Yes. All the girls wore them the nights they went missing—and they were in the tree the very next morning. I saw them myself."

When Detective Perry catches up with his notes, he looks back at me. "How do you know Dylan Unger?"

"He is a whitewater rafting guide and was a friend of my boyfriend—at least until he tried to kill me and we found out that he kidnapped Crystal. He tied flies with strands of his victims' hair in them."

"Flies? Like fishing flies?"

"Yes. Make sure the deputies take all of Dylan Unger's fly-tying equipment and flies for evidence. I bet you will find the DNA of all the murdered girls." I have the box of flies he left on my doorstep, but I don't want to give it up. I am sure that Amber's hair is in them, and I don't have much left of her. I will turn them in if they don't have enough evidence but based on what I saw, there will be plenty on Skid's tying desk.

Detective Perry cocks his head and lifts a single eyebrow at me. He doesn't believe me. "When Skid tried to kill me, he yanked out a clump of my hair to tie in his flies."

Detective Perry's eyes look up at my scalp.

"When we saved Crystal, I drove her to the hospital in Dylan's truck and found a fly box with Brian's name scratched into the top. My missing hair was in it." *Shit.* I left the box in my car, but I don't want to tell him. I don't want them searching for it. Once they let me out of this place, I will get it and turn it over.

"Can I get a photo of your scalp?" He stands before I answer and comes around the side of the table. "Where is it?"

I run my fingers over my head until I find the sore spot. I part my hair. "Here."

He snaps pictures of my head.

"I knew someone was killing the girls, but nobody believed me. Now that we found Crystal, there is proof. And the DNA. Make sure they get the flies."

After Detective Perry takes the pictures, he returns to his chair and sits down. "Please continue. After he injected you with a drug and yanked out a clump of hair, what happened next?"

"Brian came home, and he ran off. I think." Detective Perry raises his eyebrows again. "I was drugged. I didn't remember it was him until the next morning. And Brian wanted to confront him then. I was afraid to be alone, so I went with him. Skid's house reeks, and it is packed full of junk. He's like a total hoarder. We looked through all the rooms, but Skid wasn't there. His bedroom is disgusting. The walls are plastered with playboy centerfolds, shelves of naked barbie dolls, and a mannequin with no arms."

Detective Perry looks skeptical, like I am repeating a movie plot or something. "The mannequin was wearing Amber's bra. It was her only bra. I know it was hers because it was pink with embroidered stars—and it had a safety pin that I helped her put on when the strap broke. Make sure you confiscate that."

I stop talking and wait for him to catch up with his notes. He looks up and nods for me to continue.

"Skid wasn't home, so Brian knew he would probably be at his grandfather's abandoned house in Old Lodell. That's where we found him, too, coming out of the room where we found Crystal. She was naked on a bare mattress. There were bolts in the floor, and she was strapped to them with tie-downs."

I don't tell him that Brian punched Skid in the face to get him away from the bedroom door. I also don't say anything about how I jumped on top of him and beat the living shit out of him. Or how Brian had to pull me off.

"As Brian strapped Skid into a chair, I untied Crystal. She was so weak she could barely move. We loaded her into Skid's truck, and I drove her to the hospital. After that, I called you."

"Which hospital?"

"Rimrock, the only one in Lodell."

"Doesn't Robert Unger own that?"

"Yes, but I had no choice. Crystal needed a doctor right away. We were afraid she would die. I didn't tell the receptionist where we found her."

"When I returned to the old Unger homestead, Skid and Brian were gone. The chair was tipped over, and the rope lay tangled on the ground. That was when Sheriff Briggs and the deputies arrived."

"Anything else?"

"As the deputies were looking for Brian and Skid, Skid tried to kill himself in the river. Brian saved him and carried him back."

"How do you know he tried to kill himself?"

"Brian told me. They grew up together. Skid's family raised Brian after his mom died. Brian is a river guide, and he saved him." I don't tell him what Brian confided in me and why he turned himself in. "After that, Sheriff Briggs took me to Brian's house, where I grabbed some clothes, and then he brought me here. That's it."

He tries to get more information from me, but that is all I can think of right now. He clicks off the tape recorder and stands up. "I need a woman present while I take pictures of your ribs. I'll be right back."

He walks out and leaves me trapped in the tiny room. He is gone for at least half an hour, and I'm about to start pounding on the door to get out when there is a knock, and the knob turns. Detective Perry comes in with a round-faced deputy in a dirt-colored uniform with her blond hair pulled back in a tight bun.

"Emmy, this is Deputy Gorman."

Deputy Gorman smiles at me. She looks like one of the girls in high school who participated in all the clubs but always faded into the background, so nobody ever remembers her.

"Before we move on, can you take a look at some photos and identify the shoes you say were yours and the victims?"

I agree, and Detective Perry turns the tape recorder back on and lays out fifteen color prints of the shoe tree with close-ups of different sections. Each photo is numbered. There are so many shoes. Not all of them are from victims, but I wonder how many are.

As I point out Amber's and my green Converse, Crystal's heels, Kate's boots, and Mandy's sparkly turquoise tennis shoes, he has me say the photo number and a description of the shoes for the recorder.

I remember Kate and Mandy on the dance floor in those shoes. I hated them for the show they put on just to get attention from the boys.

"Is that all of them?"

"That is all that I know about. Brian told me that many guides stole shoes from girls they hooked up with and tossed them into the tree. I don't know which guides or if it was consensual or not."

Detective Perry stands up and pulls the camera from his shirt pocket. "Can you lift your shirt high enough for me to get pictures?" He presses the button, and the lens telescopes out.

When I lift Brian's shirt up, I look at my ribs for the first time. A large red splotch with two darker v-shaped lines is on the right side of my ribs. No wonder it hurts so much.

"I think you should have a doctor look at this when we're at the hospital," Detective Perry says.

I don't answer him. I just want to lie down and sleep.

When he finishes taking pictures, he slides the camera into his shirt pocket and clicks off the tape recorder.

"What about Brian?" I ask. "Can we wait for him to finish so he can go with us?"

Detective Perry looks at me with his dark Herman Munster eyes. "He won't be released today. They're booking him."

"For what? We found Crystal and saved her life—and Brian rescued Skid from drowning. He saved the lives of two people."

Detective Perry shakes his head, "I'm sorry...."

I don't realize that I am standing and yelling until Deputy Gorman places her hand on my arm. "Come on, let's get this done so you can relax and find a place to sleep tonight."

We ride to the hospital in Detective Perry's black unmarked car with Deputy Gorman in the passenger seat and me in the back. I thought they called a victim's advocate to help me, but we leave without one because clearly, they don't give a shit.

3

———

EMMY

THE BLOOD DRAW, PISS TEST, AND EXAMINATION GOES QUICK, which is the only benefit of going to the hospital with law enforcement. Everyone stares at us, but I keep my head up and stare right back.

When we get back from the hospital, my car is still where I parked it, and it looks untouched. Two women in the lobby stand as we enter. One looks like a teacher with glasses and mousy brown hair that comes to her shoulders. The other one is a big woman in a turquoise flowered shirt and white skinny jeans.

Detective Perry introduces the one with glasses as my victim's advocate before he and Deputy Gorman disappear into the locked area. The teacher-lady introduces herself as Janet Larson. The bright-colored woman with long brown hair parted down the center tells me her name is Erika Wheeler from Open Arms Women's Services through the Silverdale Community Church. Her eyes squint when she smiles, and they have that gleam in them that only middle-aged women have. The look that makes you want to crawl beneath their arms so they can protect you.

Mrs. Larson directs us all to sit in the uncomfortable seats along the lobby wall, right beneath the portraits of all the Sheriffs' past, and she holds out a stack of brochures and papers.

"Here are your victim's rights guide, a relocation guide in case you decide to stay in Silverdale, a brochure for Open Arms, which helps women who have suffered violence, and a list of contacts for services such as food, medical help, transportation, employment, shelter, clothing, and other things you may need." Mrs. Larson's two front teeth are a bit crooked, and she has a friendly smile. "As your victim's advocate, I will assist you with anything related to court, such as informing you of your rights, the status of your case, dealing with attorneys, filing orders, and getting restitution. We also give you referrals to public and private social service agencies, and we have 24-hour Crisis Intervention to assist you with emergency resources."

I know the drill. I've dealt with court and social services my entire life.

"I'm sure this has been a long day for you, and you must be exhausted. I'm going to pass you off to Mrs. Wheeler. She is one of the best volunteer advocates at Open Arms and will take great care of you." Mrs. Larson gives me a smile, and loops the strap of her portfolio over her shoulder. "Tomorrow is Brian's arraignment. It is not a trial and there is nothing you need to do. They will tell Brian his charges and decide if he can be released on bail or not. That's it. If you would like to be there, let Mrs. Wheeler know and she will help you get to my office where I can assist you."

Mrs. Larson nods at Mrs. Wheeler. "She's all yours. Work your magic."

"Hello, Emmy." Mrs. Wheeler says. "You can call me Erika."

She has a wide smile and big teeth and she reminds me of Carrie, my fifth and sixth-grade foster mom. Her white leather sandals look like they are from Target and they have scuff marks on the sides.

"I hear that you need a place to stay for the night," she says. "I can help you get a motel room if you like."

"Depends on how much it costs," I say. I don't want to use Brian's money. I have a feeling he will need it for bail.

"It won't cost you one red cent." Erika gives me another big smile and turns toward the door.

My car starts without a jump, and I flip on my headlights. They light up the huge wall of the Canyon County Sheriff's Office and cast the shadows of every iron letter onto the brick.

Brian is the only person who truly loves me, and here I am, driving away while he's locked up in a cell. The system has always separated me from the people I love.

I follow Erika's black and yellow Jeep onto the main highway through town. We backtrack and reel in the road the Sheriff and I took. With every streetlight we pass, the emptiness grows. Otis stares at me from the passenger seat with his eyes like empty black pits.

Erika's blinker clicks on in front of a retro motel sign that says *Railroad Inn* in large red letters. *Be Our Guest* is on a giant yellow arrow with the tip bending down and pointing at the parking lot.

If not for Brian, I would keep going and leave this town. I have no idea where I would go. Maybe toward one of the beautiful snow-covered volcano peaks of the Cascades.

The Inn is one of those two-story motels in the shape of a capital L, with the doors and windows of all the rooms facing the parking lot. I follow Erika toward a space by the front lobby. Our headlights light up the row of windows and doors. When we turn them off, there is nothing but dim lights outside each door and a neon red OPEN sign that sputters in the window like it is about to give out.

I sit in my car until Erika comes to the window. I don't want to stay in this motel. It has that terrible seedy feel of a group home where you know that everyone inside is lonely with nowhere else to go. Erika stands with a small, patient smile and waits for me to open my door. She has done this for a while. She is calm and does not rush me. The back of my throat stings as I open the door and try to swallow my tears.

I follow Erika into a lobby that smells like popcorn and some sort of a tropical air freshener. The tacky bright green walls, red velvet couches, golden chandelier, and wooden front desk make it look like an old west whorehouse—like one of the ones from Boomtown, the western I used to watch with Rod, my fifth-grade foster dad. This place even has an old player piano.

Nobody is at the desk. Behind it is a giant framed painting of a black train with dark smoke chugging across a desert. The office door is open, and a pair of feet in nylon ankle socks rest on a brown padded footrest with a black frame mechanism.

"Hello," Erika calls.

The feet twitch but do not move.

"Hello…"

The feet flex, and the toes curl, but whoever they belong to does not lower the footrest to come help us.

"Jocelyn?" Erika says louder. She glances over at me and shrugs.

"Goddamned…nobody can get a wink…" An old shaky voice comes from the office as the footrest lowers and disappears behind the angled door.

An old lady—a very old and skinny lady with a dandelion fluff hairdo and wire-rimmed glasses—appears in the doorway. She holds onto the frame with a shaky arm as she slides her feet into a pair of yellow Crocs.

Erika tips her head to the side. "Where's Jocelyn?"

"That ain't none of your business, now, is it?" She wears a bright red shirt and tan pants.

Erika's body tenses, and her back straightens. If I were that old lady, I would watch out. Erika could twirl her like a baton if she wanted to.

"We need a room."

The lady looks back and forth between us as she shuffles to the front desk. "You ain't no lesbians, are you?"

Erika's mouth opens, but no words come out.

"We're booked. No rooms," the lady says before Erika can answer.

The shock subsides, and Erika says, "I'm Erika Wheeler from Open Arms Women's Services. . .and who are you?"

She looks Erika up and down. "None of your business. We're booked."

"The parking lot is practically empty, so I do not see how you are booked."

"You telling me how to do my job?"

Erika steps to the side next to a large red and white popcorn maker and pulls out her cell phone. I haven't eaten all day, and the popcorn sounds like something my stomach can tolerate. I take a red and white striped paper bag and stick my hand inside to open it.

"The popcorn is for guests," the old lady says.

Erika stops scrolling through the numbers on her phone and looks over at me. "Ignore her and take as much as you want."

She returns to her phone, pushes the call button, and puts it to her ear. The popcorn is cold, but I need something to eat.

"Faye? This is Erika Wheeler."

Out of the corner of my eye, I see the old lady tense up. I scoop up a heap of popcorn and put it in my bag.

"I'm fine. I'm here at the Inn trying to get a room for a young lady, and your" —she seems to be searching for an appropriate word— "your new clerk...."

I put in another scoop, and several pieces of white-yellow popcorn fall to the hardwood floor. I pick them up and toss them into a trash bin.

"Yes. Yes, I see. I hope Jocelyn feels better soon. I'm calling because your clerk says there are no more rooms, and I have a wonderful young lady here who needs one."

Erika smiles and me and winks. "Thank you, Faye. Yes, I'm fine. How is Kerry?"

The popcorn is a bit mushy, like it has been there all day, but it is something.

"That's great!" Erika puts a finger up like she'll be done in a minute. "Tell him I'll keep my fingers crossed. Give Kerry my love. Thanks again."

Erika flips her phone shut and turns back to the front desk. "You may want to answer your phone," she says two seconds before it rings.

The lady gives her a pinched look before reaching for the desk phone. "Railroad Inn. Be our guest. This is Rowena." Her arms and head shake as she listens. I can't tell if she has a medical issue or if it is from nerves.

"Faye is the owner," Erika whispers, "and a good friend."

All Rowena says is, "Fine," then hangs up the phone and places several papers on the front desk. When we don't step forward, she tells us she does not have all night.

Erika fills out the paperwork, not needing anything from me except for my name, the make of my car, and license plate number. I do not know the plate number, so I step outside to get it. My electric blue Mazda, which was supposed to take Amber and me to safety in Canada but never got us out of Oregon, is illuminated by a parking lot light like some lost and dusty portal to nowhere.

Once we finish, Erika helps me carry everything I own in this world up a metal staircase to the second floor. She slides a keycard into the slot of room 216, and when the door clicks and she swings it open, the smell of stale cigarettes and musty air conditioner escapes just like an exhale of bad breath.

The walls, bedspread, and curtains are orange—not just

orange but a red blood-orange. The bedspread and curtains have beige circles that make my head spin.

"I feel like I stepped back in time to the old west." I set Otis, Brian's box of money and documents, and the duffle bag I packed for him on the dark wooden table by the window.

Erika sets my suitcase and Amber's duffle bag on the hardwood floor. "That stuffed bobcat your pet?"

She smiles a big smile, so I know she is joking.

"It's Brian's. His mom bought it for him when she found out she had cancer."

Her smile evaporates. "I'm sorry."

I shrug. "Me too. Brian was only eight years old."

She opens the drawer, takes out a pen, and writes on the skinny pad of motel notepaper. "Here is my cell in case of an emergency. It is my private number, so only call if it is urgent."

"You're leaving me here alone?"

She straightens up and gives me a warm smile that should calm me but does not. "You will be alright. This is a safe place. Nobody knows you are here except for me."

I want to say that the mean old lady in the office knows, but I don't. "My car is in the parking lot for anyone driving by to know I am here."

Erika gets a pained look on her face. "You'll be okay. I'll come first thing in the morning to bring you breakfast and get you to the courthouse for the arraignment—if you want to go."

Of course I want to go. I'd be a shit of a girlfriend if I didn't. "Yes, I want to."

"Do you like donuts? If not, I can bring you something from McDonald's."

It's always something cheap. My CASA and case manager did the same. I wonder if they have to pay out of their own pockets.

"I'll take a sausage biscuit from McDonald's," I say.

She holds her open palm toward me, and for an instant, I

think she is asking for a tip. I put my hand in hers, and she gives it a little squeeze. "I will see you in the morning. Try to get some sleep."

I crack open the blackout curtains and watch Erika walk to her Jeep. The dome light comes on when she opens the door and gets in. I know that she means well. She really wants to help people and make a difference. They all do, but when it comes down to it, they are all part of the system. She pulls her door shut, and all goes black until she flips on her headlights, backs up in an arc, then rolls forward toward the highway.

I am alone. I've never been alone, except when I was four and five years old, and I still lived with my dad. Sometimes he would not come home all night, and I had to find food for myself in the apartment. I didn't know that other parents stayed home every night.

When I said something to my kindergarten teacher, I was put into temporary legal custody and a foster home. Since then, I've been with other foster kids or sometimes with my grandmother, who never left the house—or the couch.

4

HIM

Where am I? A siren blares, and a heartbeat pounds in my ears. Someone straps me down and forces gusts of oxygen into my lungs. No...no...I belong in the river.

Ice-cold shivers wash over my body. A monitor beeps three times and a voice crackles over a radio. I crack open my eyes. Two paramedics shuffle around between me and glass cabinets filled with hospital supplies.

"Dylan? Can you hear me?" My father? He is here with me.

I close my eyes and pretend to sink away.

"Do something, goddamn it!" His voice sounds gravelly, like the earth.

A cuff tightens around my arm. I hear the tear and rip of plastic. There's a poke on the top of my hand, and warm water enters my vein. It branches off, courses through my body, and fills me with my essence—for I am the river, and the river is me.

The monitor beeps again, and something warm slides beneath my neck, armpits, and groin. The blare of the siren sounds as if it comes through a tunnel and the cold is so deep it runs like a wire through my bones.

"More blankets," my father orders. He always needs to be in charge.

Why am I here? Brian! He and Emmy found me with Crystal. They took her from me. The weight of another layer of blanket settles over me as my body sways with the turns and bumps in the road.

I escaped from Brian, and he tried to stop me from becoming one with the river. It was time for me to leave my flesh. Brian, with his great white savior complex, must have pulled me from the river.

"Why isn't he waking?" My father expects everything to happen at his command. "Dylan, do you hear me?"

Brian does not know what he has done. He does not know my power or my grace. I spared Emmy for him once, but now it is time for him to pay for what he has done. He has denied me my destiny, so I will not stop until I take Emmy and breathe in her last breath.

The ambulance slows, makes several turns, and we stop. The paramedics move around me. I want to look but keep my eyes closed. I will not deal with my father. I must free myself from this cocoon and get to the river.

"We're at the hospital and you're going to feel a couple bumps as we take you out," the paramedic says.

The gurney sways as they pull me from the ambulance. A high-pitched motor whines, and they roll me away. There is a whoosh of glass doors, and I am inside the emergency room. How will I get out of this?

The paramedic rambles off something about a twenty-four-year-old male, near drowning, multiple contusions, IV, and high flow oxygen. Bright light seeps in through my eyelids, and I feel bodies around me that move like disturbances in the current. I come to a stop. Things clang and rustle around me. An alarm beeps from another room.

"Okay, on three. One, two, three."

My body lifts and slides onto a different surface. Curtain rings swish as they slide across a rod, and a female voice asks my father to move aside and have a seat. A blood pressure cuff is wrapped around my arm, and something is clamped onto the tip of my finger.

I do not look, but by the creak of his holster, I know that my father is in his uniform. When they leave, he is still there, breathing beside me. He shifts his weight and clears his throat. "Dylan. Goddamn it."

There is movement in the next space beyond the curtain. A gurney clicks, and another curtain swishes shut.

"Mr. Thurston, your wife is on her way. I've placed your clothes and shoes in a bag beneath the bed."

"Thank you," a weak old-man voice says, barely above a whisper.

Voices fill the emergency room. Machines beep, and feet scuff on the linoleum. I calm myself and recharge. I need to remain silent and docile until it is time for me to escape. It needs to be soon before I am taken to jail, where I will dry up and die in my flesh.

"Where is he?" an angry voice booms. "He does not belong in the same hospital as my daughter."

"We had to divert her here," a female voice says. "We had no choice."

"Then take him elsewhere. Now!"

My father's chair screeches against the floor. The sound pierces through my temples. I sense him, still behind the curtain with me, while he waits for his chance.

"Move aside," the voice yells.

Feet pound on the floor and move toward the disturbance. My father slips out, and I seize my chance. I open my eyes to the fluorescent lights, flashing machines, and the silver railing of my bed. It is time. I only have seconds. In one swift rush, I rip the IV from my hand and the blood pressure cuff from my arm. I slip out of my gown and let it drop to the floor.

"Stand down," my father's command echoes through the E.R.

The curtain barely moves as I slip into the next stall. The old man sleeps in a sea of white blankets, unaware of what I'm about to do.

My fingers barely brush the bag beneath his bed when my father's voice yells from the other side of the nurse's station. "My son is innocent until proven guilty!"

"Like hell, he is innocent."

The E.R. erupts in curses and accusations, and nobody notices me slipping across the hall and into a bathroom. My adrenaline kicks in, and I focus past the pain of my flesh. Mr. Thurston's clothes are short and tight, but they fit. I slip on his shoes with no socks and pull his golf cap low over my eyes before I slide out of the bathroom and down a long corridor.

"Arrest this man right now," my father says. "Or I will do it myself!"

I press the handicap plate for an automatic door and slip out into the lobby. People sit in rows of chairs with their heads turned toward the closed doors of the E.R., where Crystal's father yells, "I hope he rots in jail for the rest of his life."

Two teens stand beside an automatic sliding door. They are skater boys in baggy jeans with their hats on backward.

"Nice high-waters," one of them says, and they laugh.

They are ignorant and have no idea who I am. The glass doors swish open, and I am released, for I am the river, and the river is me.

5

ASHLEY

THE TREES ALONG THE DRIVE ARE GREEN AND LEAFY, AND THE afternoon shadows stretch them out of shape. Dad keeps the grass hacked down with his riding lawn mower, almost to the dirt. In Spring, the grass is green and beautiful but dry brown the rest of the year. The house needs paint, and the porch stairs sag in the middle.

Thistle and Gretchen come prancing around the side of the house at the sound of our car. Dad bought them a few years back with dreams of becoming a goat farmer so he can make soaps and lotion from their milk, but the work was more than he could manage.

Grace sits at her blue plastic table in the front yard eating a red popsicle and eyeing us as we drive up. It would be nice to visit my parents without Mitchell and his family here. Stacy can be nice, but she always tells me how to parent, which is ridiculous since her one child is a demon. Grace has no grace, nor is she graceful. She is more of an anti-grace and my girls hate to visit their grandparents because of her.

As soon as Mitchell parked his travel trailer next to the house, Dad set up the old metal swing set that Mitchell and I had when we were kids. During the summer, that slide would burn our backsides, so we usually put the hose up to it and pretended like we were sliding down a waterfall.

I put my car into park and open the back door for my girls. Kia unlatches her seat belt and the belt on Calista's booster. I go around to the other side to pull Carina from her car seat. All three of my girls are dressed in spotless pink sundresses and headbands, but their tennis shoes are scuffed up and need to be thrown in the washing machine.

"Hey there, Grace," I say. "Can you come give Auntie Ashley a hug?"

Grace does not answer or budge an inch. I can't blame her, though, she hardly knows me, and that's my own fault. A refrigerator now sits on the front porch with an extension cord threaded through a gap in the living room window.

My parents sit on the couch with an old rerun of *Columbo* playing on the television. "Ashley! We didn't expect you and the girls today," Mom says. "What a wonderful surprise."

Dad reaches for the remote with his good hand and clicks it off. He grabs the wrist of his paralyzed arm and repositions it on his lap.

Kia plops down on the couch right next to my dad. She's a grandpa's girl and always has been. Calista hugs onto my leg, and I balance Carina on my hip.

Just as Kia gets comfortable in the crook of Dad's good arm, I stop her. "I need to talk to Grandpa and Grandma. Will you please take your sisters outside and play with Grace?"

Kia gets a horrified look on her face. The last time we were here, Grace pushed Calista off the swing and kept pulling her hair.

"Come here a minute." I motion to her with my finger.

Kia looks to my dad to save her, but he puts his hand in the air like it is out of his control. Kia slides off the couch and follows me into the guest room that is piled with so much junk it looks more like a storage unit. The moment I set Carina on the bed, she pulls fake flowers and ribbon from a bin.

"I don't want to play with Grace." Kia's eyebrows are pinched together. "She's mean."

"If she does anything to you or your sisters, just smack her."

Kia's eyes pop open. I hate to tell my child to be violent, but telling on Grace will do no good. Stacy and Mitchell think the world revolves around their daughter and encourage her aggression by laughing or calling her *Little Miss Sassy Pants.*

"You're the big sister. You've got to protect Calista and Carina."

"What if Aunt Stacy spanks me? Grace is only four, and I'm seven. Can't Calista smack her?"

"I'll smack her," Calista says and stands up on her tippy toes. She has a mean scowl on her face and her skinny little fists in the air. Even at a year older than Grace, Calista is still ten pounds lighter and has half the grit.

"Can we feed Thistle and Gretchen instead?" Kia asks.

"Yes. Let's ask Grandma if she has any carrots or celery you can give them."

After I supply my girls with a few limp stalks of celery and warn them to stay away from the creek, they head out the front door.

My parents know that something is up and sit patiently on the couch. I remove the basket of yarn and half-crocheted blankets from the uncomfortable armchair and sit down. Mom's dark roots are mixed with gray, and she is in desperate need of a bleach job. My sister-in-law, Stacy, flunked out of cosmetology school, but she does well enough to keep the family trimmed and dyed. She seems to be slacking though because dad's hair curls up at the collar of his shirt.

"Where's Mitchell?"

"At work," Mom says with her chin in the air and her eyebrows raised. "He got a job at Timberland Mill. He's part of a new department making wood pellets. You know, those things they put in the stoves?"

Maybe he can get his own property and tow his trailer onto it. "Is Stacy here?"

"Yes, she's in their trailer doing God knows what. That woman hardly comes out and leaves us to watch Grace all the time. I would like to clip their electricity so she can't sit in front of the television all day long."

"When did you put the refrigerator on the porch?"

"It looks godawful, doesn't it? Mitchell put it there. The one in their trailer is too small, and Stacy doesn't want to come into the house whenever she wants something. I told her she still needed to come on the porch, so a few more steps shouldn't matter. If you ask me, it is because she's stingy and doesn't want to mix her food with ours."

"Or she doesn't want you complaining about how much room their beer and Dr. Peppers take up," Dad says, then changes the subject. "I can tell you didn't just come for a visit. What's up, Baby Girl?"

I used to hate it when Dad called me Baby Girl, especially when I was Kia's age. I wanted to be a big girl and thought he was making fun of me. Now, it makes me feel treasured even though his baby girl is grown and has her own baby girls.

I take a deep breath and realize that every muscle in my body is strung tight. Maybe I just need to figure things out on my own. My parents do not need another adult child who can't function.

Several blinder slats are missing from the sliding glass door, and the faucet in the kitchen drips onto a pile of dishes. Ever since Dad's accident, the house has sunk into disrepair. It's hard to see my parents living like this.

"Since Mitchell and Stacy live on the property for free, maybe you can get her to earn her keep with some house-cleaning."

"I can clean my own damn house," Mom says. "When you get my age, you realize there is more to life than dusting and vacuuming. Plus, do you think I want Stacy nosing around all my stuff?"

I stand up and head toward the kitchen. The dishes are piled in the sink so high that I can't find the scrub brush. When I stack enough cups and plates on the counter, I see the handle beneath a frying pan.

"Just spit it out," Mom says. "You came to ask something, so ask it."

I close my eyes and shake my head. "It's nothing. We're fine."

Outside the window, Kia helps Carina feed Gretchen. Carina clutches the celery in her pudgy little hand while Kia steadies her arm and encourages her. Behind them, Calista and Grace swing back and forth on the old swings. The high-pitched creak of the chains brings back many memories of a time when life was easy.

I need to do it, so I take a deep breath. Without turning around to face my parents, I let it out. "I was wondering if I could borrow a hundred dollars. I need school supplies and some clothes for Kia and Calista. I can work it off. I can do some chores around the house for you...."

"We want to help you, sweetie." Here comes Mom's usual *We would help you if we could, but we can't* response. "What about the life insurance annuity from Chris?"

"It's barely enough to live on."

"You should've taken a lump sum. You could have a nice car and plenty of cash."

"I need to make the money last until my girls are all in school, and I can go back to work." I want to remind her that Mitchell took a lump sum from his auto accident and blew fifty-thousand dollars in six months on alcohol, drugs, and baseball cards—but I hold it in, so she doesn't lecture me about being jealous of her precious boy. Plus, if I had a lump sum, they would all have their hands out to me. I need to take care of my girls.

"You know we will help any way we can, just like we do for Mitchell and Stacy, but we can't give you cash all the time."

"All the time? I hardly ever ask you."

"We just can't keep doing for you like we used to. Ever since Dad's accident, we no longer have a man's income. We got the house and the land, and that is about it."

"We can put another trailer on the property," Dad says.

"I want to be independent."

"Then you need to get yourself a job," mom says, "or find a new husband."

I ignore the new husband part of her comment. "I will pay more for childcare than I can earn. I'll be worse off than I already am. Once Carina is in kindergarten, I can get a job or go back to school. I still want to go to nursing school."

"You're smart enough for that. I wish you would've gone to college instead of getting married right out of high school," Mom says.

"Then I wouldn't have my girls."

Mom eyes me as she takes a drink of her Pepsi. "Maybe you can ask your grandpa."

"He's on Social Security and barely has enough to live on." I put the plug in the sink and squirt in some green dish soap.

"I have known that man all my life, and he always weaseled away his money. I bet he's got a whole mattress full of cash," Mom says.

The sink foams with suds. "I just need a hundred dollars to get school supplies and some new clothes for Kia and Calista."

"You need to find yourself a man to help support you and the girls. It's been two years, and it's time to move on. Chris would've wanted you to."

She has no idea what she is talking about. Chris would never want another man beside me in our bed.

"He should have provided for you better, so you don't need another man. He went wildland fire fighting with a thirty-thousand-dollar life insurance policy that was barely enough to bury him and get you situated."

"Never mind. I'm sorry I asked." I turn around to keep myself from screaming at her, and I say, as calmly and I can, "I need to get back home."

"You don't need to run off just because the conversation got tough. Your girls need you to make the right decisions for them. Come home. We will help you with childcare, and you can go back to school. You can go into nursing like you've always wanted."

Calista lets out a blood-curdling screech. I run for the door and make it just in time to see Kia smack Grace upside her head. "Don't you touch my sister!"

Calista's hand is pressed to her left eye, and Grace stands there with a stick. She raises it up to hit Kia, but Kia yanks it from her hand. Grace screams, and the door to the trailer flies open. Stacy races down the metal steps so fast that she's a blur. I get to Calista just as the blood starts to seep through her fingers, and she lets out another hysterical scream.

"Let me see," I say, but she shakes her head and screams louder. I scoop her up and take her to the porch. Stacy yells at Kia and asks what she did to Grace.

"Grace hit Calista with the stick." Kia's voice is shaky. "I took it from her."

I sit on the steps with Calista and pull her hand away. It is filled with blood, and there is a gash next to her eye. "Get me some paper towels," I say to Mom.

"You're the only one I see with a stick," Stacy says.

Mom rushes into the kitchen and reappears with a washcloth and a first aid kit. We try to clean Calista up, but she screams and pulls away.

"She's going to need a stitch in that," Dad says.

I stand up with Calista in my arms and walk toward my car just as Stacy grabs hold of Kia's arm and yanks her away from Grace.

"We're leaving," I say. "Let her go."

Dad struggles to get Carina into her car seat with one arm. I put Calista into her booster and hand the washcloth to Kia. "Make sure she keeps it on the cut."

Dad stops me at the far side of my car. "She will be okay. I'm sorry."

"Mitchell and Stacy need to discipline her. She's mean."

Dad reaches into his pocket with his good hand and pulls out some twenty-dollar bills. "This is for school supplies for the girls."

"Mom said you didn't have the money...."

"Grandpa Hudson isn't the only one who knows he needs to weasel money away around here. If I didn't, we'd be on the streets."

My chest tightens, and tears slip down my cheeks. "Thank you, Daddy."

"I love you, Baby Girl." He puts his arm around my shoulder and pulls me to him for a hug. "I'm proud of you. You're a good momma, and I wish I could help you more."

I get into my car and pull the door shut. Carina is already asleep, and Calista sits there whimpering with the washcloth pressed to her eye.

Dad taps on my window, and I lower it. "Think about moving back home," he says.

Out on the lawn, Stacy comforts Grace and shoots dirty looks at my girls and me as I pull forward enough to turn around.

6

EMMY

THE ROOM IS PITCH BLACK, AND I CANNOT SLEEP. A MAN AND A woman argue in the next room. The neon red numbers of the alarm clock laser 2:45 onto my eyeballs. The air conditioner clicks off, and without its loud drone, I hear every word through the wall.

"If you didn't dress like a slut, he wouldn't a been staring at you."

"I dress like this for you. I can't control what other men do."

"I don't need you to dress like a whore for me. I know exactly what your cunt and tits look like."

Something bangs against the wall.

"Bitch! You're lucky that didn't hit me."

"Or what? What you gonna do, Kyle? You gonna hit me and get yourself thrown back in jail? You like being fresh meat?"

"Fuck you!"

"I'll send you a package of KY if you're nice."

Something big crashes to the ground, and they fight for another half an hour before the headboard bangs against the wall in time with her moans.

It finally stops, and it is quiet. Just as I start to doze off, a diesel engine rumbles in the parking lot. I peek through a gap in the blackout curtains and see two men in a jacked-up truck with an American flag strapped behind the cab. I can't see their faces, but they are stopped behind my car with their headlights shining directly at the rooms across the lot.

In their beam of light, a motel door opens. A barefoot girl in short shorts and a belly top steps out. It looks like she is being beamed up by a UFO as she runs to the front of the truck. She goes around to the driver's side. The door opens, and as she climbs over, he slaps her ass. She settles into the middle front seat, and his door closes.

I turn up the air conditioner for some background noise, climb back into bed, and pull my pillow over my face. The next thing I know, the room has a morning glow, but it is still dim with the curtain closed. I roll over and reach for Brian's side of the bed, but he is not there. Across the empty sheets and pillow, I see the red numbers on the alarm clock: 6:23. My stomach grumbles. Erika did not say what time she would come with breakfast.

I go to the bathroom and search through my suitcase for a hairbrush. Once I find it, I head toward the window, open the curtain, and let the light wash in. My brush snags in the tangles of my hair, so I start at the tips and work my way up.

Through the gauze of the white sheer, I see two men sitting inside a black car parked next to mine. Their windows are down, and both have their elbows sticking out. A white to-go coffee cup sits on the dash, along with crumpled-up wrappers. I would bet a hundred bucks they are cops. My stomach flutters, and it feels like a swarm of moths are beating their wings up my throat. Are they here to arrest me?

Erika's Jeep pulls into the lot, and she parks next to the black car. Her door opens, and she steps out with a McDonald's bag and a drink. She slams her door shut and turns to the men in the car. Her smile quickly disappears, and she starts to nod—

not a good nod but the fatal type that people give when they realize they need to do something they don't want to.

The men step out of their car when Erika heads toward the stairs. Both men have badges clipped to their belts and guns in shoulder holsters. Either they are here to arrest me, or something terrible happened to Brian. The back of my throat stings, and I can't swallow. As Erika climbs the metal stairs, each step echoes down the corridor. My air conditioner clicks back on and drowns everything out until she knocks.

I open the door. Erika stands there with my food and a fake smile.

"Good morning. I brought breakfast." She sets it on the little round table beside the window and pulls out a chair.

I do not move. I think I am keeping it together until my brush drops from my hand and clunks to the floor. Erika's smile disappears, and she gives me that tender, motherly look.

"What happened?" My voice comes out with a wet sound. I swallow and brace myself.

She reaches out and places her hand on my arm. "Dylan Unger has escaped."

7

EMMY

A TRAIN PASSES SOMEWHERE IN THE DISTANCE AND BLOWS TWO long whistles just as Deputy Gilbert opens the back door of his patrol car. He looks like a skinny high school boy in a uniform. Erika stands there with a forced smile. I can't ride in her car because of Skid. They are worried he may come after me. Erika brought me a white button-up blouse and a blue skirt for court. They are not new and have that funky smell of a thrift store.

The doors to the other motel rooms are closed, and the curtains are shut, but I feel eyes watching me through the gaps. One of the housekeepers, in purple scrubs, backs out of a storage room with a yellow laundry cart. She looks over at me but turns away when I stare back.

Whichever dumbass was supposed to detain Skid should be fired. They knew, at the very least, that he kidnapped a girl and strapped her to a mattress with tie-downs. Once they test the DNA on the hair in his tackle box, they will know he is a serial killer. I told them, and nobody listened.

I lower myself into the back seat. The deputy shuts the door, gets behind the wheel, and latches his seatbelt. A black grate separates us, and I feel like a caged animal.

Today is Brian's arraignment. The charges are felony charges, and Brian has no assets or property to put up for a bond. Erika gives me a reassuring smile before she gets into her yellow and black Jeep that reminds me of a bumblebee.

Two officers have the hood of my Mazda up, with jumper cables going from my battery to the battery of a patrol car. I have given them permission to take it to an impound lot to hide until they find Skid. Now, I can't go anywhere, even if I want to.

As we pull out of the parking spot, I can't take my eyes off the orange *Do Not Disturb* sign that hangs on the door to my room. I don't want anyone going in there even though I have all of Brian's money in his black duffle bag beside me, mostly in wads of hundreds and twenties, folded over and held with rubber bands. Erika doesn't know we have this, and I pray it is enough to get Brian out of jail.

In what seems like forever but could not have been more than minutes, Deputy Gilbert and I pass by the front of the brick courthouse with ivy creeping up it and a white wooden bell tower. Long cement stairs rise up to the front door. The grass is newly mowed into stripes, and water sprays up from a fountain. We pass by the jail that looks eerily similar to one of my elementary schools and circle around a little park to the backside of the courthouse.

Deputy Gilbert reaches for the door handle, but Erika says something, and he stops. They both look toward the side door of the jail. Brian! It feels like a bird is caught in my throat and flapping its wings. I cannot breathe. He walks with cuffs around his hands and feet. They are shackled together with chains. Not my Brian. I want to scream that he is a good man. He saves lives. A guard holds Brian's elbow, and another guard follows behind. Brian wears a dark blue suit and white tennis shoes that I have never seen before. He looks unnatural in them.

Brian's hair and skin are brownish-red, and his eyes are the same deep greenish-blue and white as the churning river. I wish he would look up at me so I could see them, but he does not. Brian needs to be free. He should be beneath the sun and clouds, bare-chested in shorts and water sandals. He does not belong in a cell with men who control his every move.

The inside of the car heats up, and a bead of sweat runs down my spine as they lead Brian into the back door of the courthouse. Erika's mouth is moving, and I can hear her voice but not what she is saying to Deputy Gilbert. They left me in the car. If I was a dog, they would at least crack the windows. I tap on the glass, and they ignore me. I tap again, and Officer Gilbert turns his head toward me. A look of shock washes across his face when he realizes that he has left me in the oven of his patrol car.

The door swings out and lets in a blast of warm air, only ten degrees cooler than the car, but it feels better.

"Oh my gosh," Erika says and puts her hand to her mouth. "I'm so sorry, sweetie. We got to talking and…some advocate I am."

Deputy Gilbert looks between the jail door and the back door to the courthouse. "Let's get her inside."

I put the long strap of Brian's duffle bag over my head and across my body. The morning is already hot. It's going to be a scorcher. I also take hold of the handles of the duffle bag, and we head straight for the same door where they took Brian. Please, God, let him be right there inside the door. I will wrap my arms around him before they know what happened, and they will have to peel me off. What can they do to me? Loving someone is not a criminal offense.

Just as Deputy Gilbert reaches for the courthouse door, a loud "Get your fucking hands off me" comes from the side of the jail.

The door opens, and I turn. Jake is behind us, shackled and

throwing elbows at the guards, but Erika's hand presses on my back and ushers me into the back of the courthouse. Brian is not there. There is nothing but a linoleum floor, a closed door, an elevator, and a long dark wooden staircase leading straight up. I didn't expect to see Jake today.

"Keep me away from him," I say and hurry toward the stairway. I can't face Jake and his anger. He hates me. Everything turns fuzzy. My foot slips off the first step. I fall forward and catch myself with both hands.

"Whoa there." Erika grabs my arm and pulls me to my feet. "You okay?"

I nod my head. "I don't want to see...."

Jake's voice booms just outside the courthouse. I grab the handrail and take another try at the stairs. This time, my foot gets traction, and I climb up.

"Let me help you."

The strap of the duffle bag lifts off my shoulder and releases the weight.

"No!" I grab hold of the bag and press it against my body.

She lets go but stays so close that her body is a solid wall behind me.

The stairs lead to the courthouse's main entrance with its shiny white floor and dark wooden door frames and doors. Several American flags and Oregon State flags hang limp on poles on either side of the entrance and the outside of several office doors.

"Over here." Erika leads me to a door with *Victims Advocate Office 201* in dark lettering on a frosted window. Everything on the other side of the window is blurry and nothing but blended colors and shadows.

Erika opens the door to a tiny lobby the size of a storage closet. Two red padded chairs face a glass reception window and a door. She steps in behind me, and I realize that Deputy

Gilbert is no longer with us. My heartbeat thumps in my ears, so I take a slow breath in, count to ten, and blow it out.

Behind the window is an office packed with desks, filing cabinets, a copy machine, and papers. All government offices have the same feel—they just have different accessories. Randall, my eighth-grade foster brother, used to say it was like putting the same pig in different dresses.

Mrs. Larson rises from a desk chair and opens the door to an inner office. "It's nice to see you, Emmy. Come back here. It is much more comfortable."

Mrs. Larson wears a black business skirt and jacket with a burgundy blouse and looks ready for court. She leads Erika and me to a waiting room with a big window that looks out over the grass in front of the courthouse.

A young couple walks by with a golden retriever on a leash. The man says something that makes the woman laugh, and the dog sniffs at a light pole. Life keeps on going for some people while others deal with horrible things. Erika takes a seat in a wooden chair, and Mrs. Larson shuts the door. Children's toys, folded quilts, picture books, and novels fill a bookshelf along one of the walls.

"Would you like something to drink?" Mrs. Larson opens a mini fridge filled with Shasta soda and water bottles. "A ginger ale or lemon-lime would be good for your stomach."

"Lemon-lime will be fine. Thank you." I lift the duffle bag and set it on my lap. "Will Jake be at the arraignment?"

Mrs. Larson nods her head instead of saying it out loud. "Mrs. Wheeler and I will be with you every moment. If he gets out of hand, he will be removed from the courthouse. Judge Bateman will not tolerate it."

Mrs. Larson sets a Lemon-Lime in front of me and a Diet Cola in front of Erika. "We can wait here until it is time for the arraignment. As I told you before, you don't need to be here today."

"I need to be here for Brian."

Mrs. Larson glances at Brian's duffle bag but does not ask me about it. Erika lifts her arm to check the time. She has thick wrists and a silver watch. "We should head upstairs."

"Would you like to leave your bag here?" Mrs. Larson asks. "I will lock the office."

I clasp it to my chest. "No." This money is all we have, and there is no way in hell it will leave my side.

"We will need to run it through a metal detector, and they may search it."

My stomach flutters. What will they do if they find all this money? It's not illegal to have cash, is it? If they see we have so much money, they may not help us.

"It will be safe." Erika gives me a reassuring smile. "I promise."

After I put Brian's duffle bag in a cabinet and Mrs. Larson locks it, they take me up a massive wooden staircase. When we get to the landing, I freeze in my tracks. Rose Unger stands at the top of the stairs talking to someone out of my view. She is all dried up and leathery with her long dirty blond hair with the sides pulled up in a clip. She wears a flowery sundress and strappy sandals. I can't see who she is talking to, but I would bet everything I own that it's her husband, Police Chief Russ Unger, or her brother-in-law Doc Unger. Or both.

Rose sees me now. She has her usual hard-ass expression with deep-set eyes and high cheekbones. I can tell she used to be beautiful, but life and the sun have hardened her. She looks more drained than usual with her son on the run and her nephew, Jake, about to appear before a judge for date rape.

A hand touches my back, and I flinch. "It's okay," Erika says and adds pressure and presses me forward.

When we get to the top of the stairs, I see Russ and Doc Unger, just as I guessed. Russ is in his uniform and stands like he is in charge instead of the father of an escaped killer and uncle of a rapist. All of them stop talking and stare at me. The hall is long, with doors on both sides and wooden benches that look like church pews against the walls. We head toward two enormous wooden doors with windows to the courtroom. All the way to the doors, I feel the Ungers' eyes on my back.

The first time I went to court, my grandmother made sure I wore my best Sunday dress—the one with the pink roses and sash. I cried when she pulled the brush through my hair and made a ponytail so tight it hurt. When we all filed into the wooden pews, I thought we were in church and wondered why the choir sat there, not singing.

I knew my father had done something bad when he had to stand before the priest who was dressed in a long black robe. I waited for the priest to stand, come around his big desk, and put his hand on my father's head to forgive him. Instead, they took him away. For the longest time, I thought my father was in hell with the devil, and that was why I had to live with the Brandts.

My father was called daddy or Peter—just like Peter, Peter, pumpkin eater. When my mother died, I thought he had locked her away in a pumpkin shell. That first Halloween without her, our carved pumpkins sat on the front stoop until they grew hair and caved in. I imagined a giant pumpkin with my mother turning to mush inside it.

I suck in air, but it feels like no oxygen is in it. Nothing good has ever happened to me in a courtroom. Mrs. Larson leads us into a front pew. Erika gets in first, and I only scoot down far enough for Mrs. Larson to sit because I do not want the Ungers trapping me in. So far, it is only the three of us in the big hollow of the courtroom.

All I hear is my own breathing until the Ungers enter. They fill the room with their presence and their voices to the point that it feels sacrilegious. Courtrooms are like churches or libraries, where you are supposed to be silent or whisper.

I'm halfway surprised that Erin is not with them. She and Jake have been a couple since middle school and friends for their entire lives. She is not sticking with him through this one, and I don't blame her. Jake is accused of date-raping girls for years. I bet she realized he drugged her to get her out of the way. I remember several times when Erin got wasted off only a beer or two, and we would practically have to carry her home. She should file charges against him—but who am I to say anything?

Just think how many criminals could be stopped without family loyalty or a code of silence between friends. Plus, Brian had joined them once. His guilt and conscience would not let him continue. Still, it was enough to keep him quiet. Until now. Until Skid took things too far, and now Brian is willing to face the consequences to stop them—which is why he now must appear before the judge. He turned himself in. He wants to pay for what he did and make sure that Jake and Skid do also.

An older man with thick gray hair and a dark suit opens the courtroom door and holds it for a woman. She is young with dark hair that comes to her shoulders. She wears a cream-colored jacket with a matching skirt and a purple blouse. Her briefcase has a shoulder strap, and it hangs right beside her hip. You can spot them as lawyers from a mile away. The woman walks past the Ungers without acknowledging them, but the man sets his briefcase on the pew before them and slides in. He turns to talk with his arm stretching across the back of his seat.

The lady lawyer sets her briefcase on a long table, the one closest to the empty jury seats, and unlatches the top flap.

"Is she Brian's lawyer?" I whisper to Mrs. Larson.

"No, she's the prosecutor for the state. Her name is Veronica Gray. She's tough but fair."

"Where's Brian's lawyer?"

Mrs. Larson shrugs and gives Erika a sideways glance. My

throat closes so tight I cannot swallow. Jake has a lawyer, but Brian does not?

"The male lawyer is Sheldon Tate," Mrs. Larson says. "He's one of the best attorneys in the county."

Of course, he is. Jake will have the best, and so will Skid if they ever catch him.

8

———

EMMY

A SIDE DOOR OPENS, AND A DEPUTY STEPS THROUGH, FOLLOWED BY Brian, who does not look like himself in that suit. He is no longer in handcuffs and has another deputy right behind him. Veronica Gray looks up from the papers she is organizing on the table and gets her first look at a man she wants to lock behind bars. Maybe she will determine her strategy by Brian's appearance.

I want to run to Brian and throw my arms around him. I know he is a good man and regrets what he did. He saved my life, and he has saved many lives. Brian's head is bent, and he keeps his eyes on the floor. I don't look at the Ungers, but I feel the tension radiating from where they sit. When Brian's mom died, they raised him as a family member, and he betrayed them.

Brian barely sits down when Jake bursts through the doorway, still in handcuffs and jerky defiant movements. The moment he struts through, he gives a defiant nod toward his father, Uncle Russ, and Aunt Rose.

Jake sits at the end of the pew directly behind Brian. He leans forward and whispers something to the back of Brian's head. Brian gives a single, almost unrecognizable nod of his head.

Even trying to whisper, Doc's voice booms through the courtroom. "Why is my son in handcuffs? That could unduly influence the judge."

Jake's attorney says something and then stands up and sets his briefcase on the chair of the other long table, the one closest to the door that Brian and Jake came through. He is big and square-shouldered, just like Doc. Mr. Tate looks like one of those men who was class president in high school, elected for nothing but his popularity. He approaches the deputy with a confident walk but keeps a respectful distance.

The deputy's expression is unreadable. He keeps one hand on his radio and the other on his belt buckle, and it looks like Mr. Tate is trying to convince him to take the cuffs off, but the deputy does not do as asked. Jake sits there like a docile human being for the moment, probably because his father and uncle are in the room. He is just like the kids in school who are rude and aggressive to the teachers and principal but act like angels the moment their parents show up so they can act like victims.

Mr. Tate returns to the Ungers and tells them that the deputies will keep Jake cuffed for everyone's safety. He tells them the deputy said Jake has been aggressive and lashing out.

"You're his attorney," Doc says. "This is his first time in court, and he's not used to anyone restraining him."

Of course he's not. His uncle is the police chief, and his family runs Lodell. Jake is an arrogant and mean asshole. I hope Jake gets what he deserves. A lady with short brown hair and glasses comes and sits at a small desk at the front with a laptop and keyboard.

"Who is that?" I ask Mrs. Larson.

"Her name is Stella, and she's the court reporter."

Stella opens the laptop and arranges her desk just as a group of people enter the courtroom. It feels as if I was just sucker-punched in the stomach. The Rhodes family—no longer in their matching red t-shirts with Crystal's photo on the front—look haggard in their expensive dresses and suits.

"Are you okay?" Erika whispers, and I feel her hand on mine. "Who are they?"

"Crystal's family." The words flutter from my mouth. "Crystal is the girl who was kidnapped. The one Brian and I saved. Why are they here?"

Mrs. Larson shrugs. "I'm sure we will find out."

There are six of them here, all with blond or gray hair, except for Crystal's dad, whose hair is light brown and has a scraggly beard. A dark-haired man in a black suit leads the family to a pew right in front of the Ungers, and they file into the seats one by one. Two blondes in their twenties who look like they are Crystal's sister and brother scoot in first, followed by her mother and grandmother holding onto one another, then finally, the grandpa and dad.

The Ungers do not greet them, and the entire Rhodes family acts as if the Ungers are not there. Russ Unger instantly stiffens. He whispers something to Doc and Rose. The three of them stand and move to the last row of seats directly behind Mrs. Larson, Erika, and me.

Once the Rhodes are settled, the dark-haired man walks to the front and talks to Veronica Gray, the prosecuting attorney. She smiles and holds her hand out to him. He shakes it and takes a seat next to her.

I look to Erika and do not need to say a word before she says, "He's probably their attorney."

Why would the Rhodes family need an attorney here for the arraignment? Unless they suspect Brian and Jake are involved in some way. The light in the courtroom starts to fade, and the sounds turn fuzzy when the bailiff announces we all should rise.

Jake stays in his seat with a scowl on his face. One of the

deputies grabs Jake's arm, and it looks like Jake will resist, but he looks over at his family and gets to his feet.

Once we all stand and the judge enters, the bailiff says, "The court of General Sessions, Seventeenth Judicial District, is now in session. The honorable Judge Paul Bateman is presiding."

The sheriff's deputies stand beside Jake and Brian with their hands crossed in front of them. I want to catch Brian's eyes, but he will not look up. I'm sure it is his guilt for what he has done. It is not fair that this judge, who does not know Brian, will decide his fate.

Once Judge Bateman sits, so do we. He shuffles things around on his desk and opens a folder. "We are here for the arraignment of Jacob Carl Unger. Will the attorneys announce their names for the record?"

All the attorneys stand.

The Unger's attorney speaks first in a booming voice. "Good morning, your honor. Mr. Sheldon Tate, on behalf of Mr. Unger."

The lady attorney says, "Ms. Veronica Gray, on behalf of the state of Oregon."

And the young dark-haired attorney says, "Mr. Antonio Ramirez, on behalf of the Rhodes Family and Crystal Rhodes."

As the judge flips through papers on his desk, Crystal's mom sniffles and wipes her red-rimmed eyes with a tissue. She has white-blond hair with dark roots, and the grandma beside her trembles when she whispers something to her. The grandpa, in black-rimmed glasses, sits with his mouth clamped shut and his arm around his wife.

I remember when they all arrived in Lodell in red t-shirts like a swarm of ants. Crystal's father came like a man in charge. He demanded to speak with the police and found rooms for his family and friends who came to help search for his daughter. Now, he sits unshaven with a scraggly brown beard and circles beneath his eyes. None of them look like they are here to thank

Brian for saving Crystal's life. They seem to be here for someone to pay for what happened to her. The brother looks in his early twenties and stares straight at Jake and Brian with a vein bulging out on his forehead.

Judge Bateman has short peppered gray hair and a creeper mustache. He looks like a male librarian glancing over the top of his glasses toward Jake. "Mr. Unger, you have been charged with ten counts of first-degree rape, ten counts of first-degree sexual abuse...."

"That's bullshit!" Jake's voice explodes and echoes through the courtroom.

"You will refrain from interrupting, or you will be escorted from this courtroom," Judge Bateman says.

The deputy standing next to Jake shifts and places his hand on the butt of his gun. Brian can't see Jake unless he turns around. He glances over at me with a nervous look, and I can tell by the way his body shakes that he is tapping his heels on the ground like he does when he is nervous.

"Mr. Unger," the judge continues. "You have been charged with ten counts of first-degree rape, ten counts of first-degree sexual abuse, ten counts of first-degree kidnapping...."

The sound of Jake's handcuffs and chain rattles as he pulls at them like an animal. "You're full of shit. You can't prove none of that."

"Mr. Sheldon, will you please speak to your client and explain that he must refrain from interrupting this courtroom. I will remove him if he doesn't."

"I'd like to see you remove me!" Jake springs to his feet. His full-moon face is red beneath his mutton-chop sideburns. He takes a wrestling stance and braces himself right behind Brian. Brian leans forward and rests his forearms on his thighs, probably trying to be out of striking distance.

Someone shuffles directly behind me, and I turn. Russ Unger scoots out of his pew, and a deputy steps to the end with one hand on his radio and the other on the butt of his gun.

The judge strikes a mallet three times and says in a stern but calm voice, "There will be order in this courtroom. Have a seat, Mr. Unger."

Jake does not sit, and neither does his uncle. One deputy reaches for Jake's arm, and he pulls away. Russ gets to the deputy at the end of his pew and can't pass by him.

"The public in the gallery will also remain seated, or you will be removed."

"I'm Chief Russ Unger, his uncle…."

"I don't care who you are. You will sit down."

"I can help…."

"This court does not need your help. Mr. Unger will control himself."

"Sit down," Doc says. His deep voice rumbles through the court, and Jake, still red in the face, lowers himself into his seat.

"Mr. Unger," the judge continues in a steady voice. "You have been charged with ten counts of first-degree rape, ten counts of first-degree sexual abuse, ten counts of first-degree kidnapping, ten counts of sexual penetration, and possession of a schedule-three controlled substance, all first-degree felonies punishable by imprisonment. How do you plea?"

Jake's attorney stands and says, "My client pleads not guilty on all counts."

Of course, he pleads not guilty. Jake never admits when he is wrong. Even if someone watches him do something, he denies it.

"A plea of not guilty shall be entered on the defendant's behalf on all counts." Judge Bateman looks down at his desk. "I will set the case on the calendar for Friday, October twenty-fourth. Does that work for everyone?"

The air is thick in the courtroom while Jake shifts and rustles in his seat, and the attorneys check their calendars and agree on the date. After that, Jake's attorney asks for bail, but it is denied until Jake serves three days in jail for contempt of court. The deputy leads a red-faced and tightly wound Jake from the courtroom.

There is only one moment of relief before I realize Brian is next. He stands, silent and without handcuffs. He finally looks up and meets the judge's eyes. Oh God, what will Brian do without an attorney? He is truly alone as he stands there and waits to hear his fate.

The judge opens another folder. I cannot breathe. I know Brian will plead guilty and take what is coming to him.

"We are here for the arraignment of Brian Joshua Cobb. Will the attorneys announce their names for the record?"

I close my eyes and brace myself for Veronica Gray's voice, stating that she will prosecute my Brian for the state of Oregon. Instead, a deep voice says, "Sheldon Tate on behalf of Mr. Cobb."

I hear the tone of the prosecutor's voice followed by the sound of the victim's attorney, but their words do not make sense to me.

"Is he a court-appointed attorney?" I whisper to Mrs. Larson.

She shakes her head. "Not Sheldon Tate."

I look over at Erika, and she rubs her thumb across the side of her pointer finger, indicating that he is expensive.

How does Brian have an attorney? Jake's attorney? And what does that mean?

Judge Bateman sounds like he is at the end of a tunnel. "You have been charged with one count of first-degree rape, one count of first-degree sexual abuse, one count of first-degree kidnapping, one count of sexual penetration, and possession of a schedule-three controlled substance, all first-degree felonies punishable by imprisonment. How do you plea?"

I look over at Brian, but he does not turn toward me. I wait for his mouth to open and say *guilty*, but he does not. Instead, Mr. Tate says, "My client pleads not guilty on all counts."

What? My hand flies to my chest.

Erika puts her arm around me and whispers, "It will be okay. It is almost done."

Brian's trial is set for the same day as Jake's. The same day. The same attorney. Brian needs to be separate from Jake. We finally got away from Lodell and away from the Ungers, but here we are, getting wound around them again.

A gasp comes from the direction of the Rhodes family, and I feel Erika's arm tighten around my shoulder. I look over at her, and she is smiling.

"What happened?" I ask.

"Brian's bail has been set."

"What does that mean?"

"He will be released on bail until his trial and will probably be with you tonight."

I want nothing more than to be with Brian and have him free, but something is wrong. This is not what Brian said he would do.

$$9$$

HIM

THE RIVER AT NIGHT IS AS BLACK AS GLASS. I SHED THE OLD MAN'S clothes with every step toward my destiny until I am on the bank and the water laps at my bare toes.

When they find my body, they will think they are safe. They are ignorant and do not know my power. Once I am the river, I can return to my town. They ridiculed me in the flesh, but they will worship me as the fluid. The river is the lifeblood of Lodell. I am the lifeblood, born, raised, and embodied.

The townspeople, children, tourists, and fishermen will all have fun when I am merciful and when I allow it. They will be unaware of the thunder that rages beneath my surface and will float around in their artificial bubbles and think they are safe and invincible. They will not realize that I can rage and snatch whoever I want at any minute. I will keep them until they are nothing but meat and bone. In the end, everyone will gather to pay tribute and leave their crosses and flowers to mark each occasion along my banks. After I rage, their strongest men will doubt themselves and fear their own weakness.

My ankles twist, and pain shoots up my calves when I slip over the mossy rocks beneath the surface. The flesh is weak, and everyone clings to it like it is their only worth. Cool and ever-living water rises up my calves and thighs and lifts me from the tethers of the earth.

I wade deep, lie back, and allow my waters to cradle me beneath the glow of the moon and the stars. We will finally be one, no longer the flesh and the fluid, but one single entity finally at peace and free from my human restraints.

10

―――

EMMY

WHEN I OPEN THE DOOR TO THE MOTEL ROOM, BRIAN LETS OUT A low whistle, and the stink of stale cigarettes and musty air conditioner washes over us. He looks around at the blood-orange bedspread and curtains. "How do you sleep in this place?"

"I don't," I tell him and let the door slam shut behind us.

We have not had a moment to talk since they released him. Erika and I waited in the victim advocate's office until she got a call that they had finished the paperwork. We met Brian at the side of the jail. When the door opened, I saw the green uniform of a deputy, but he stayed in the doorway. Brian walked out with no handcuffs and dressed in his own shorts and *Rimrock Outfitters* t-shirt.

He looked just like my Brian, but something felt different. I did not run up to him and fling my arms around him the way I thought I would. We held hands in Officer Gilbert's patrol car as I explained that my car was in storage somewhere to keep me safe from Skid. Brian did not look surprised when I said that, so he must have already heard that Skid escaped.

Brian goes straight to Otis on the top of the dresser and runs

64

his hand down his fur from the top of his head and down his back, then kisses his fingertips and puts them on the top of his mother's ashes. I stand by the closed door with my arms wrapped around my chest. I don't know what to do. I have so many questions, but I also want to be here to support Brian in any way I can. The air conditioner kicks on and lets out a noisy whir of cold air.

Brian stands with his back to me. His head is bowed like he is saying a prayer to his mother's ashes.

"Thank you for bringing Otis and my mom," he says before turning around. "You get some new clothes?"

I look down at the white blouse and dark blue skirt. "Erika brought them to me."

"Erika?"

"My advocate from a church group."

He lets out a breath, drops his head, and whispers, "I'm sorry."

"It's not your fault."

When he looks up, his eyes are damp and defeated. "It is my fault. I knew, and I didn't turn them in."

A shiver runs across my shoulders. "You knew that Skid. . ."

"No. Oh, no." Brian shakes his head back and forth. "I had no idea that he would hurt anyone."

I stare at him and rub my shoulders. "Isn't rape..."

"Yes, of course. I'm sorry. I'm not thinking straight. It's just that. It is hard to believe that someone I knew my whole life... someone who was practically my brother since I was eight years old would do anything like..." Brian's chest heaves, and he clenches and unclenches his hands.

I take a step forward, and he opens his arms to me. I go to him and press my face into his t-shirt. He wraps me up in his arms, and I can feel the beat of his heart and the whoosh of air going in and out of his chest.

Beneath Brian's scent, I still smell the river. This is the same shirt that was wet from him saving Skid and the shirt he wore when they handcuffed him and drove away in the deputy's truck. Was that just two days ago? It feels like forever.

I slip my hands beneath his shirt and lift it over his stomach and chest until it is bunched around his neck. He pulls it over his head and drops it to the floor. I run my hands around his waist and press my cheek to his bare skin. His chest hair tickles my nose, but I do not pull away. I just wanted to be rid of the scent of the river, but Brian gets hard, and he presses against my belly.

He unbuttons my blouse, slowly working each tiny button with his big fingers until it is undone. He slips it from my shoulders, bends down, and kisses me as he unhooks my bra. It drops to the floor. He runs his hands over my breasts before he scoops me into his arms and steps toward the bed.

I lift my skirt and slide my panties down my thighs, and he lowers his shorts just enough to slide inside me. We make love slow and smooth and warm. The weight of Brian's body presses me into the mattress until we both cum and he rolls off. When I turn onto my side, he pulls me against him, and we fall asleep.

Brian runs his hand over my shoulder to wake me.

"Thank you," he whispers. "Thank you for being here for me and bringing my things."

"Why wouldn't I? I love you."

He pulls me tighter against him. There are things I want to ask, but this is not the right time.

He turns his head toward the clock on the nightstand. "Oh God, it's seven o'clock! I haven't eaten anything all day. I need something. What about you?"

"I haven't had an appetite."

Brian rolls off the bed and pulls his shorts on. "I'll go get us something. I saw a few fast food joints around here."

I wiggle out of my skirt and pull my panties up. The side of the bed sinks when Brian puts a knee on it and leans over me. He kisses my breasts and puts his warm mouth over my nipples.

It seems like he wants to make love again, but then he stands up. "To be continued…" he says, with a slight smile—the first one I've seen on him in a while.

When Brian leaves, I want to shower, but Skid is on the run, and scenes of slasher movies with a woman in the shower flash through my head. I peek out the gap in the blackout curtains. A cop sits in a dark unmarked car. He is there to protect me, so I go into the bathroom and turn the water on.

When I get out, Brian sits at the little table by the window with a bucket of KFC and a six-pack of Hamm's, which the guides used to call a Hamm's Canwich.

"You got a whole bucket for the two of us?"

"We have a mini fridge." Brian has the blackout curtain open a few feet with the thin gauze of the white sheers letting in the last of the daylight. He does not turn to look at me.

"Is everything okay?" I go to my suitcase to get some of my own clothes.

"Did you know there is a cop sitting in the parking lot?"

"Yes." I do not say anything more. I pull on my t-shirt, then rummage through my clothes to find some underwear. My fingers brush past something hard and cold. A chill washes across my shoulders. It is the box of flies with my name scratched into the top. The ones that Skid tied with Amber's hair in them.

I sit down in nothing but a t-shirt and panties, and the chair is cool on the back of my thighs.

Brian pulls a Hamm's from the plastic ring, cracks it open, and sets it in front of me.

He takes a drink from his beer. "Fucking Skid. Leave it to him to turn all of our lives into a shitstorm."

A folded newspaper sits on the table next to the red-and-white striped bucket of chicken. The front page lies face down, and all I can see is the bottom half with a black and white photo of a parade float filled with little girls in sashes and crowns and various headlines, *Truck Wreck Closes Highway*, *Spring Salmon Return*, and *Fire Damages Barn*.

Brian was hungry, but the bucket sits unopened. I don't know if it is the deputy in the parking lot or what is on the other side of that newspaper, and I'm afraid to ask. He didn't bring any paper plates or sides or plasticware. There is nothing but chicken, beer, and a pile of napkins. I set a napkin in front of Brian and one in front of me before I remove the cardboard lid of the bucket.

"You want a breast, thigh, or leg?"

Brian shrugs. "Just give me whatever."

Normally, he would say he wants all three and whisk me into the bedroom for another round. I take out a thigh for Brian and set a leg on my napkin.

The smell of chicken and beer fills the room, which is much better than the stale cigarette air of this non-smoking room.

"What made you plead not guilty?"

Brian's head snaps toward me and finally meets my eyes. His jaw clenches, and it is not from chewing. I clamp my lips together but do not take my eyes off him.

He takes a deep breath and says, "The lawyer advised me to do it. He said that is what everyone does at an arraignment, then we will have time to discuss my options."

"You and Jake have the same attorney? Erika said he is one of the best in the county and that he is very expensive."

Brian flings his uneaten thigh into the bucket. "He's the Unger family attorney."

"And he is representing you?"

Brian slowly turns his head back to me and glares for a moment before his eyes go dead, and he nods.

I don't want Brian linked to Jake and Skid. They are both

criminals. If they have the same attorney, he will seem as guilty as them.

"Are the Ungers paying for your attorney?"

He nods.

"Why would they do that? You are the one who turned them both in."

"I'm like family to them."

"Like family is not family. Trust me…I know that for a fact."

Brian doesn't take his eyes off me. They are not angry, but they are also not filled with love.

"I thought you wanted to face what you did and get past it."

"I do, but the attorney told me what would happen. I will forever have to register as a sex offender. I will not be able to live near schools or have certain jobs. It will affect my life forever. If we have kids, I will not be able to go on field trips with them or enter their school for any reason." Brian put's his hand on my cheek, and I can smell the chicken. "I am not a threat to anyone. I made a fucking stupid decision, and I regret it with every ounce of my being. I never did it again and will never do it in the future. The courts don't know that, and I'll be in the same category as every fucking predator in Oregon."

"I don't trust the Ungers or their attorney. They may sacrifice you to save Jake and Skid."

"You may be right. I don't know what I'm going to do. All the cops have is my statement. No girls have come forward about the rape charges. I may be the only one who does time or has any punishment." Brian taps his heel, and his leg shakes the entire table. "Jake can deny it. It is only my word against his. I can't afford an attorney, and the public defender won't give a shit about me."

"What about Skid? Will you testify against him?"

"They think Jake and I helped Skid kidnap Crystal. That's why they won't drop the charges. That's why Crystal's family was there with a victim's attorney."

"Crystal knows what happened. She can testify that it was only Skid."

"If she remembers. My attorney thinks she was drugged the whole time. She may or may not recognize Skid, but even if she does, that doesn't mean he's the only one. The detectives think Jake and I helped him kidnap her...and in a way, we did."

My throat swells shut, and I cannot swallow—or breathe. I gag and cough the bite of chicken into my napkin. "What about Amber and the other girls? The ones they found in the river? The ones he killed?"

"I bet there's no evidence pointing to Skid. It could just as easily be Jake or me—or you, for that matter. Or the girls could have just drowned. They were drunk. Each time a girl went missing, so did a raft. The rafts were found downriver, so they could have taken them."

"Seriously? What girl would do that? I know Amber wouldn't. She was terrified of water, and after our rafting trip when she fell in and almost drowned, there is no way in hell she would do that." My face feels hot, and I can't get enough air. "What about the hair in Skid's flies? That is DNA. What about my testimony that he tried to kill me?"

I don't realize I am trembling until the legs of my chair scrape across the floor when Brian pulls me toward him and wraps me tight in his arm. "That's what we need to navigate. That's why I need a good attorney. Maybe the evidence will point to Skid without my testimony. And without yours."

My insides turn to rock. That is it. Our silence is the price of Brian's freedom. That is why the Ungers will pay for his defense.

Brian reaches for the newspaper, pulls the thin front page from the rest, and places it over the top of my half-eaten chicken leg.

A photo of Skid stares up at me. He has a slight smile that sends a shiver across my chest. He looks scrappy with his hair overgrown and a wispy mustache and beard. It must have been taken when he was guiding on the river because he wears a yellow life jacket.

SUSPECTED KIDNAPPER ESCAPES FROM E.R.

Suspected kidnapper, Dylan Unger, escaped last night from Good Samaritan Hospital in Rockland. During a confrontation in the emergency room between the father of the victim and Dylan's father, Police Chief Russ Unger, the suspect fled.

A local K-9 search and rescue dog tracked Dylan Unger's movements through an empty field behind the hospital and to the banks of the Deschutes. A stolen bicycle was found next to the river in Wildwood Park, along with the clothing he allegedly stole from another patient.

The search is still on, but it is assumed that Dylan Unger has drowned in the river. He attempted suicide the day before by trying to drown himself in Steelhead Rapids in Lodell, but was saved by his long-time friend, Brian Cobb.

Grease from my chicken leg soaks into the paper and creates a dark spot on Skid's cheek.

Brian is currently in the Canyon County jail, awaiting arraignment on felony charges related to his participation in drugging and raping girls who went to Lodell for white-water rafting. It is unknown at this time how many girls are involved. If anyone has any information, they are asked to call the Canyon County Sheriff's Office.

"They don't mention anything about Jake. Not a single word," I say.

"What do you expect? Jake will probably get out of this with nothing. He's an Unger." Brian wads up his napkin and drops it into the bucket of chicken. "Skid would too if we hadn't called the Sheriff's department and they found Crystal alive."

"Do you think Skid is dead?"

Brian turns both palms up and shrugs. "He seriously tried to kill himself the day we saved Crystal. He was out of his mind and rambling something about being one with the river and taking all the nymphs he wants—like he thinks he is some sort of a river god. It was fucking creepy!"

The chicken grease covers half of Skid's face and bleeds into the print. "You think he's dead?"

"I don't know. I was in jail."

"What do you feel? Do you feel it in your gut that he is gone?"

Brian doesn't answer, but he clamps his lips together and gives one slight shake of his head.

11

HIM

THE RIVER LIFTS THE WEIGHT FROM MY BONES. AN ALMOST FULL moon hangs above, surrounded by a million twinkling stars. It casts a pearl-colored light on the rocks, long grasses, and willows along the banks. The entire river is washed in the glistening light with the dark silhouettes of houses like cutouts on the shore.

I lie back and surrender my breath. The water wraps around my body, cradles my flesh, and rocks me in perfect measure to the beat of my heart. "Now I lay me down to sleep. I pray the River my soul to keep. Let me die before I wake. I give the River my soul to take."

Rocks scratch against my back, and my blood rises as I feel the weight of my flesh on the shore. I wade back out, submerge my face into my waters, and scream, but my body will not breathe the fluid in. The flesh is disgusting and weak. It involuntarily spasms and coughs trying to save itself.

My mouth opens, and the single word, "Why?" thunders from my lungs in a long and anguished howl. It ripples across the surface like a shock wave until it dissolves, and the only sound left is the water that laps on the shore.

"Why do you forsake me?" I stand naked in my flesh, heavy and earthbound. "Am I not worthy?"

When I take a step upstream, a single thread of electricity shoots up my spine. I take another step and unleash another charge. Something awakens and pulls me forward.

My feet slip on the rocks, and my ankles twist, but there is no pain this time. When I wade deeper to get around the grasses and the brush, the current pushes against my thighs, but this is the way. I feel it now. The moonlit river is my path. Instinctively, I know that I must go upstream. I am called to my headwaters, where I originated—where my waters seep up from the ground, born again into the river.

I slowly move up past the dark houses with dim yellow lights in the squares of their windows. I turn away and focus on the water that glimmers before me. It froths white over rocks and lies black in the eddies.

I have no idea how long I walk until my thighs burn and my energy drains away. I stop and scan the shore. I am almost to the downtown lights. Music from a band drifts toward me on the breeze. It is time to rest.

The moment my feet touch the gravel of the shore, my consciousness returns to the flesh. I have escaped, and they will come for me.

I need to find a place to rest. I am as silent as the river as I cut across lawns. I slip by in the dark past people asleep in their houses. They think they are gods with their money and expensive cars.

Several pairs of shorts and a string bikini hang over the railing of a deck filled with padded furniture and strings of patio lights. One of the pairs of shorts looks my size. I pull them down and step in, tightening the string at my waist. I am still in the flesh, so I must blend in.

The deck couch looks comfortable, but I cannot be found, so I make my way back to the river and move up, toward the familiar sounds of the bar, with the band and deep-throated and high-pitched laughs and screams.

I slip behind a rafting shop with piles of kayaks, rafts, and paddle boards tethered down for the night. The dark shell of a restaurant is lit by a single light inside that illuminates the shelves of glass bottles behind the bar.

I miss the energy of the river. On land, I am a sleepwalker with heavy feet. The high-pitched laugh of nymphs calls me toward a riverfront bar. Strings of lights sway in the breeze, and people dance with beers raised above their heads. Girls shake their asses in shorts so short their butt cheeks hang out the bottom. The smooth muscles of their asses contract and relax with the rhythm of the music. They fling their hair, giggle, and call to me to take them into my depths and breathe in their last breaths.

I back away toward a willow brush where I can lie down and rest my bones. When the band takes a break, I crouch in the brush and breathe in the sweet smell of the earth, sagebrush, and juniper.

Two girls, hand in hand, with bubbly-drunk laughter, start down the stairs of the deck. At the bottom, one of them stops and pulls the arm of the other. She prevents her from stepping onto the dirt.

I can't hear them or make out their features, but the glow of the moon lights them up like glass dolls. The hesitant one stays on the steps. The other pulls away until their arms are stretched out and linked only by their hands. They let go, and one comes toward me. She twirls and dances in the moonlight like an offering.

She comes so close I am afraid she will hear my breath. I could reach out and grab her ankle, but instead, I close my fingers and withdraw my hand. As she steps away, tufts of grass sweep across her bare legs and gather her scent on their blades.

I am weak, but she is drawn to me like a gift, and I cannot

deny her. I just need to get her deep into my dark waters where she will surrender—and where I can breathe in her last breath, and we will be one.

A branch snaps beneath me, and she freezes. Her head slowly turns my way. She cocks it to the side and listens. Her hair is thin, ash blonde, and catches the moon with a silvery glow. She came to me to live in eternity.

I do not move and keep my breaths shallow and silent. The girl is appeased and crouches down with her bare knees spread apart and unbuckles her sandals. She slips them from her feet and steps barefoot into my waters until I rise around her ankles. She takes another step and bends down to sink her hands into me.

This is my chance to have her for myself. To make love to her, take her nipples into my mouth, let her breathe my fluid into her lungs, and take a clump of her hair for my flies. I shift, ready to slip out from the bush, when another twig snaps. It is not from me.

"Ella?" my nymph calls out into the dark. There is fear in her voice

At the bar, people cheer when the band starts up again and plays the intro to *Let It Rock*.

She rises and looks around. I do not move, but she senses me.

"Lexi..." the girl from the steps calls into the dark.

Lexi looks around one more time before she grabs her sandals and scampers off, back toward the lights and the music.

I missed my chance, but I am weak. I will return to my headwaters, where I was born from the rain and snow—and to my source, where I trickled from the earth. Every spring and creek will nourish me until I return and rage through the canyon stronger than ever before. For I am the river, and the river is me.

12

―――――

ASHLEY

When I'm unloading the shopping cart, Kia yells, "Put that down! Mom…Calista is stealing Skittles."

I turn around and Kia has a death grip on Calista's arm. Thanks to Grace, Calista has two stitches beneath a butterfly bandage next to her eye. I must look like a wonderful mom.

"Let go," Calista yells and kicks Kia's shin.

Kia lets out an ear-piercing scream that resonates through the entire Walmart. Everyone turns toward us. My heartbeat races and I want run from the store. Carina starts to cry and drops her beanie baby from the shopping cart. The pink bear falls face down on the dirty linoleum floor with one leg twisted up behind it. The conveyor belt moves, and half our items slide toward the cashier.

"Let her go," I tell Kia. "You unload the cart, and I'll take care of it."

I get dirty looks from the people behind us as I kneel down to Calista. "If you don't behave, we will go straight home after this instead of McDonald's."

"Can I have the Skittles?"

"No, put them back."

Calista frowns but sets them on the display rack.

"You should never negotiate with a child," the woman behind us says, like she is disappointed in me. "A quick smack on the behind will fix it."

The woman looks to be in her fifties with dark circles beneath her eyes and chain-smoker wrinkles around her lips. If I had the energy, I would explain that the shopping took longer than I expected, and my girls are just hungry, but I don't. Instead, I smile and push the empty cart to the cash register.

Calista picks Carina's beanie baby up from the floor and makes it dance on the shopping cart handle. It soothes Carina and life is good again.

"That will be one hundred and twenty-three dollars," the cashier says.

No…Crap! I only have one hundred dollars and enough for two happy meals and a quarter pounder.

"I'll need to put some of the items back."

The cashier nods and looks annoyed. The required school supplies took over half the money my dad gave me. I separate out one of the binders and a pack of notebook paper. Kia can use her binder from last year.

"I'll take care of it," a voice says from behind me.

The chain-smoking lady steps toward me with her debit card out.

The back of my throat stings as I try to swallow my sobs. "Thank you."

"You're welcome. I've been there," she says. "I was a single mom and raised three boys. It will all turn out fine."

I feel like I am looking into the worn-out face of my future self, and the tears spill out.

13

EMMY

WE USED A BIG CHUNK OF BRIAN'S CASH FOR A NEW CAR. WELL…
new to us. It is a used four-door Ford Taurus—a true tan-
colored grandpa car. The idea is to be as inconspicuous as
possible and blend in with the scenery until Skid is behind bars
or dead and buried. Since he has already escaped once, I hope
he is found dead in the river, just like he did to Amber and the
other girls, Shawna, Mandy, and Kate. May God forgive me for
wishing someone dead, but Skid is evil.

It is already eighty degrees and only eight-thirty in the
morning. Brian sits behind the wheel and the cool air blasts
from the vents as we follow Erika in her yellow Jeep.

We rented one of the units of a duplex without ever seeing
it. Erika knows the owner and put in a good word for us. The
unit is not ready for occupancy, so we got in with the first
month free and no last month or security deposit required.
Brian didn't want Erika's help, but since we had to buy the car
and own no furniture or kitchen supplies, we had no choice.

Everything we own in the world is in the trunk except for
Otis, who is propped against the back seat with the center seat-

belt across his base. I have no idea where we will sleep. We don't even have blankets to put on the floor.

I wanted to get as far away from Skid and the Ungers as possible, but Brian is out on bail, and we need to stay close until his trial. Brian thinks the district attorney won't dismiss the charges, so they can use him to catch Skid and force him to testify. Erika said that does not happen, and it sounds like a conspiracy theory to her...but she lives a life where she can still believe that everyone in authority has good intentions.

Brian makes a left at a red brick library with a beautiful green lawn and shady trees. Hopefully, the house is close by, and we can come here to use the internet. I put my hand on Brian's leg, and he takes one hand off the wheel to place over mine.

"We will get through this," he says. "Then we'll get the hell away. Maybe to Idaho or Wyoming. Do you have a preference?"

"I don't know. I've never been out of Oregon."

"Maybe we can stick some money away and get a truck and travel trailer. Then we can hit the road and figure out where we want to be."

It all seems so impossible. My entire life is like one of those dreams where you are trying to get somewhere but the journey is constantly interrupted by problems. Every time I had a dream of a forever home or made friends in a school, my foster family changed their minds or the system pulled me out. Maybe Brian is my forever partner, and we can be free together. "Why Idaho or Wyoming?"

"They both have gorgeous country with whitewater rafting and fishing. Idaho has many rivers. I've been on the Salmon and the Snake. The Snake also goes through Wyoming, but I haven't been on that part of the river. I've rafted in Wind River Canyon in Wyoming and it was beautiful. You would love it."

I see a spark in Brian's eyes for the first time since Skid tried to attack me. He belongs on a river. I used to think he belonged in Lodell because he physically looks like the landscape. Maybe he will become part of any land and river he goes to.

With every turn, we move further from the nice part of town. Here, the houses are smaller, and the lawns are dirt or full of weeds. The turn signal on Erika's Jeep blinks. She makes a right and pulls into the first driveway of a duplex with green siding and fake brown shutters. It has a dirt yard with two pine trees.

The duplex is on the corner of Juniper and Dobbs and connected to the next unit by the garage. Brian pulls to the curb next to a street sign that says DEAD END. Not a good omen.

The porch light is on in broad daylight, and the side yard is knee-high with brown weeds. A long wooden fence goes down one side of the back yard all the way to what looks like an alley.

Brian puts the car in park and turns the key without taking it from the ignition. He stares forward, down the dead-end street lined with older cars and a couple of basketball hoops rolled to the curb. "I'm sorry."

Erika steps out of her car and stands in the shade of the garage. The house looks much nicer than Brian's tiny little house in Lodell.

"Sorry for what?" I ask.

"For everything. I should have just turned Skid over to the Sheriff and kept my fucking mouth shut. Now, I have Jake and the Ungers breathing down my neck and I may need to register as a sex offender. That will affect us forever. Plus, we need to stay in this town where no one gives a shit about us."

Erika waits while the sun beats in the car windows, heating it up. "Erika cares."

Brian turns his head to look at me with flat eyes. "Really? She is only doing her job. And part of that job is protecting you from me."

I want to tell him that she is really not that bad. She didn't need to help us find a place to live. She could have walked away as soon as Brian got out. She wants to keep both of us safe from Skid.

I put my hand on Brian's leg. "Maybe we will have more resources once they realize Skid is a serial killer. Doesn't the FBI come in to help find serial killers? Maybe there will be a witness protection program, and they will set us up in another state."

"I'm not waiting around for fucking handouts. First thing tomorrow, I'm looking for a job."

"I'll look, too," I say. "With both of us working, we can buy a travel trailer sooner and get out of this state."

Brian looks over to me, and his face relaxes enough that I can tell he is letting the stress subside enough to move forward.

A line of sweat trickles down my spine. "Let's get the keys from Erika, then she will leave."

Brian doesn't say anything but pulls the key from the ignition and opens his door. When I open mine, I expect a blast of cooler air, but it is hot and filled with the smell of pine and dirt. The street is silent except for the cicadas buzzing like electrical wires.

The unit on the left looks vacant, with newspaper taped in the windows and an old toilet, and broken floor tiles piled on the porch. We step up to Erika, and I expect her to turn toward the door to let us inside, but she only shifts and shares her shade.

"Dale should be here any moment. He wants to meet you and bring the keys himself."

I assume she is talking about Dale Shaw of Elite Rentals LLC, the name written at the top of our rental agreement. A dark red truck with silver along the bottom pulls up to the curb along the side of the house. The truck's bed has a big cardboard box and several long strips of lumber sticking out above the tailgate with a red flag tied to the end.

A tall and handsome man in his fifties steps out. He looks

like one of those ex-high school football players who now has bad knees. He's balding with salt and pepper hair and a goatee.

"Dale!" Erika steps out of her shade to greet him with a hug. "Thank you so much for helping these kids."

Brian and I join them in the dirt yard.

"Nice to meet you." He holds his hand out to Brian, and he shakes it.

When he smiles, Dale has deep dimples and lines in the corners of his eyes.

"And you must be Emmy," he says with a wink.

"I'm happy to help. Both units are empty because I'm renovating. I'm sorry the one I'm putting you in isn't in the best shape, but it was the better of the two to begin with. I didn't expect to have anyone living here, but when Erika said you needed a place, I couldn't let her down." He keeps on talking and pulls a wad of keys from his pocket. "She's a tough lady to say no to. You're welcome to stay in unit two until I need to get in there. If you like it here, pay your rent on time, and don't bother the neighbors, we can move you over to unit one while I renovate the one I'm putting you in now."

"Thank you, sir," Brian says.

He raises his head and looks at Brian. His eyes crinkle when he smiles. "Dale," he says. "Dale is good enough."

He turns toward the little front porch, where an old metal chair is folded and propped next to the door, and opens his hand and plucks out two keys on a ring with a small manila tag tied to them.

"I haven't had a chance to clean this unit out, so that's why I'm giving you the first month free." Dale slides one of the keys into the lock and pauses. "You can keep anything the last family left and toss out the rest. If there are any big items you don't want, go ahead and put them in the yard of unit one, and I will have my crew haul it away."

He unlocks the door and hands the keys to me. On the tag in

blue ink and small print, it says Dobbs Ct. Unit #2. Dale steps aside and lets me enter first. The living room and kitchen are one big room divided by a counter and the back side of the kitchen cabinets. Straight through is a sliding glass door to the back yard with an air conditioner in the wall right next to it. Luckily, the floors are wood and not old and smelly carpet.

"What do you think?" Dale's voice echoes in the hollow of the empty room. He seems to be the sort of man who doesn't like quiet, so he fills it every chance he gets.

"This is great. Thank you." I reach out and take Brian's hand. Dale keeps apologizing for the condition of the unit, but it is much nicer than our house in Lodell. I squeeze Brian's hand, so he knows that I love him.

"The old tenants were clean, so it shouldn't be too bad," Dale says.

There's an old round kitchen table with three chairs and scraps of trash along the wall.

"This will be fine for us, thank you," Brian says. I can tell he just wants Dale and Erika to leave and give us room to breathe.

"The refrigerator and stove are old, but they work great. So does the air conditioner." Dale leads us down a hallway and points out a laundry room with no washer or dryer. "There's a washer in the next unit. I'll have my crew bring it over. I think I have a drier in my workshop. I'll make sure it works, then bring that over too."

He keeps referring to people as his crew, which I assume is a work crew, not a boat crew.

"This is the first bedroom," he says, waving his palm toward the open door.

First? We will have two bedrooms? I've never had so much space to do whatever I want. Brian's house was the first home I ever lived in without adults monitoring me and giving me a small space to call my own—like half of a bunk bed and half of a dresser. Which is funny since this is a duplex and half a house.

When I moved in with Brian, he already lived there, and I just settled in. This time, we can make a home together.

I peek into the first bedroom, littered with tiny pink and purple Polly Pocket accessories, some Shrek and Littlest Pet Shop Happy Meal toys, and a few mismatched little girl socks. We move down the hall, and Dale points out a bathroom with two doors. One opens into the hall, and the other must go to the master bedroom.

A loud thump comes from the kitchen. We all turn to look down the hall. Erika is not behind us.

"You alright in there?" Dale calls out.

"Just bringing a few things in," she says in her usual loud and cheery voice.

Brian tenses, and I squeeze his hand again. He gives me a little smile, then brings our hands up and kisses the top of mine.

"And here is the master. It's not that big, but it has a nice window that looks out to the back yard."

The rod has no curtain. I go to the window to look out. The back yard is divided in half by an old wooden fence. A trampoline sits in the back corner of our side. I always wanted a trampoline, but none of my foster families ever had one.

"I can have that taken out if you want," Dale says.

"No," I answer before Brian has a chance. "I would love to keep it here."

"It's all yours then." Dale smiles and gives me a wink.

When we return to the kitchen and living room area, the air conditioner blows dusty air full blast into the room. Erika enters the front door with a box so big it bumps into the door frame.

Brian hurries over to her. "Here, let me help."

He takes it from her and sets it on the little round table that is now filled with two more boxes.

"I have a couple more. Will you give me a hand?"

We all follow her to the back of her Jeep, where she hands

me a blow-up mattress and a folded pile of sheets. Brian and Dale take the last two boxes and turn toward the house.

"Where did all this come from?"

"Most of it is from Sophie's House, which is a place that takes donations to help families in need."

I try to keep the tears down and smile up at Erika. "When I set these down, I'm giving you a hug."

She answers back with a huge smile. "I'll take it."

Once everything is in, Dale asks Brian for a hand unloading the back of his truck into the other unit. When the men walk out, Erika and I unload the boxes onto the counter. There are pots and pans, dishes and silverware, cleaning supplies, toilet paper, paper towels, bath towels, canned and boxed food, and all the things we need to get started on our own.

After the boxes are empty, Erika breaks them down, then hands me a roll of paper towels and a bottle of Windex. "You better clean those cabinets before you put your new stuff in them."

I smile, and when I turn away, the tears start streaming down my face. My insides are all jumbled up. I am happy to have the help, but at the same time, I don't want to need it. Amber and I tried to escape the system, but it keeps sucking me back in.

When Brian and Dale return, I am still wiping out the cabinets and breathing in the smell of Windex and dirt.

"I'm going to head out," Dale says. "It was nice meeting you, Emmy. And Brian, if you want to make a little extra money, you can help my crew next door."

He leaves and pulls the door shut behind him.

"Oh," Erika says. "I almost forgot...I talked to Faye Strickland."

She must see the confused look on my face because she adds that Faye and her husband Kerry own the Railroad Inn.

"Rowena is just not working out for them, and Jocelyn wants the night shift again. If you want the day shift, it is yours."

"At the front desk?"

"Yes," Erika smiles. "You'll work with Faye. She likes someone dedicated to the front desk so she can do the paperwork and manage the motel and employees. You will love Faye. You interested?"

It feels like I am filled with a million tiny bubbles, and I want to jump up and down. I look over to Brian to see what he thinks before I answer. We are a team now and need to make decisions together. He gives me a smile like he is proud of me.

"Yes, I'm interested," I say and hug her.

"One more thing," Erika says and heads back out the door.

When she returns, she is carrying a bouquet of flowers in a blue glass vase shaped like a bubble of water. "You need something colorful for your new home."

Brian and I spend the rest of the day getting settled. I make us a box of mac & cheese for lunch and a can of beef stew and creamed corn for dinner. We put everything away, and our mattress is blown up with the bottom sheet and the thin bedspread over it. Brian draped the top sheet over the curtain rod for some privacy. We don't have pillows, so we added those to our list.

The sun sets and turns the sky orange, and we head out to the trampoline to lie on it and wait for the stars.

I rest my head on Brian's shoulder and feel like I can breathe for the first time in weeks...no days. It feels like weeks, but it has only been a few days since our life was turned upside down.

"What was Skid like as a boy? Did he show any signs that he could do this?"

"No. I never thought he would have the balls to do anything like this. He's always been a bit of a dumbshit and an ass-kisser."

"Did he ever do anything creepy?"

"Skid is obsessed with the river. He was very close with his grandfather, who died while fly fishing. Skid found him floating in the river. I never really thought about it until now, but ever since, he has a fascination with dead things he finds in the water or along the bank.

Brian is quiet for a long time, and we both lie there looking up at the stars. We must have fallen asleep because when I open my eyes, it is dark, and the sky is filled with stars.

"You awake?" I ask, and Brian gives me a mumbled *mmm hmm.*

A rumble comes from the alley between our back yard and the houses on the street behind us. It is going slow, and its headlights become brighter and brighter until they light up the leaves of the tree in the other half of the yard. As it moves forward, each slat in the fence glows with light.

"We need to put a lock on that gate," Brian says.

The truck moves past the back fence, turns onto Juniper, and slips slat by slat along the side fence until it gets to the corner and stops. It idles on the corner of Juniper and Dobbs for a long time before the engine shuts off.

"Do you think that is a deputy coming to check on us?"

"No," Brian says. "That sounds like an old pickup."

A creaky truck door opens, then another. Brian sits up. The doors slam shut, and it sounds like footsteps on dirt, not the road. Brian scoots to the end of the trampoline.

"Stay here," he whispers before he hops off.

He starts toward the side fence, and I climb down to follow. There is no way in hell I am being left alone or leaving him to face anything by himself. He is halfway to the fence when someone pounds on our front door. Brian peeks over and turns toward me.

"Shit!" Even in the moonlight, I can see his face is drained of color. "It's Jake."

14

———

HIM

The willows and grasses glow in the morning light, and a fine mist rises from the surface of the water. Three deer drop their heads to drink on the opposite bank as birds trill in the pines. My flesh shivers, and my head throbs with the rhythm of my heart. Once the river and I are one, the pain of the flesh will be gone.

A lone fly fisherman in tan waders and black fingerless gloves makes his way down the dirt path next to the bar. He sets a small red cooler and camo backpack beside a boulder and wades into my waters, up to his knees. I lie still in the willows with my cheek resting in my palm, and he does not see me. His rod is rigged with a San Juan worm, and he has a wooden trout net hanging down his back. He pauses to read the water and looks for seams and where the fish may be holding. He comes with piety and respect.

Most people come to the river in ignorance. They come without honor or appreciation, only for entertainment or a thrill. I take their phones, hats, and shoes when they come without offerings to appease me. Sometimes, I flip their rafts and spill their bodies into my raging waters. All they need to do is respect me, but they do not.

With their unbalanced belief in science, the ignorant only see my bare elements and deny the spirit within me. Occasionally, someone will come to my banks to pray, burn their incense, or wade into me naked to let my cool fluid run across their skin. They know that the river gives life and takes life. They are devout and take the time to observe and respect.

When the fisherman wades upstream to find a nice riffle for his fly, he leaves his cooler and backpack as an offering. Even in my flesh, the river provides for me.

Inside the cooler are two homemade sandwiches in Ziplock baggies, thick with deli meat, a red and white can of Coke, two dark long-neck bottles of Hefeweizen, and large navel orange. I take one of the sandwiches and the Coke.

Through the willows and grass, I watch him stand thigh-deep in my waters. As he casts upstream, I unzip his backpack and empty it. I take my offerings of a t-shirt, camo baseball cap, granola bar, and old tennis shoes with a clean pair of socks rolled and tucked into one. After putting on his cap, shirt, and shoes, I stuff the sandwich and Coke inside the backpack and slide my arms into the loops. His gifts will be rewarded, and the fish will be plentiful.

I slip downstream, away from the fisherman, and step up onto the deck of the outfitters. The piles of yellow, blue, red, and orange kayaks, rafts, and paddleboards will provide cover. The button on top of the baseball cap rubs against a lump on my head, but I cannot let anyone see who I am, for I am the river, and the river must flow free. I take a bite of the sandwich to nurture my flesh.

Halfway through my meal, two big doors at the back of the shop swing open, and a longhaired dude in cargo shorts and a tie-dyed t-shirt steps out. His shirt has a peace sign with mountains and a giant pine tree inside it.

He is startled when he sees me. Does he recognize my face from the news?

"Dude!" he says, half laughing. "You scared the shit out of me."

"Sorry." I take another bite of the sandwich and try to keep my hands from trembling.

"It's all good. You hiking the PCT?"

It takes me a moment to realize he is talking about the Pacific Crest Trail. It starts at the border of California and Mexico and goes all the way across the tops of the Sierra Nevada and Cascade ranges, and eventually ends in Washington at the Canadian border. I nod my head as I swallow my bite.

He runs his hand through his hair. "Cool! I've always wanted to do that. I've hiked portions of it, but I want to thru-hike it. You heading into Rockland or returning to the trail?"

I need to get higher into the mountains, to my headwaters. "Back to the trail. You know anyone who can give me a ride?"

"Dude…I can do it. I'm heading up to Hosmer Lake as soon as my kayakers get here. I pass right by Elk Lake."

"That would be great. Thanks." The guy's face lights up as if I am doing him a favor. He must sense who I am to my core and does not judge me in the flesh.

"Can you help me throw the kayaks on the trailer? The other guides aren't here yet."

I agree and follow him through the shop that is filled with t-shirts, sunscreen, and water shoes. As I pass by a rack, I grab a pair of sunglasses and slip them into my pocket. A girl with long blond hair twisted up into a messy bun comes in the front door. "Sorry I'm late. Long night." She ignores me and heads straight toward the checkout counter.

Her hair is more of a pearl than a golden blonde. A black choker necklace encompasses her throat, and it has a silver triangle charm that sits right in the V of her collarbone.

"That's Heidi. She's not rude, just scattered. By the way, I'm Zack."

I do not give my name. The store reminds me of Rimrock Outfitters, where I am a...where I *was* a guide. I know I cannot return. It is time to shed that life and transcend.

I follow Zack outside to a white church van with Riverbend Kayak Adventures in big blue letters. He turns toward me with his big smile. "What's your name?"

When I don't answer him, his eyebrows arch up, and he gets an understanding smile. "Oh yeah...what's your trail name?"

"River," I say.

As soon as we finish loading the kayaks, a silver Volvo pulls into the parking lot with a young couple in shorts and water sandals. I get into the van's back seat while Zack talks with them.

Once they load in and pull onto the road, Zack cranks *The Sweet Escape* on the radio. The woman's long auburn hair whips around in the wind from her open window. It flies around the interior of the van and wraps around the back of her seat. Several tendrils stream out the window like they want to be free. The sunlight makes them look almost bronze or caramel, but my bet would be auburn.

I need to replace my hair color charts. Mine are probably in evidence with the FBI. Her hair would be perfect for one of my flies. Maybe a caddisfly or a stonefly. I reach for it. She must sense my intentions because she gathers her hair in her hands and pulls it back into the front seat with her.

She knows me. Some women have strong intuition, almost psychic. They are the ones who shrink away from my power. Maybe they all have it but do not trust it. This one, her name is Alyssa, has it strong. When we loaded into the van, her boyfriend headed for the front passenger seat by the guide, but she took hold of his arm and whispered something in his ear.

He glanced over at me. He did not look concerned, but he let her have the front seat.

In my hat and sunglasses, they cannot recognize me from the news. She just feels me and my power. She knows I am the river, and I take what I want. I may follow them to Hosmer Lake and wait for her to be alone so I can pull her under.

The first stage of drowning is shock. Her blue-green eyes will widen, and her lips will part, then clamp shut. Involuntary breath-holding is the second stage, and she will try to prevent my water from entering her lungs. The third stage is unconsciousness, then hypoxic convulsions, and finally, death. She will be mine forever. I will strip her bare, run my mouth over her tits and enter her.

"Dude!"

An elbow taps me on the arm. I look over at the man next to me. I didn't catch his name, and I do not care. A thick black seatbelt runs across his chest, and behind him, out the window, is a stationary wooden building. We have stopped.

"Dude!" The voice is not the man next to me this time. His lips are shut and curving up into an amused smile.

The driver is talking. Zack. It is Zack, the guide in the peace sign t-shirt. He has a big smile. "Dude! You were totally zoning out. We're here at Elk Lake."

The girl continues to stare straight forward and does not turn around. I want to see her face one more time, but I am denied.

"Thanks for the ride." I unclasp my seatbelt and open the door. Once I am out, I reach in and take hold of my backpack.

"How are you hiking the Pacific Crest Trail with that day pack?" Alyssa's boyfriend asks.

I look up into his face. Why is he questioning me? I don't owe him an explanation, but I cannot let them suspect me. What if they watch the news tonight? "I left my gear with a friend here."

"Cool, cool." He nods at me, and Zack flashes me a giant smile.

They make a U-turn on the dirt road and drive away with two yellow kayaks and a red one on the trailer behind them. They kick up a trail of dust, and once it settles, I turn toward the lake.

Cars pack the parking lot that ends at a marina with small sailboats tethered to the dock. People swarm everywhere in bathing suits and shorts. They go in and out of a restaurant or stand in line at a walk-up window that sells ice cream. A black and white husky sits in the driver's seat of a blue SUV with a terrier mix in the back that yelps out an open window.

Elk Lake is deep blue and surrounded by ponderosa and lodgepole pines—with the snow-covered peaks of South Sisters and Mount Bachelor on the far side. Sailboats line the docks, and a cabana rents out kayaks. The wind blows ripples across the lake that is dotted with orange and yellow kayaks whose paddles sweep through the air in irregular loops. A toddler in a saggy diaper and floaties wobbles along the shore with a yellow bucket.

I am drying up in the dirt and the air. I need to submerge myself in the water and soak it in. This lake will sustain me until I can get to my source at Little Lava Lake. It is not far. I feel it. Once I reach it, I will be reborn.

"Hermit, Hermit," some girl calls out behind me.

A gray Trailblazer backs a small sailboat down the boat ramp. The mast is so high it brushes the branches of the trees and causes pine needles to rain down into the boat.

"Hermit..." The sound comes right behind me, and a hand touches my arm.

I flinch and turn around. A girl stands there, and her eyes pop open. She retracts her hand. "Oh, my God. I'm sorry. You look just like someone I know."

Her short brown hair curls up on the ends beneath a red

bandana, and she hugs a medium-sized Priority Mail box. Her hair looks dark chocolate—maybe good for tying into an elk hair caddisfly or an Adams dry fly. A strip of pink packing tape with white stars is wrapped around the middle of her box with *HOLD FOR PCT HIKER. ETA: LATE AUGUST* written in sharpie in the corner.

"I can't believe how much you look like Hermit. You could be brothers. Is he your brother? I was hoping we would meet up here. He went off on his own and left the bubble of hikers behind him. Some people are loners and want to meditate on their hike. Well, that's him."

Her lips keep on moving. I should hold her beneath the surface and let my waters fill her with something of substance.

"I just got my resupply box," she says. "It has my organic and homemade dehydrated Thai Curry Chicken and Rice that he almost died over. Not literally. He loved it. I made all my own organic food from scratch before I left and put it in shipping boxes. It is so nice to have food that is good fuel for my body, and I don't have to depend on pre-made foods at the trail towns."

Her tits are bigger, and her waist is thicker than I prefer, but it is time to replenish my nymphs, and I need to be open to what is provided for me and be grateful.

"Hermit may have already gone through. What about you? Are you a hiker? My trail name is *Yapper*. I'm sure you can tell why. I just can't help myself. I'm a people person."

She finally clamps her lips shut and looks up at me like she is expecting an answer to her shitload of questions.

"I'm just here for a swim. If I see anyone who looks like me, I will let him know you're looking for him."

She turns her head and locks her eyes on a group of three girls with their hair wrapped up in towels like they just came from the showers.

"Thank you. Nice meeting you," Yapper says. She takes three

steps toward the girls and then turns back. "If you're still here around dinner, stop by my tent, and I'll feed you. It's the white one with the lime green hammock."

"Maybe I will," I say. She smiles and scampers off toward the girls with her thick legs and tight ass.

I am still in the flesh to fulfill my fate. I cannot deny my destiny or ignore the gifts bestowed upon me.

15

———

EMMY

BRIAN AND I STAND IN OUR EMPTY LIVING ROOM, HESITANT TO open the door. My throat feels so tight I cannot even swallow the air.

Jake is on the other side, pounding with the side of his fist. "Open the door, Brian. I know you're in there."

"Should I grab a knife?" I whisper.

"He's not going to hurt me."

He may not hurt Brian, but that does not mean he will not attack Brian. I've seen the two of them go at it in our house in Lodell. It was like the clash of the titans. Their bodies slammed against the wall and flipped furniture as things crashed to the floor.

Brian braces himself, ready to block a blow, then reaches for the door knob.

Crap! We have nothing to defend ourselves with besides Brian's fists and dull thrift store knives.

When Brian opens the door, it is not only to Jake's round mutton-chop face. Standing beside him with a fake smile is Rose. She looks so much like Skid that my heart freezes mid-beat, and I feel sick.

Brian stands in the crack of the door with one hand on the inside knob, and the other gripped on the doorframe.

"What's up, dude?" Jake asks with a flat expression. "Nice place."

"How did you find us?"

"What? I didn't know you're in witness protection now." Jake lets out a harsh laugh.

Brian doesn't answer, and he doesn't move. The muscles in his arms are tight as he grips the door.

"We just want to talk," Rose says.

"Go ahead." Brian does not budge.

"Can we come in?" Rose asks in a sarcastic tone like Brian is the one with the problem.

Brian thinks for a moment, then steps aside. They enter and look around at our empty place. Jake has a look of amusement, like we are silly children who have run away from home. "You going to offer us a place to sit?"

"You're capable of figuring it out." Brian clenches his teeth so hard the muscles in his jaw bulge out.

"Calm down, you two. Stop trying to piss all over each other," Rose says.

Rose wears a tight yellow tank top and blue tennis skirt, always showing off her boob job. Jake goes to the little round table, takes two of the chairs, puts them in the middle of the living room, and holds his hand out for his Aunt Rose to sit down. Jake sits in the other while Brian and I remain standing.

"Can you get me a cup of water?" Rose asks and glares directly at me. Her hard-ass glare always intimidates everyone around her, including me. It is hard to believe that she had a heart big enough to raise Brian when his mom died.

On my way to the sink, I open the silverware drawer, grab a steak knife, and slip it into my pocket. I don't know what I'll do with it, but I feel better just having it.

"You don't seem very appreciative," Rose says.

"Thank you for the attorney." Brian's voice is low and deep. "And for posting my bail."

I open the cupboard to our new mismatched dishes and take out an old mustard yellow Tupperware cup that probably came from an estate sale.

"I'm not just talking about now," Rose says.

I fill her cup until the water runs over the rim. I pour a bit out without wiping down the sides.

"Russ and I took you in when your mom died. What would have happened to you if we didn't?"

I return with the water. Brian stands there with his head down and does not say a word. Rose and Jake sit in the chairs in the middle of the room with pissed-off expressions.

"I treated you like my own son." Rose takes the water from me, inspects the cup, and sets it on her knee without taking a drink.

Brian continues to stare at the floor. I can't imagine how scary Rose must have been when he was a child.

"You fucking turned me in for something I didn't do," Jake says. "Friends don't do that kind of bullshit."

Brian finally looks up and glares at Jake. We all know that he is full of crap. Typical Jake. He never admits to anything. He is the golden boy—the only child of Doc Unger. Jake gets a free ride wherever he wants to go. His daddy bought him Rimrock Outfitters and several rental homes in Lodell...as well as an all-expenses paid trip to the university each year.

"You need to tell them you lied," Rose says to Brian.

Brian looks her in the eye for the first time.

"You lied about Jake date-raping girls, and you don't remember anything about that day with Dylan except that he slipped into the river and you saved him," Rose says. "That's your story."

"They found the girl in the house with him," Brian says.

"You could have put her there."

"Skid tried to rape Emmy."

Rose looks over at me and raises her eyebrows. "And you believe her? She has done nothing but lie and drag her drama into town."

"You need to leave." Brian walks to the door and opens it.

"Good luck with a public defender." Jake stands and steps close to Brian. "You'll be the only one going to jail. There's no proof I did anything. There's not a single report from a girl. Nobody claimed to be raped. Not one. Do you have their names? Their addresses?"

"I know you did it, and you know you did it," Brian says.

"Bullshit. I didn't do anything. You may have, but I don't know anything about that...or maybe I do. You already admitted you date-raped a girl, so all I need to do is give them a few stories about all your middle-of-the-night walks and what you were really doing."

Brian's entire body tenses, and he looks like he's going to throw a punch. He does not say a word but stares Jake down. Brian needs to tell Jake that he is full of shit. He needs to deny it, but he doesn't.

Rose puts her hand on Jake's shoulder and moves him away from Brian. "Think about it," Rose says. "Talk to Sheldon Tate and let him explain your options. If you agree to tell the Sheriff's department you lied, Sheldon will represent you. If not, you're on your own."

Jake gives Brian a very self-satisfied smile before he turns and steps out the door. At the edge of the porch, he turns back. "And you will owe us ten-thousand dollars we paid for your bail."

Rose slides past Brian and out the door.

"Tell Erin I said hi," I call to the back of Jake's head.

He stops and turns to glare at me. "Fuck you."

Tiny shivers of happiness ripple over my skin. Erin finally left Jake. Maybe more people than we know believe Brian.

Brian stands in the doorway and watches them walk to Jake's jacked-up silver truck. The engine turns over and rumbles like it is trying to catch its breath. That is the same truck that pulled up to Amber and me when we were about to turn around and not go to Lodell. Rose now sits in the passenger seat where Brian sat the first time I laid eyes on him. I knew at that moment that Brian was my person. As Jake makes a U-turn, his headlights scan across the houses and trees of our new neighborhood until they drive past our duplex. We watch until their taillights turn bright red, and Jake turns left down the back alley.

Brian shuts the door and presses his forehead against the wood. I want to wrap my arms around him and tell him we will make it through this, but I have no idea how. I think about Brian's middle-of-the-night walks and what he was really doing. I can't remember how many times I woke up, and his side of the bed was empty, or I heard him slide out and pull some clothes on to leave me alone in our bed.

16

———

HIM

Her campsite is easy to find with the white tent and green hammock, but she is not there. I wait in the trees and watch a giant swarm of gnats. The angled light catches their wings and reveals their erratic dance through the air. Little black birds flit around, and squirrels scamper from tree to tree. Once the night comes and stars fill in the dark gaps between the treetops, murmurs of conversations come from other sites—both male and female.

At one of the small cabins, a man lights a giant campfire with something combustible. It blares and lights up the side of a SUV and a picnic table filled with people. They get louder and louder as they play Yahtzee and fill the campground with the sound of dice shaking in a cup, over and over, that erupts in laughter and screams.

Yapper finally emerges from another campsite and squats down to unzip her tent. I step toward her and pine needles crunch beneath my feet. She pauses and looks toward me into the dark trees. I stop. She glances around, then climbs in and zips her tent shut.

A light clicks on inside, and I watch her silhouette sort and organize her stuff. She pulls off her shirt. The outline of her tits bounce as she wriggles her shorts down her hips. Adrenaline courses through my veins and reenergizes me. Her lamp clicks off, and I step forward past her hammock.

"Hello? Is someone out there?"

"It's me. You invited me to dinner."

"Oh…" Her voice is filled with excitement. "Just a minute."

She shuffles around inside. The zipper finally rises, and her head pokes out. Without her bandana, her hair is full and wavy.

"I didn't think you would come. Give me a minute." She clicks the light on again, and like a shadow dancer, she gets dressed.

She comes out with her pack and food box. "I'm so glad you decided to come. I thought you would be back home by now. Do you live in Rockland? I don't know the other towns around here."

She digs out a small hiking stove. "I have some homemade granola bars with nuts and some turkey jerky we can have for appetizers."

"That will be great," I say. "I'm starving."

She assembles and ignites her backpacking stove—not as graceful and delicate as most of my nymphs, but she will do. In death, all bodies move with the rhythm of the water.

"Ever go skinny dipping?" I ask.

She sets a small pot on top of the burner and glances up at me with a sly smile. "It's my favorite way to swim."

17

———

ASHLEY

"Kɪᴀ," I ᴄᴀʟʟ ᴅᴏᴡɴ ᴛʜᴇ ʜᴀʟʟᴡᴀʏ. "Hᴇʟᴘ ʏᴏᴜʀ sɪsᴛᴇʀs ɢᴇᴛ ɪɴᴛᴏ their bathing suits."

I lay out four slices of bread and scoop out a knife full of creamy peanut butter. I like chunky, but my girls hate the bits in their sandwiches and spit them out like I put rocks in there.

Oreo, our border collie mix, runs around all hyper and excited. I don't know how, but he knows we are headed out, and he gets to come with us. I haven't even taken his leash from the laundry room, but he knows and turns in circles at the front door.

The girls and I need to get out of the house and do something fun. School shopping was like herding cats, and now the girls need to get their energy out.

"Stop," Kia whines. "Mommy, make her stop. She won't let me help. That's her old swimsuit. It's too small and goes up the crack of her behind."

Calista prances into the living room in her tiny swimsuit so low on her chest that it doesn't cover her nipples and the butterfly bandage is beginning to lift at the corner of her eye. Calista hugs her Baby Kristy doll that wears the bathing suit she

104

should be wearing. It is so baggy that the crotch hangs lower than the doll's feet.

"I'll take care of it," I tell Kia. "Can you finish making the sandwiches? All they need is the jelly, then cut them in half. Put half a sandwich in each baggy.

I step into the living room and look down at Calista. "Maybe you and Baby Kristy can trade bathing suits."

"I want to wear *my* swimsuit," Calista says.

"You're getting to be a big girl, and it doesn't fit you anymore."

"I don't want to wear Kia's old bathing suit. I want to wear *my* bathing suit."

I can't do this alone. Chris was so good with the girls, and they listened to him.

I take a deep breath and blow it out. The big family photo we took just before Chris died hangs on the wall, surrounded by all the framed snapshots of us and the picture of Chris in his yellow shirt and silver hardhat.

Please, Chris...I need you to help me raise our girls. I cannot even get them out the door today. I try to think how he would have handled this. I take another breath and try to remain calm.

I lean back on the couch like I have all the time in the world. "Okay, do as you please, but we are not going to the lake until you are in the bathing suit that fits you."

Calista was only three when she lost her daddy. Only Kia remembers him. I got pregnant with Carina four days before he died. I should frame and hang more photos of Chris with the girls so they can see how much he loved them.

Calista has not moved.

I shake my head at her. "That's fine. We don't need to go anywhere. Maybe we can stay home and get the apartment all nice and clean."

She stands there, not knowing what to say for thirty seconds, then opens her mouth. "I don't want to clean."

"That's up to you. I want to go to the lake with the ice cream window."

"Can I get a rainbow one?"

"Yes, and I bet there are lots of ducks. You can feed them your sandwich crust. Oreo is excited for you to throw his ball into the water so he can fetch it. He will be sad if we don't go."

Calista furrows her eyebrows and presses her lips together in a pout when she strips off her bathing suit and trades with her baby doll.

Twenty minutes later, we are all situated in the car with Kia strapped in the back between Carina's car seat and Calista's booster. Oreo sits up front with his head out the window. When we hit the Cascade Lakes Highway to Elk Lake, the wind blows Oreo's ears back and flaps his lips into a ridiculous smile.

18

HIM

YAPPER'S MOUTH OPENS IN A SCREAM THAT RISES AND BUBBLES TO
the surface—flat and muffled. She thrashes, but I pin her
beneath the surface with my arms and knees. I prefer to spare
my nymphs of the fear and let them sink into eternity in peace,
but I have nothing to sedate her.

Moonlight shimmers across the lake and illuminates the
black outlines of Mount Bachelor, Broken Top, and South Sister
in a quiet beauty that sings to my soul in an ancient earthborn
hymn. I feel the earth calling to me to fulfill my destiny so that I
may become one.

When her muscles relax, I dip my face into the water, put my
mouth to hers, and take in her last exhalation. Her convulsions
cease. She is free and sinks into death.

The lake is so quiet and still that I hear the distant crackle of
logs on a fire and the tussle of wind in the forest boughs behind
me. We will all return to the earth, either through water or in
the soil. I envy Yapper in her peace and silence, one with the
lake, the moon, and the stars.

Her hair is shorter than I like, but I wind a lock of it around my fingers until the tips become numb, and I pull them from her scalp.

19

———

EMMY

UP AHEAD IS THE RETRO RAILROAD INN SIGN, LIKE ONE OF THOSE from the nineteen-fifties. Its giant yellow arrow points down like a limp dick with *Be Our Guest* written across it, and *We're Open* on the tip. Brian pulls into the parking lot and turns the steering wheel with the palm of his hand until we stop in a spot near the lobby.

We sit in the car while the air conditioner blows out a musty smell that gets warmer the longer we sit. Brian puts both hands on the wheel with a blank stare out the front window. He wants to say something, but he apparently won't. Two farm boys in camo t-shirts and cowboy hats come out of one of the rooms.

"Are you okay?" I ask.

He slowly turns his head toward me, and I cannot stand the look in his eyes. I have never seen Brian so defeated. When he was a river guide, he was free and doing what he loved. He could face any whitewater and know he would bring himself and his customers safely through. Now, he sits here, out of his environment, all because of Jake and Skid. They think they can do anything to whoever they want just because they are Ungers.

Brian lets out a gush of air just as the two farm boys pass by the front window of our car. "I don't know what to do."

"About what?"

"What do you think?"

"I don't know. Are you talking about this instant? Or overall, with the court crap?"

"The court crap. The Ungers. Us."

Us? Before I can ask what he means, Brian shuts the engine off. "You better go in. It's not good to be late on your first day."

The sun blares through the windows, but I can't move. The car heats up, and a line of sweat drips down my cheek. I love Brian so much it hurts, but I'm half afraid he will drop me off, pack up all his shit, and take off. "What are your plans for today?"

"Got to look for work."

I don't know why he turned the engine off. Maybe he wants to sweat me out of the car. I open my door and glance back before I step out. He stares at me with a flat expression.

"I love you," I say.

His lips form into a slight smile, and he gives a single nod but does not say it back. It feels like Brian has my heart in his hand and squeezes it so tight it will burst. I want to beg him to reassure me and to tell me how much he loves me, but that will sound needy. Neediness pushes people away. Neediness will land my ass on the curb, so I shut the car door, and Brian starts the engine.

He stares at me through the window with his eyebrows pinched together. I turn toward the lobby door and hear him back out of the parking spot behind me.

A sob catches in my chest, and I try to keep it down. I need this job. When I open the door, the smells of popcorn and tropical air freshener make me nauseous. I turn to look one more time and catch the back of our tan-colored grandpa car turning onto the highway.

The neon red open sign still sputters, but not as vivid in the light. I don't know how I will function today.

A lady steps out from the back office to the desk. Her medium brown hair is pulled back into a tight bun. "You must be Emmy." She looks to be in her forties with a kind face and smooth skin. There is something Russian about her features, but she doesn't have an accent.

"Are you Faye?" I make myself smile.

"I am," she says. "Erika highly recommended you and said you have hotel experience."

"I do, but not behind the desk. I was a housekeeper."

"Oh…" her smile drops. "I need a front desk clerk. Would you rather clean rooms?"

"No!" I say a bit too forceful. "Sorry, I didn't intend for that to come out like that. I am excited to work at the front desk."

"Good." Her smile returns, but she looks down at my legs. "Do you have any dress slacks?"

"No. I have a skirt that Erika brought me. I wore it to court."

"The skirt is fine. We usually wear dress slacks or trousers. Jeans won't cut it. Come back and pick out a couple of shirts."

I follow her into the back office and recognize the brown recliner that Rowena slept in the night Erika brought me here. A horrible vision of Rowena's bright red shirt and tan pants flashes through my mind. Please, not another ugly uniform. At the Whitehorse Inn in Lodell, I had to wear a disgusting polyester dress that was dark blue with a white collar, cuffs, and apron—and of course, a name tag. The housekeepers here at least look comfortable in purple hospital scrubs.

Faye sits at a desk with a giant painting of a train chugging through the old west behind it.

"Have a seat." She points at a chair in front of her desk then swivels her chair around to a stack of cardboard boxes. Their lids are folded instead of taped. She pulls open the top one, then folds it shut again before taking it from the stack and dropping it to the floor.

The faint sound of a train in the distance makes it feel like the painting has come to life. It gets louder as Faye digs through the next box, and I half wonder if the sound is piped in through some speakers. "Are there tracks nearby?"

She pops her head up and turns toward me. "What?"

"Train tracks. Is that a real train?"

"Yes." She smiles big. "Isn't it wonderful? I love trains. They give me a feeling of the past, when this land was rugged. The depot used to be just behind the motel. That's how it got the name and why the lobby is decorated like a fancy old west hotel."

I would say more like an old west whorehouse, but my only references are the movies I've watched. Framed photos of her and a bald man hang all over a side wall. There is a large professional photo of them by a river and several taken all over the world. One is with the Grand Canyon behind them, and another with the Golden Gate Bridge. I recognize the Eiffel Tower and the Leaning Tower of Pisa. Another photo shows them on camels with pyramids behind them.

"Is that your husband?"

Faye looks up toward the wall and smiles. "Yes, his name is Kerry."

Faye stands up and lifts the box from the stack.

"Do you have any kids?"

Her smile fades away, and she plops the box on the edge of her desk. "Find your size in here while I find the button-ups."

I should have known better than to ask. Obviously, they don't have kids or their photos would be plastered all over the room. The box is filled with burgundy polo shirts. An exact likeness of the motel sign, including the limp arrow, is stitched onto the left side of the chest. I'm usually a woman's small, but sometimes a medium. "Are these men's sizes or women's?" It is hard to tell with polo shirts.

"Those are women's. I hate it when women are made to wear men's styles. They try to get around it by calling them unisex, but they are really designed for a man's body. Women's bodies are shaped like hourglasses, and men are shaped like sausages, so they are fooling nobody but cheap people who only want to buy one style for everyone."

I lift a small out and ask if I can try it on.

Faye points me to a closed door at the back of the office. "That's the employee bathroom."

The sound of the oncoming train vibrates the linoleum and porcelain in the tiny bathroom. It reminds me of Lodell and the life Brian and I had in his tiny bachelor house. We would cuddle in the nest of our bed, skin to skin, and listen to the train chug through town. Back then, Brian stroked my cheek like I was the most precious thing in the world to him…nothing like his face staring at me from the car this morning.

The shirt fits and makes my boobs look bigger than they are. It also comes in at the waist, hourglass instead of sausage-shaped, as Faye called it. I take it off, pull my t-shirt back on, and head back into Faye's office.

A different box sits on top of her desk. She pulls out a gray long-sleeve button-up and turns toward me. "It didn't fit?"

"I need a medium." I have no desire to stand behind the front desk in a tight shirt and being hit on by every asshole who thinks I am fair game just because he is a customer.

Faye puts her hand on the middle stack of polo shirts. "These are medium. Help yourself."

A high-pitched ding-dong comes from the lobby.

"That's the entry alert, so you know someone came in. It helps if you're here alone," Faye says as she heads toward the front desk. "There's nothing worse than coming out of the bathroom to someone at the desk, staring at you."

I'm not sure what to do, so I follow Faye to the lobby. A young deputy in a tan shirt, green khakis, and a black bulletproof vest stands in the middle of the lobby. He holds onto the neckline of his vest like he is trying to keep it from choking him. He looks to be in his late twenties and already losing some hair. His hairline looks like the beginning of McDonald's Golden Arches…except dark brown.

"Hey, Jesse," Faye says. "Everything okay?"

"Yep," he says.

Faye waits for him to say something more, but he just stands there and looks around like he is casing the lobby. I know he is here because of me, but I don't say a word.

"You need a room?" Faye asks in a humorous voice that sounds a bit sarcastic.

His eyes squint, and his mouth forms a perfect rectangle when he smiles. "Just checking to see if everything is okay here."

"I appreciate that," Faye says. "Any chance you can ask the Sheriff to send plainclothes deputies and unmarked cars? I don't want customers to think we have problems here."

"I will, ma'am."

"Ma'am?" Faye lets out a laugh. "How's your momma? I heard she wasn't feeling well."

"She's fine. Her blood sugar went low and we had to call an ambulance, but she was fine once they got it back up."

After they discuss all their family members and their health, Deputy Wright leaves the lobby with another high ding-dong of the door chime. Faye tells me to change into my new polo shirt or button-up, then she will train me. When I come out of the bathroom, both boxes of shirts are packed up and back on the floor. Faye sits on the edge of her desk with a look on her face. It is not an angry expression, but a motherly, *we need to talk* sort of look.

"I don't know what your situation is, but I assume it is domestic violence. That is why Erika brings women and children to our motel, and why we give her a discount. I also noticed that a man dropped you off this morning."

"You saw us?" Brian did not park in front of the lobby windows.

Faye turns her computer screen toward me. There are ten squares of videos. Two of the stairwells, two with different angles of the parking lot, four down the corridors of rooms, one that looks like it is in an alley behind the motel, and one of the front lobby with an empty front desk. The back of a man in shorts and flip-flops disappears from one frame, then appears in a stairwell video. He carries a duffle bag in one hand and a small cooler in the other.

Video surveillance? I wonder how many times she watched me when I stayed here. She knew when Brian got out and when deputies sat in the parking lot to keep me safe.

"It is none of my business as long as you don't bring your problems here. But I also feel a sense of responsibility woman-to-woman. An abuser does not change. An abuser does not get better the longer you know them. It usually gets worse once you have children because it is harder to get away."

The pit of my stomach churns. "Erika didn't tell you why she brought me here?"

"She can't. There are privacy issues."

"That's not what's happening. Brian has never abused me."

Her lips form a tight line, and I can tell she doesn't believe me. She knows I stayed the night here alone and then showed up in a police car with Brian. I need this job. I have no idea what would happen if I told her that I escaped a serial killer, and he is after me. Or that a prominent family wants me to keep my mouth shut and is willing to destroy me.

"He hasn't." I look directly into her eyes. "I promise."

"Alright." She gives me a sad smile like she has heard it a million times. "If you ever need anything from me, please ask. Kerry and I have made it our mission to help women and children. Even if you just need a little advice, I hope you will learn to trust me and ask."

"Thank you," is all that I say.

We go out to the front desk, where there is a computer with a black keyboard. A container with pens and a candy dish with red and white individually wrapped peppermints sits out for customers.

Faye slides a typed list over to me. "These are your responsibilities. We will go over them one by one. For the first week, we will work together, and you can take on more and more each day as you feel comfortable. Go ahead and read through them, so you have the big picture before we start going into detail."

It's nice to have a list, so I know what is expected. At the Whitehorse Inn, they threw me in with Mary. It was full immersion, sink or swim. Most of the time, all I could do was tread water.

The door chimes again, and an older man in a t-shirt and dirty jeans walks in with some newspapers.

"Morning, Faye," he says. "You got a new girl?"

He has scraggly gray hair, big wire-rimmed glasses, and a mouth full of bright white teeth.

"This is Emmy," Faye says. "Today is her first day. Emmy, this is Herb. He brings the paper for us every day and will come once a week to collect payment."

"You already got sick of Rowena?" Herb asks. "Don't know why you gave her a chance in the first place. What a nasty bitch she is."

"Everyone deserves a chance," Faye says.

"Whatever you say." Herb sets the papers on the front desk and then takes a peppermint before leaving.

"Herb has been delivering papers ever since he was a boy. He just loves it and knows everybody in town. Why don't you put the papers on the end table by the couch? I like to leave them there for the customers."

I grab the stack from the counter, and my heart leaps into my chest. Skid smiles up from the cover with **No Trace of Escaped Kidnapper Found** above his photo. It feels as if everything in me has drained out onto the floor. When I look up, Faye stares at me with big eyes and no color on her face.

20

ASHLEY

MOM-LIFE IS DRIVING WITH THE WIDOWS DOWN, THREE GIRLS seat-belted in the back, a dog in the front, the London Town Nursery Rhyme CD on full blast, and the smell of Cheetos swirling around the interior. Oreo pulls his head in and lets out a whine.

"We're almost there, boy." He's going to have to hold it. The highway is too busy, and I worry about the girls trying to climb out.

This is my favorite drive, and I already feel rejuvenated. The road winds through the forest with something beautiful around every bend—like the peaks of Mount Bachelor, Sisters, and Broken Top, still with traces of snow in the shady spots. I love when we get to the break in the trees where a pile of sharp black lava rock stretches back for miles. It is from an ancient eruption, but so barren it looks like it just crumpled up from the ground. We pass the turquoise water of Devil's Lake and the grassy marsh of Sparks Lake, with Mount Bachelor rising up on the far side of it.

I feel better just being here, but a stinging line of pain runs from my throat to my stomach. Chris and I dreamt of exploring nature with our girls, where they would learn to be self-sufficient and outdoorsy. Now, once they are old enough, it will be up to me to teach them to camp, hike, and Kayak all by myself.

Just like my girls, there are three peaks named North Sister, Middle Sister, and South Sister that the pioneers called Faith, Hope, and Charity. I will tell my girls that there is a peak for each of them.

I check the rearview mirror. Carina sleeps with neon orange Cheeto dust smeared around her mouth. Her head leans against the side of her car seat as the wind flaps her tiny ponytail around. Kia sits strapped into the middle seat belt. She stares out the window at the scenery and recites *Little Miss Muffet*. Calista sits in her booster with her hand out the window twirling her fingers in the wind.

Brake lights flash up ahead, and I slow the car.

"Are we there?" Kia asks.

"Yep, it's just ahead." Shit. A line of cars slowly inch forward, with nobody turning onto the dirt road to Elk Lake. I should have known better. It's Labor Day Weekend. Of course it is packed with no parking.

As we get closer, I see two orange-and-white-striped barriers with ROAD CLOSED and a Sheriff's truck. A deputy stands at the barricade and talks to people as they pull up. When our turn comes, I inch up far enough to see down the road. It is filled with emergency vehicles, and people gather in groups. Something terrible has happened.

"The lake is closed," the deputy calls toward my open window.

I eject the CD and stop *Humpty Dumpty* right in the middle.

"What happened?" I ask, and before I know it, Kia tumbles over the seat and sits up front with Oreo and me.

"There's been an accident. You'll need to keep moving. Sorry for the inconvenience."

He has probably said the same thing over and over and is

tired of people who roll up to him, frustrated that their plans will need to change.

I drive forward and pull to the side of the road. I have a terrible feeling, and a shiver runs across my shoulders. Whenever I shivered as a child, Grandma Ava always said, *Someone must have walked over your grave.* That scared the crap out of me back then and still does. Oreo whines again. He needs out.

"What happened, Momma?" Kia asks.

"I don't know." With that much police activity, it must be a missing person or a drowning, but I don't say that to Kia. "Get in the back and put your seat belt on. We can try Lava Lake."

Kia climbs back over, and Carina laughs when she gets stuck with her foot in the air. She has Chris' sense of humor. He would have said, *Smooth move, Ex-Lax.*

"Put London Town back on," Calista says.

"Just a minute." I need a break from Georgie Porgie, Jack and Jill, and Mary with her little lamb. "How about if I tell you a story?"

When Kia's seat belt clicks, I put on my blinker and ease back onto the highway. Lava Lake is only about ten minutes up the road.

"I don't want a story. I want London Town," Calista says.

"We can make our own London Town. I'll go first, then Kia, Calista, and Carina." The car in front of me pulls over, and I pass. It flips a u-ey behind me, probably heading back to Devil's Lake or Sparks.

"Hey diddle diddle, the dog had to piddle, the girl jumped over the seat: the littlest one giggled to see such fun, and the momma drove away in defeat."

"You drove away on your feet?" Calista starts laughing.

By the time Kia explains what defeat means and makes up her own nursery rhyme, we are at the turn-off for Lava Lake. I roll up the windows, and we bump down the gravel road toward the marina. It is packed, but I find a spot in the fifteen-minute parking area next to the store.

The lake is filled with kayaks, motorboats, canoes, and small sailboats. Mount Bachelor, Broken Top, and South Sister rise behind the trees on the opposite shore.

My dad used to bring Mitchell and me here to rent a fishing boat and spend the day bobbing on the water. Mom hated fishing, so she never came. I half think dad did it to give her a break from us.

Before I know it, Calista is free from her booster seat, and Kia opens the back door. I snap the leash on Oreo before he follows them out. "Take Oreo for a pee while I get Carina out."

Oreo pulls Kia to the lawn in front of the old-time store, with Calista right behind. Several kids sit on the steps and eat ice cream. As a kid, I thought the store was built with giant Lincoln Logs, and I used to build a replica of it at home.

I pull a wet wipe from the container and clean the Cheeto dust from Carina, and she moves her head from side to side, trying to stop me. Just as I lift her from her car seat, a high-pitched scream erupts from where my girls are. My heart stops, and a wash of fear runs through me. I look up and relax. She is fine. Oreo pulled Kia into a sprinkler. Before I get to them, Calista runs in behind her and dances in the spray. God, help me.

21

EMMY

Brian pulls up in front of the lobby ten minutes before the end of my shift. Ever since Faye realized I am a victim, not of domestic abuse, but associated with a kidnapper who escaped custody, her entire demeanor changed. It does not help that the newspaper named Brian.

I know when someone does not want me around. I don't blame her. I'm sure she wants to protect the reputation of her motel, and she does not want a psychopath showing up.

I bet she searched online when she returned to her desk to work on her computer. I'm sure she knows that Brian is also accused of rape.

"Nice shirt," Brian says.

"I know! Much better than my old uniform."

"I don't know. I think I'm turned on by polyester now."

Brian is in a much better mood. Maybe his lawyer gave him some good news.

"Guess who got a job?"

"You did?" I plaster a big smile onto my face and do not tell him I think I will be fired. "Where?"

"Timberland Mill."

"A lumber mill?" I picture Brian out in the forest, hot and sexy in a hard hat and with a chainsaw.

"Yep. It's good money. Want to see it?"

"Am I dressed okay?"

"It's not like I can take you on a tour or anything. They just hired me. We'll just drive by."

A drive sounds terrific. Ever since I got to Silverdale, I have spent all my time inside the motel, the courthouse, or in our duplex. I have only seen parts of the town, and that is all a blur of fast food and businesses, one blending right in with the next. I would not even be able to find a grocery store on my own. It will be wonderful to get out of the city and into the woods. Maybe we can pull over and take a walk.

We pass a restaurant with an outdoor barbecue that pumps out the smoky smells of ribs and brisket. My stomach growls so loud that Brian hears it and laughs. "We'll get dinner on the way home."

"Barbecue?"

"That exact restaurant if you want. It's a good day to celebrate, but we need to order it to go."

"Why?"

Brian glances over at me with *that* look in his eye. "Because there is something more that I want to devour other than dinner."

"Is it the uniform?"

"It's the sexy girl in the uniform."

I'm already getting wet just thinking about it. "We can go home now."

"Nope. We will wait until we can no longer stand it and want to rip each other's clothes off."

"That will be difficult to explain to Faye."

"Okay, rip is a bit much. I will gently remove your gorgeous new shirt."

We pass by a farm supply and feed shop. I used to go into

one with my second-grade foster parents. I loved when they had baby chicks in giant silver bins with heating lights over them. And I loved the smell of the feedbags and the feel of the leather boots and hats.

Brian turns up a road with a cemetery, which is surrounded by a brick wall, and an archway with Pine Grove Cemetery cut into the metal. The entire thing is shady and filled with pine trees. Brian slows the car, and I expect him to pull into the drive. Instead, he pulls over on the opposite side of the road, alongside a giant chain-link fence with barbed wire at the top. He stops the car before we get to a guard shack with a cement barrier and two yellow warning signs.

Behind the chain-link and through a large field of dried weeds, a group of faded yellow buildings sit with clouds of white steam above them. It looks like a prison camp, and my head starts to spin. Is Brian trying to tell me that he is going to prison and that will be his new job?

"I thought you said you're working in timberland."

"I am. This is Timberland Mill. I'll be working here, processing the wood."

Brian is not an inside sort of a man. I can't imagine him at a machine in this prison of a job, right across from a cemetery.

"I thought you'd be happy." Brian's excitement fades.

"I am," I lie. "Will you be okay working indoors? I can't picture you inside. You belong on the river."

"I'll be fine doing anything I put my mind to." I know he sees the expression on my face because he adds, "It's temporary. Once we get everything settled, we'll get the hell out of here and go to Wyoming or Idaho."

When we get home, Brian plops the bag of barbecue on the counter and pulls me to him. He kisses me hard like he needs to show me that we are okay—and to prove how much he loves me. He does not look into my eyes, so instead of feeling reassured me, I want to cry.

Afterward, Brian pulls me to him. We lie on our blow-up mattress in the empty room with a sheet for a curtain and our clothes scattered all over the floor. Time stops, and there is nothing but our heartbeats. It is just the two of us. Alone.

"I went to see my lawyer today," Brian says.

I get a sour taste in my mouth. "Your lawyer or the Unger's lawyer?"

"I need to do what they want."

"About Skid, too?"

"I will tell them I lied about the date rapes, and I will refuse to give any more information or testify against Skid."

If I open my mouth right now, the scream trapped inside will escape.

"I need you to refuse also."

I pull away and sit up. "I can't. Skid needs to be caught, or he will do it again."

"It is the only way. If we don't, I will go to jail, and you will be all alone. We just need to get out of this situation then move out of state. Maybe even to Montana. It's the only way. There is probably enough evidence in Skid's house and their old homestead where they found Crystal."

It was a nightmare when Brian and I broke into Skid's house looking for Crystal. I close my eyes and see the mannequin with deep blue eye shadow and coats of red lipstick smeared around the edges of her mouth, and at his grandfather's house with the stained mattress and Crystal naked and spread-eagle across it. She was skinny and sweaty, with her blond hair spread across a dirty pillow so weak that all she could do was mew like a kitten.

"I can't do it," I say.

Every muscle in Brian's body tenses. "If you don't, I will go to prison."

My teeth begin to chatter, so I put my tongue between them.

Brian puts his hand on my knee. "I will be used as a pawn for them to convict Skid. They will keep me as long as possible to make deals and make me testify for a reduced sentence. Plus, the Ungers raised me after my mom died. I had nobody. Rose took me into her home."

"I think I'm…" I can't stop shaking. "…having a heart attack."

"You'll be okay," Brian says. "It's just a panic attack."

22

———

HIM

I FINALLY MAKE IT TO LITTLE LAVA LAKE, WHERE MY HEADWATERS rise from the volcanic rock beneath the earth. It is where I am formed and where I will rejuvenate and regain my power. No… it is where I will surpass my former power and become the river god I am meant to be.

With Yapper's razor, I shaved off every bit of hair from my head, face, and body so that I am clean and ready for purification. The sapphire blue lake is deep and calm, like a palmful of holy water. The three volcanic peaks rise on the far side, and my waters spill out like a small pulsing vein right here where I sit on the south shore. It is like witnessing my own birth—not in the flesh but in the fluid as a god and a conscious being.

"Oreo…" a tiny voice calls from around the bend of the lake just before a black and white border collie comes dragging a blue leash. He stops before me with hackles raised and a low growl that gurgles in his throat.

A tiny sprite of a girl, who looks to be about six or seven years old, chases behind him. When she gets to the end of the leash, she grabs it and tries to pull the dog away, but he does not move. I pull the baseball cap down to shade my eyes.

"Are you a water sprite?" I ask.

She is beautiful with silky white blond hair and big green anime eyes. She gives me a shy smile. "No, I'm Kia."

"Do you live here in the lake?" She gathers up the leash until she is next to the dog and puts her hand on his back.

"No." She giggles again like I am being silly. "I live in Rockland at the Juniper Grove Apartments."

She strokes the dog and tries to soothe him. I have never taken a nymph so young, but she has come to me at this exact moment when I have come to purify myself. She is innocent and virginal, like the ancients required of their sacrifices. Is she a messenger, come to guide me down a deeper course?

"Kia..." A nymph appears from around the shoreline. Warmth rises and fills my body at the sight of the delicate goddess.

She has two more little water sprites younger than the one before me. The nymph is tiny, maybe five foot one and under a hundred pounds. She is an exact image of this little Kia, except grown, and her hair is a bit darker, more of a Champagne blonde.

My heartbeat quickens. She is divine, and she is the one. "Is that your sister?" I ask.

Her smile fades, and the edge of her lip trembles. She senses something about me, but her intuition is immature and undeveloped. Out of politeness, she answers. "She's my momma."

"What is your momma's name?"

Before she can answer, they all stand before me.

"I'm sorry," the momma nymph says. "I don't know what has gotten into him."

I know what has gotten into him. He knows their destiny, and he brought them to me, even if it was against his will. The dog lets out another growl deep in his throat. It bubbles in there but does not rise up.

She reaches for the leash with one hand while she balances

the youngest sprite on her hip. Her hands are small and thin, with the nails bit down to the skin. "I'm sorry we bothered you."

"You're not bothering me."

The middle girl hides behind her mother's legs and watches me from the corner of her eyes. She knows. She fears me. She may not understand why, but she knows just as she knows that the wind will blow, fire will burn, and the water will rise.

"Come on, Oreo…" The momma nymph pulls the leash and dislodges the growl that had been trapped. "Oreo! No! I'm so sorry. He never…"

She hands the littlest one to Kia and takes both hands to pull the dog away. She is so tiny that it is hard to believe she can manage all three girls and a dog. I want to pull her into me and take care of her. She will be my nymph and her daughters my sprites. My heart races, and a flush prickles my skin and burns my cheeks.

"What is your name?" I ask.

She looks hesitant but answers like most nymphs do, not willing to be rude.

"Ashley."

"Nice to meet you, Ashley. Want to hang out here with me? I can help you keep an eye on your girls."

"No, thank you. We need to get going…what is your name?"

Without thinking, I say, "Hermit."

The color drains from her face, and she takes a tiny step backward.

I give her a smile, "It's my trail name. I'm hiking the Pacific Crest Trail."

"Oh…cool," she says. "A friend of mine did that a few years ago."

Kia and her sisters move down the shore with their feet beneath the surface of my waters. Ashley turns her head to check on them and looks back to me. "I gotta go. Nice meeting you."

Every nerve in my body tingles as I watch Ashley walk away. Her ass and tits are tight and sleek—meant for the water.

When she and her girls disappear around a bend in the shore, I turn back to the lake and follow it to my headwaters. My heart freezes then begins again and pounds in my chest. There he is, delivered to me in the flesh right where my river begins. Hermit. His name rises and slips from my lips. It is like I spoke his name out loud and brought him into being. He looks just like Yapper told me. It is like I am released from my body and watch myself from a distance.

He squats down at the junction where Little Lava Lake ends, and the Deschutes River begins. Where I begin. He fills a bottle with my fluid and presses it through a filter so he can consume me. He tips the bottle to his lips and takes me in before he turns toward the trees and starts down a woodsy trail.

I glance around. Nobody is here. Ashley has taken her girls to where the tourists crowd the beach. I turn back to where Hermit disappeared, and I follow. As I pass through my headwaters, I dip my hand in and run it down my forehead, nose, and lips. He and I will merge and become one, stronger than either of us could ever be in the flesh.

23

———

EMMY

"WE NEED A SECOND CAR OR GET YOURS OUT OF IMPOUND."
Brian's hair sticks up in little wet tufts, curled at the ends.
Before we headed out the door, he threw on his jeans, without
underwear, and pulled a t-shirt over his head. "I don't like not
knowing how you will get home from work."

He knows it is unsafe to drive my car with Skid on the loose.
"Maybe Faye will let me change shifts, so you and I work the
same hours."

Brian puts the blinker on and turns into the parking lot of
the Railroad Inn. It's almost seven in the morning, and the
streets are filled with school buses and people on their way to
jobs that start at the butt crack of dawn.

Today is Brian's first day of work. They have given him
swing shift from two o'clock until ten at night. "If Faye lets me
switch, my shift will be from three o'clock until eleven. We
could work that with one car. You can drop me off early, then
pick me up once you get off."

Brian turns into a spot in front of the lobby and shifts into
park. He turns toward me and rests his forearm on top of the
steering wheel, just like Rod, my fifth- and sixth-grade dad,

used to do. Rod usually had a funny story or a dad joke when he did it, but Brian's face looks grim.

"I don't want to tell you what to do, but I would rather you did not work at night. That is when the crackheads come in... plus, as long as Skid is out there, I don't feel safe having you in the lobby alone." Brian reaches out and takes my hand. "Is there someone you can ask for a ride home?"

"The housekeepers work until four. I'll see if any of them can give me a ride. I'll only have to wait an hour, and maybe we can throw them a few bucks for gas."

"Okay," Brian says, "and I'll let the mill know I would like the day shift as soon as possible."

I lean across the console and give him a kiss. It is going to suck working different shifts. I get off at three, and I'll be home alone until Brian gets home around ten-thirty at night.

Brian waits until I open the lobby door before backing out of the parking spot. A girl with long black hair parted down the middle stands behind the counter with her purse hanging over her shoulder. She is thin with big eyes and a broad nose.

"You must be Emmy," she says with a smile.

I smile back and give her a nod. "And you are Jocelyn?"

"Yes." She moves to the end of the desk. "Faye told me that she hired you, and you know your shit."

Oh, thank God! Maybe she will not fire me.

"I know you don't start until seven, but if you could be here five to ten minutes early, that would help. We need to count the cash drawer, and I will catch you up on anything that happened overnight. I don't mind staying a few minutes late, but if we can split that time, I would appreciate it. I sleep when my kids are at school, which by the time I get home, have breakfast, and fall asleep, only gives me about five and a half to six hours each day. Today, I'll be lucky to get five."

"Of course." I feel like it would be polite to ask her how many kids she has, but since she is in a hurry to leave, I keep my mouth shut.

She pulls a spiral coil with a key off her wrist and unlocks the cash drawer. "We had a hectic night. The cops were here at two o'clock. They arrested a lady from room 206. Deanna checked her in at ten. She was from victims' assistance and not on the *Do not rent* list—but she will be now."

Jocelyn hands me the key. "Keep it on your wrist, so you don't forget where you set it down. Trust me. I know from experience."

Jocelyn counts the twenties, writes the amount on a form, and tells me to recount them. We continue to count and initial the form for the tens, fives, ones, and change to verify how much money she will leave me with.

"The lady was out of it and looked like her old man...or someone...beat her up pretty good. Deanna thought she would just sleep it off, but the lady woke up around one-thirty and started trashing the room." Jocelyn puts the cash back in the drawer and slides it shut. "Other guests called in, saying it sounded like a bar fight with furniture flying. I thought maybe her old man got out and was back for more, but when cops got here, it was just her."

"Just her? Destroying things for no reason?" I lock the cash drawer without taking the coil from my wrist.

"It happens more than you would think. Faye already knows. Jason will start clearing things out, and Faye will handle the rest when she gets in around eight o'cock." Jocelyn inches toward the door. "There are holes in the wall, and she shattered the bathroom mirror. Sucks for her! She's got seven years of bad luck now."

I have a million questions, but I don't want to keep her from leaving. I will ask Faye about the *do not rent list* and where it is.

"Oh, and the man in 102 had people coming and going all

night. It looks like he might be dealing. Will you tell Faye so she can check the video?"

I tell her I will, and she reaches for the door.

"See you at two."

"Two?"

She turns her head back toward me and rolls her eyes. "Faye called an all-employee meeting for two o'clock today."

"About what?"

"Hell if I know."

"Is it about the lady trashing the room?"

"No, Faye called and told me about the meeting before that happened. I hope it doesn't run late. My kids get off the bus at three fifteen."

My stomach drops. Faye didn't call me. Maybe because she is going to fire me. But then again, how could she call? We don't have a phone.

The high-pitched chime on the door dings and Jocelyn leaves me alone and in charge of the motel. Please, don't let anyone come to check in or have any issues in the next fifty minutes before Faye gets here. I will not know what the hell to do.

The popcorn machine sits cold with a bed of yellow popcorn that needs to be refreshed, and the player piano is silent. Those are two things on my list of responsibilities, but Faye still needs to show me how to do them. I'm supposed to change the music roll in the piano, but I can't imagine having it play all day, and it wasn't on at any time I came in.

My list was on the desk, right next to the computer, but it is not there. I slide open the drawer beneath the computer. It is filled with Railroad Inn pens, notepads, rubber bands, and paper clips. Stacks of tourist brochures fill the next drawer.

Amber and I sat in the Portland hostel looking through brochures just like these, and the whitewater rafting one detoured us from our escape to Canada. I wish I had never touched that brochure.

Maybe Jocelyn put my list in Faye's office. The office is tidy with no papers on the desk. Maybe she slipped it into a drawer. I slide open the middle one, which is the most organized drawer I have seen in my life. There are dividing bins for everything. Not just a mix-match of pens and pencils. Each type of pen has its own space, and each size of rubber band does, too. There is no bin for my list, and it is not in this drawer.

I put my fingers in the handle of the righthand drawer and pause. It feels like an invasion of privacy, so I step away. Back at the front desk, I search everywhere and can't find it. I will look like crap if I can't do what Faye asked on my first day. Back in her office, I go behind her desk again and look around. Nobody is here, and the security cameras do not film this room.

I slide the drawer open, and right on top in a yellow cover with red print, is, *What to Expect When Adopting: A Guidebook for Adoptive Parents*. It feels like a moth flutters in my windpipe. Shit! I can't believe I asked her if she had children yesterday. I should have kept my mouth shut. They want to adopt a baby.

My entire childhood, I wished someone would adopt me, but by the time my dad lost his parental rights, I was nine years old. I lived with my grandmother for a year…who was more strung out than my dad. They finally took me from her when I was ten, already in my awkward years, and too old. Everyone wants a baby.

I set the book on her desk and open to the table of contents. Several sheets of printer paper are folded and stuck in the pages. I set them aside and turn to the contents: *Misconceptions About Adoption, Choosing the Right Agency, Representing Yourself Well, Paperwork, Types of Adoption, Cost and Ways to Get Funds, The Emotions of Waiting, Myths About Adoption, It's Not Going to be Easy, Children with Trauma and PTSD, What if…Questions and Fears, Involving Extended Family and the Community.*

I accidentally bump the mouse, and the screen comes to life with a wall of little video squares from the surveillance cameras. One of the frames shows a red beater truck pulling into a spot at the back of the lot. The numbers in the upper left corner say 7:49 AM. Both doors swing open, and two housekeepers in their purple scrubs climb out. I feel like a creeper, but I can't help myself.

Faye said the housekeepers are Mindy and Izel. The driver, who I assume is Mindy, has thin shoulder-length white-blond hair, and the lady in the passenger seat is Hispanic with her hair parted to the side. I'm sure she is Izel. They both look friendly. Maybe I can get a ride home from them.

A white boxy four-door car pulls into a spot, and the maintenance man gets out. He looks about thirty and around six foot two, with longish brown hair and a short beard. He's not thin or overweight, but he is one of those naturally big guys. I think his name is Jason. When I stayed here, I watched him drop wads of sheets and towels from the second story into a red laundry cart below. When he saw me, he gave me a smile that made his eyes squint so tight I wondered if he could still see.

The housekeepers wait for Jason to get out of his car. When he does, the three of them stand in the parking lot and talk. Maybe Jason is telling them about the lady in room 206 and what happened. A silver SUV pulls into the top video, and all three of them glance toward it, stop talking, and head toward the laundry and storage rooms.

The SUV pulls just to the left of the lobby, and Faye gets out. I shove the papers back into the book, drop them into the drawer, and shut it before hurrying back to the front desk.

"Good morning." The door chime sounds, and Faye comes in with a box of donuts and sets them on the counter. "Nothing like starting the day with a trashed room, huh? Help yourself to a donut."

"Sorry, but there is another thing that Jocelyn asked me to tell you."

Her shoulders drop, and she waits for it.

"The man in room 102 had people coming and going all night. She wondered if he may be dealing."

Faye nods. "I'll check the video."

She slips past me and into her office. There is silence, then, "Emmy, will you come here for a moment?"

She stands at her desk and stares at the glowing computer screen. It had been asleep when I came in.

"Were you behind my desk?"

My face feels hot and starts tingling. "I was looking for my list of responsibilities. They weren't at the front desk where I left them, so I came to see if someone put them here."

She looks around to see if anything is missing, opens and closes drawers. When she opens the one with the book, she pauses and raises her eyes to me. I don't speak. If I start blabbering and defending myself, I will look guilty. I didn't take anything from her.

"Were you going through things in my desk?"

"I was looking for my list. I saw your book. I shouldn't have, but I looked inside. I accidentally bumped the mouse, and the computer screen came to life."

Before she answers me, the lobby door chimes, so I walk out of her office and to the front desk. My entire body feels heavy like it is filled with water.

Herb comes in with the newspapers and a huge big-tooth smile. "Morning, Emmy." He sets the papers on the top of the front desk and opens the lid of the donut box.

"Good morning." My voice sounds thick.

"Heard that someone caused a ruckus here last night. I hope nobody was injured." He sticks the end of a maple bar between his teeth and bites down.

"Just the room."

He chews and cocks his head toward the open office door. I know he is waiting for Faye to come out, but she doesn't.

"Tell Faye I said hi," he says, and finally leaves.

When the door chimes, Faye appears in the doorway with her lips pressed together, and her arms crossed over her chest. She stands beside me at the front desk, and we both stare at the newspapers Herb just brought.

BODY OF GIRL FOUND IN ELK LAKE is printed in giant black letters across the top of the paper. Beneath the headline, it says *foul play is suspected*, and the smiling face of a girl with short brown hair and a red bandana.

"Trust is the most important thing to me," Faye says.

Her words sound fuzzy, like she is speaking through water. "If I trust an employee, I will do about anything for them. If I can't...well, let's say this is my business. This is my livelihood and how I pay my bills. I will not keep an employee I don't trust."

I can't take my eyes off the girl smiling up from the newspaper, and tears run down my cheeks and drip onto the front desk. I place my hand over the shiny drops to hide them.

"Trust is the most crucial aspect of any relationship," Faye says.

Words will not rise to my mouth, so I nod.

"The things on my desk are my private business. They are not for you to touch, whether it is a book or a hundred-dollar bill. If it is not yours, don't touch it."

I manage to squeak out, "I'm sorry," but the words are muffled. I cough to clear my throat. "It won't happen again."

"Thank you," Faye says. I about jump out of my skin when I feel her hand on my shoulder. "While we are on the subject of trust...I want you to know that I'm aware that the escaped kidnapper has something to do with you."

Oh no, here it is. I'm fired.

"Did Jocelyn tell you I called a meeting?"

I nod but can't pull my eyes away from the girl on the paper. Deep down, I know. It is one of those intuitive things. I know that Skid killed her.

"I need to keep all of us safe," Faye says.

"I understand."

"Jesse…I mean, Deputy Wright will be here for the meeting. I'm giving the Sheriff's department access to my live video feeds so they can check on you anytime without having to come here and scare our guests." She takes her hand from my shoulder, and it feels like there is an empty spot now. "When cops hang around, people assume there is trouble here. He will also bring pepper spray and personal alarms for everyone. It is something I should have done long ago anyway."

I lift my chin and turn to meet her eyes. "I'm not fired?"

Her eyebrows pinch together. "No. I'm going to make sure that you are safe while at the same time protecting my business and the other employees. But back to the trust issue." She pulls a tissue from a box and hands it out to me. "Do you trust me enough to tell me what is going on with the escaped kidnapper?"

I search her eyes. Trust is as hard for me to give as it is for others to give to me.

She puts her hand on the face of the girl with a red bandana. "And how that is associated with this girl? I want to help you, but you need to let me know what I am dealing with."

I take a deep breath and close my eyes. "How much time do you have?"

"How about the Cliffs Notes version now? I have to get that room repaired. We can talk more at another time."

"He is more than a kidnapper. He is a serial killer. I told the Sheriff's department, and they have the proof. They may be checking DNA before they tell the public." It all comes spilling out, just like when I was a kid and got caught. "He killed my best friend and tried to kill me. There are at least four girls, maybe more. My gut tells me he killed this girl in Elk Lake, also. He drowns them."

The more I talk, the better I feel. Faye's eyes are wide, and her lips are pressed tight. Some of the worries drain from me and fill Faye.

"Oh, my God. Oh, my God," is all that she says and raises her palms to me. "That is good for now. I need to digest that."

She reaches out and puts her hand back on my shoulder. "Oh, my God. I am so sorry." Her hand trembles, and she pulls it away before she turns back to her office.

"I'm sorry about your book. I always wanted to be adopted, and I…"

She slowly turns back around. "You were an orphan?"

"Foster care," I say. "I prayed that someone would adopt me, but it never happened. I aged out."

Tears spill from her eyes, and before I know it, she wraps her arms around me in the type of hug only moms know how to give, and it feels good. My body trembles. I don't want to break down, so I pull away from her just as the door chimes, and the maintenance man walks in.

"The room is trashed. We need a drywaller and…" He notices us all emotional and freezes. "Oh…"

He looks around and tries to find a place to put his eyes, and Faye laughs. "It's okay. I need to get focused. Show me the damage."

24

———

HIM

HERMIT SITS CROSS-LEGGED ON THE SHORE, BARELY LIT BY THE flames of his stove. Most people have gone, and only a few campfires and trailer lights twinkle in the campground across the lake. I leave him alone to enjoy his last meal.

As the sun sinks lower, stars shine on the lake and in the night sky as if they are one continuous loop above and below. Hermit finishes his meal and sits in perfect stillness as if he knows what is coming and has accepted his fate. A frog croaks with each beat of my heart, and a squirrel scurries up a tree trunk. A silvery wash of starlight glistens on the lake and washes over his body.

I take Yapper's black folding knife from my pocket, unbutton my shorts, and let them fall to my feet. I drop my hat and shirt on top of them until I stand naked. The wind slides across my body that is fully shaved and as sleek and shiny as a salmon.

I unfold the silver blade of the knife. My palms sweat, and static pulses in my ears.

He lies on his side and faces the lake with his chin raised and his throat exposed. He is positioned upon my altar. It has been determined. It is divine.

I move to him like slow-rising water. He will not know I am there until he feels the chill of my blade at his throat. I do not like the messiness of flesh and blood, but he has been presented, and I must prove myself worthy.

I crouch behind him. He does not stir. I wait and listen to his deep sounds of sleep before I lie alongside his body and inhale and exhale with the rhythm of his breaths. In one quick movement, I throw my leg over him, sink the blade into his throat, and draw it across.

He flails and gurgles, but I pin him to the ground. His arm pops out of his sleeping bag and slaps at the ground like a wrestler who tries to tap out, but I do not release my hold. I clasp him to my body as his blood seeps out and puddles like black water in the night.

He smells unwashed and earthy, nothing but flesh. The coppery scent of his blood on the earth makes my stomach churn. He stops moving, and I no longer feel his pulse.

25

ASHLEY

CARINA FINALLY SLEEPS, AND I HAVE TIME TO MAKE DINNER. SHE has been cranky with a low-grade fever all day. Kia and Calista sit on the floor in front of the television and watch Fairly Odd Parents on Nickelodeon. What a great mom I am. Carina has been so fussy that I haven't had a chance to look in their backpacks to see if they have any homework.

The fridge is almost empty because I had to use the entire social security check on rent. Quesadillas it is. Quick, easy, two ingredients, and a favorite with the girls, so it won't be a fight to get Calista to eat.

"Noooo!" Calista screams. "Mom, Kia turned off my show."

I run into the living room. "Shhhh. Carina's sleeping."

"It changed to iCarly," Kia says. "That's a teenage show, and Calista is only five."

"You chose the last show," Calista screams.

"Keep your voices down, or I'll shut the TV off." I hope they listen because it will be a hassle to keep them entertained while I make dinner.

"Get off me! Mom!" Calista jumps on top of Kia and tries to

yank the remote from her hand. Oreo joins the fun and starts licking Kia's face.

Carina screams from her crib. "Look what you two did."

They don't even hear me while they wrestle over the remote. Kia grabs Calista's hair, and she lets out an ear-piercing screech. I want to scream too, but I am the mom, and I need to keep calm. I pull the remote from them and click the television off.

Carina stands at the bars of her crib and wails. Her cheeks are bright red, and her diaper hangs down wet and full. A high-pitched brawl erupts from the living room. I lift Carina from her crib. She is burning up. I grab a diaper and head into the living room. *Oh, Chris, I don't think I can do this. I'm a failure.* I had a bad feeling when he applied for Woodland Fire Management, but it was good money, and he promised me he would be safe.

Calista has Kia by the hair, and she howls. "Both of you, stop it now, or you'll get time out."

Carina continues to scream as I lay her on the floor to change her diaper. It is soaked and hot. "Kia, go in my bathroom and get the Tylenol drops. It's the grape ones."

She does not respond. I grab Calista's wrist and squeeze until she lets go of Kia's hair. "Time out!" I point to the timeout chair.

Calista scrunches her face and stomps her feet all the way to the chair as she tells me how unfair I am. I grab Kia's arm to get her attention. "Go in my bathroom and get the Tylenol drops. The grape ones."

Kia crosses her arms in front of her and heads toward my bedroom just as someone pounds on the door and sends Oreo into a volley of barks.

"Just a second," I yell and slide a new diaper under Carina. I fasten it without wiping her down and hurry to the door.

Mrs. Simpson stands on my welcome mat with her lips

clamped tight and her long gray ponytail hanging over her shoulder. "Having trouble with the kids?"

"Yes. Carina has a fever, and the girls are bickering. I'm sorry. I'll try to get them quiet."

I keep the door barely cracked, so Oreo does not run out. Mrs. Simpson peeks her head around me like she is trying to assess the damage. Carina's screams have turned to whimpers, and she lays her head on my shoulder. The heat from her little body radiates up my neck.

Oreo pokes his head between my legs. Behind Mrs. Simpson, the door to Mr. Wade's apartment swings open, and he stands there in a dirty wifebeater t-shirt and black sweatpants.

"You need help?" Mrs. Simpson asks me.

"No, thank you." The first and last time I accepted her help, she lectured me about the proper way to manage my kids with a paddle. She said they had too many toys, and my apartment was too modern.

Mr. Wade stands frozen with the typical old man scowl on his face. He never says a word to me. If he is angry, he scowls. If all is well and I say hi, he gives me a single nod.

Kia appears with the Tylenol and takes a protective stance at my side.

"Hello, Kia," Mrs. Simpson says.

"Hello."

"It's hello, Mrs. Simpson. How are you today?" She puts her hands on her hips. "Kids have no manners anymore."

"Thank you," I say to her and swing the door shut. "I need to get dinner going."

"Please, let me help." She takes a step forward.

"I've got it. I'll keep the kids quiet." I close the door so that only a sliver of her face shows in the crack. "Thank you."

She shakes her head in disappointment, and I shut the door, turn the deadbolt, and cry. I am a failure. I can't even manage my own kids.

Kia and Calista come to my side and wrap their little arms around me. "I'm sorry, Momma," they both say.

Instead of comforting me, it makes it worse. My chest heaves as I gasp in air. Another knock comes on the door.

"Go away," Calista yells.

"Calista!" Kia reprimands her.

"It's me," a deep and muffled voice comes from the other side.

I unbolt the lock and swing it open.

"Uncle Mitchell," the girls yell and jump into his arms.

Mrs. Simpson appears on the landing behind him, then slinks back into her apartment. Mitchell's shirt, baseball cap, and goatee are covered in wood dust.

Mitchell peels the girls off of him. "I'm all dirty," he says and dusts himself off on the landing. He is skinny and all elbows and shoulders. "I just got off work."

He looks down at me, and his face collapses. "You okay?"

"It's been a rough day. Carina has a fever, the girls are bickering, and I can't even make dinner."

He clears the door and just before he shuts it, Mr. Wade's door swings open again and he glares out.

"Mind your own fucking business," Mitchell says and shuts the door.

I start laughing and crying at the same time. I've wanted to say that to Mr. Wade for years.

Mitchell puts his hand on Carina's face. "You need to get her to urgent care."

"I know," I say. "I'm a terrible mother."

"No, you're an overwhelmed mother."

"I need to wash up so the tickle monster can get Kia and Calista," he says and waves his fingers toward the girls. They laugh and screech as they run to hide behind the couch.

"Yes, but I'm trying to get them quiet. The neighbors are complaining."

"It's only five-thirty. Fuck the neighbors."

"Language…" I warn him. Chris and I promised never to swear in front of the girls.

"Sorry." He gives a shrug and a smirk toward the girls. "Uncle Mitchell forgot the rules. Screw the neighbors."

After Mitchell cleans up and looks more like my red-bearded brother, he calls Stacey and tells her that he will be home late because I need to take Carina to urgent care. I can tell that Stacy is not happy and gives him a hard time because he holds the phone to his ear, rolls his eyes, and makes faces.

"Go ahead and get her to the doctor. I'll feed the girls as soon as the tickle monster is done with them."

Another giggling shriek comes from behind the couch.

I hold Carina with one arm and pack her diaper bag with the other. By the time I get back to the living room, all three of them scream and laugh as the girls climb on Mitchell's back, and he reaches around to tickle them.

I grab my purse and keys and step onto the landing. When I get to the top of the stairs, Mrs. Simpson's door swings open.

I look back and just as her mouth starts to open, I say, "Carina's sick. If you need anything, talk to my brother," and I head down the stairs with a sense of satisfaction. That felt good.

When I get home from the urgent care, the girls are asleep, and Mitchell sits on the couch watching an action movie with a car chase. He mutes it and waits for me to put Carina in her crib. As soon as I do, I plop down on the couch next to him. On the television, someone has a gun out the window of a speeding car and blindly shoots at another car behind it.

"Have you eaten?"

I shake my head, and Mitchell starts to stand up. I put my hand on his leg. "I'm not hungry."

He sits back down. "You can't keep going on like this."

"I know, but I can't move back home. I need to live my own life." I don't tell him it's mostly because of his wife, Stacy, and his spoiled brat of a daughter. My girls and I don't need to be tortured like that.

Mitchell leans over, sticks his hand into his pocket, and pulls out a small wad of twenties. "Here's some grocery money."

"I'm okay. I don't need it." I do need it, but Mitchell has been out of work and just started his job. He needs it for his family.

He gives me a blank look, then raises his eyebrows. "I looked in your fridge and cupboards." He tosses the money onto the coffee table.

"Thank you." I tip my head onto his shoulder.

"You think it's time to start dating?" he asks. "You need to find love, and your girls need a father."

I lift my head and scoot away from him.

"I can't. There will never be another Chris." Chris and I met in middle school and I was pregnant with Kia by my senior year.

"It's been over two years. Nobody will replace Chris, but the girls deserve a dad, and you cannot keep doing this by yourself."

"Only Kia remembers Chris. Calista knows him mostly by his pictures and the stories I tell her. If I bring another man into our lives, he will replace Chris for the girls."

On the television, the car with the gunman rounds a curve in the road. The car goes up on two wheels, rolls, and crashes in a field.

Mitchell picks up the remote, clicks it off, and pulls me into a hug.

26

EMMY

WHEN IZEL OPENS THE PASSENGER DOOR OF MINDY'S TRUCK, TWO soda cans roll out with a hollow aluminum clunk. The truck's tires and wheel wells are coated in dried mud like someone went off-roading. The back is speckled with bits of hay and oats.

Izel picks up the cans and walks them to a recycling bin. The cab has one long bench seat and a manual gear shift. I climb in and scoot to the center with my legs angled toward the passenger door, so Mindy doesn't need to reach between my legs to shift.

Mindy, still in her purple scrubs, tosses something into the bed. She has thin white-blond hair with long bangs that fall across her eyes as she climbs in. She sweeps them aside and tucks her hair behind her ears before she puts the key in the ignition.

"Where do you live?"

"Over by the library on the corner of Juniper and Dobbs. I can direct you when we get closer."

"I know exactly where it is. My grandpa used to live on Dobbs."

When Izel returns to the truck, she takes her tote bag from her shoulder, climbs into the passenger seat, and places it on her lap. It's a canvas bag with coral, yellow, and brown geometric designs. "You threw your purse into the bed of the truck?"

"There's nowhere else to put it." Mindy rolls her eyes, presses in the clutch, wobbles the gear shift, and turns the key. The truck sputters and rumbles to a start.

We back up in an arc and stop, and she shifts into first. With a lurch, we roll forward toward the Railroad Inn sign. Mindy coordinates both hands and feet to put on her blinker, shift, and steer.

We pull onto the highway next to a pickup with three barking dogs in the back. With the windows down, the smells of exhaust and gasoline fill the cab.

Mindy pushes in a cigarette lighter and pulls the sun visor down. A red and white pack of smokes drops into her palm. "Do you mind?"

I shake my head. I don't like smoking and don't want to breathe it in, but it is her truck, and I need to arrange a way home every day.

She taps one out, then holds the pack to me. "Want one?"

"No thanks."

She doesn't bother offering one to Izel. Mindy puts the cigarette to her lips and pulls the lighter from the dash. The coils glow red as she holds it to the tip and inhales, a thin line of smoke rises.

She says, "You should have seen the shit that guy in 102 left for me to clean."

"Did he check out?"

"Nope. It's your turn tomorrow." Mindy takes a long drag and blows it out. "There was a torn open sack of McDonald's with half a Big Mac and four squeezed-out packets of catsup. He squirted the catsup all over the table like blood spatter. I found an empty coke cup on the floor in a sopping wet puddle and empty beer cans all over the room."

"Remember what Rhonda did that time?" Izel asks.

"Yes! That was legendary!"

Mindy downshifts and takes a right and another drag of her cigarette. She blows the smoke toward the open window and says, "This guy was a complete dick, talking down to us and calling us bitches. Every day, he left a shitstorm of crap in his room and used condoms on the floor and in the sheets—like three condoms a day. Who needs that many?"

Izel's soft voice comes from the other side. "Maybe they were too big and kept slipping off."

Mindy and I both burst out laughing. I did not expect that to come from Izel. We pick up speed, and Mindy shifts again.

"Well…Rhonda found his stash of condoms and poked holes through the packages with a needle. Then, she swished his toothbrush into the dirty toilet. I miss Rhonda! She was a crack-up!"

"Now that we got these"—she pats her container of pepper spray clipped to her waistband—"maybe we can just spray the shit out of assholes. I wonder what the acceptable level of harassment is before we can use them."

"Probably only if we are attacked," Izel says and changes the subject. "How do you like working at the Railroad Inn?"

"So far, so good," I say. "I think I screwed things up with Faye, though."

"What happened?"

"I was looking for something and opened her desk. I found her adoption books, and she caught me."

"Yikes!" Mindy says. "Faye and her husband Kerry…have you met him yet?"

"No."

"He's great. You'll like him. They have been trying to have a baby for a long time. Faye got pregnant twice, and both times, she lost the baby very late in her pregnancy. It devastated her."

Now, I really feel bad.

"I hope they find a baby. They will be awesome parents," Mindy says.

"You'll be fine with Faye. She comes across as harsh, but she's fair. She truly cares about her employees and will do anything for you as long as you're honest with her."

Mindy downshifts and turns into a one-story apartment complex with cars pulled up to the front doors of each unit. As soon as she comes to a stop, Izel's door creaks open, and she hops out.

"Thanks. See you tomorrow." She slams the door shut.

Izel walks up to an apartment with two little kids in the window, excited and waving to her. I scoot toward the door as Mindy shifts into reverse, and we pull away.

Once we are back on the road, Mindy takes one last drag and flicks her cigarette out the window. The atmosphere in the truck has shifted. All the fun and lightness went out with Izel.

"So what's your story?" Mindy asks.

She sounds friendly, but there is an edge to it.

"What do you mean?" I ask, mostly to avoid the question, but I can see she is not having it. "I grew up in Alder Creek, and I just moved to Silverdale."

"Directly from Alder Creek?" she asks.

"No…" I say. "I lived in Lodell for a year."

She nods her head like she is testing me, and I have given a correct answer.

"What's up with all the security?"

Does she know it's because of me? Or maybe she thinks I know since I work at the front desk. She doesn't seem like the type of girl I should lie to, but I don't want to spill my guts to her, either. "It's about that guy who was arrested for kidnapping the girl. The one who escaped from the hospital."

Mindy slows and downshifts when she gets to the corner by the library. The gears grind, and the truck almost stalls. "You mean Skid?"

My heart about stops, and my throat clamps shut. As Mindy turns the corner, the red bricks of the library slide past the truck window. She stares straight out the front and waits with her lips pressed together.

"You know him?"

Mindy glances over out of the corner of her eye and shrugs.

"Yes, it is because of him. It's worse than they are saying. You need to watch out."

"Worse, how?"

"He killed at least four other girls. They found them in the river."

Mindy pulls to the curb and puts the truck in neutral. We sit there idling with the cab filling with exhaust. She slowly turns toward me. "How do you know?"

"He killed my best friend and tried to kill me."

We sit there in the truck for what seems like forever. She doesn't take her eyes off me and stares like she is summing me up and wondering if I am full of shit. Finally, without a word, her hand quivers and she reaches for the gear shift.

When we roll up to my duplex, I say, "It's the blue one on the corner."

Mindy pulls to the curb and stops. The door gives a loud metal creak as I open it. I climb out, and before I shut it, I say, "Should I arrange another ride for tomorrow?"

She is ash white. Even her lips have no color. She shakes her head, but no words come out. I start to shut the door, but when I hear her speak, I stop. "I'm sorry about your friend. Do you need me to pick you up in the morning?"

"No, I need to be there earlier than you, and my boyfriend can drive me."

It looks like she wants to ask more, but she does not. I shut the door and walk away. Behind me, her truck grinds and rumbles as she drives away.

I look around to see if anything seems disturbed before I put the key in the door and open it. Our duplex may be sparse, but it is ours, and we are together. We now have an actual mattress that sits directly on the floor and a tall dresser, couch, and coffee table we bought from a store called R & R, which sounds like rest and relaxation but really means recycle and reuse. When you start with nothing, two bedrooms, a living room, and a kitchen is a lot of space. We still need a television, and I can't wait. The hours drag by with me here alone from four-thirty until ten-thirty when Brian gets home.

I sit down at the table where I have a two-hundred-piece puzzle called Misty Pines that I completed last night. The image has trees in the mist with two tall mountain peaks behind them. This is my second time putting it together. There is something haunting about it that gives me the creeps, but I have nothing better to do than work on it. I start at the corner, lift it up, and pull the pieces apart.

I am sleepy and half-conscious by the time Brian gets home. He brings the earthy scent of sweat, grease, and sap as he leans over the bed to kiss me.

"What a shitshow of a day today," he says. "The guys were all fired up, much worse than normal."

He usually has stories of the guys chucking knots of wood at each other or referring to the supervisors as *Yellow Hats* or *Foreskins.*

"When Jimmy, the Hyster driver, was on break, they waxed the forks of his forklift." In the dim light of the room, all I see is Brian's silhouette. He stands next to the mattress and stretches his arms and neck. "After his break, Jimmy lifted a whole stack of wood twenty feet into the air. As he backed out and turned, the entire stack slipped off and crashed to the ground. They all thought it was funny as hell, but the Yellow Hat made Jimmy take a piss test. He could have lost his job."

From what Brian tells me, most men hate working at the mill, but they need a paycheck. It is hot and loud. Forklifts rip around, lathes peel logs, and belts and chains run all day long. It is physically exhausting, and they get wood slivers in their hands, even through their gloves. I've had to help Brian get several deep ones out. On top of all that, their supervisors are complete assholes. As soon as their shift ends, most of the men head straight to ice chests of beer in their trucks or hit the bars on the way home.

Brian does not go to the bars but frequently slips outside in the middle of the night to lie on the trampoline and watch the stars. He's always done that, but in Lodell, he would go to the river.

The bathroom light casts a glow, and I turn toward it to watch him strip off his dirty clothes and drop them to the ground. His muscles are thick and defined from years of hard work and whitewater rafting. When he pulls his underwear off, his ass is bright white compared to the rest of his tanned body, still a deep brown from Summer. Last winter, his tan lines faded but never went away. Brian belongs on the river, not in a hot and dusty mill.

I must have dozed back off because I wake to the feel of his skin, still sweet and syrupy from the shower. He runs his hand up my belly and pulls me tight against him. I feel him get hard. His breath is warm on my neck as he kisses it and sends shivers through my body.

"Want me to stop?" he breathes into my hair.

"No."

He takes hold of my breast and kisses me all along my shoulder. "Are you sure?"

Brian slides his hand over my hip and between my legs.

"I'm sure."

He slips his fingers inside me. "Mmmm. You're already wet."

I roll onto my back, and Brian puts his mouth to mine. He kisses me soft and slow before he moves down to my breasts, my belly, and between my legs. Nothing feels more natural to me than making love to Brian—he is wild and primitive, just like the land, the river, and the canyon.

I cum twice before Brian pushes himself up and climbs on top of me with a smile. I can never resist his smile. There is a sadness to it that pulls me in and holds me under so deep I can't breathe.

PART 2

27

———

HIM

THE TIRES OF A MAROON FORD PICKUP CRUNCH ON THE GRAVEL when it pulls off the road. Finally, someone has stopped. I lift my pack and peek into the passenger side window. A man in a cowboy hat sits behind the wheel. He is beefy with steely gray hair and looks about sixty. He reminds me of my Uncle Russ, only more weathered.

"I'm headed into downtown Rockland," I say.

"Hop in."

I reach for the handle, and a wash of apprehension runs up my arm. I hesitate.

"You can sit in the back if you'd rather, but it's dirty back there."

The bed is filled with chunks of tree bark and dried leaves. I ignore the feeling, swing my backpack into the bed, and open the passenger door. The front cab smells of cigarettes and fills me with memories of my grandfather, fly tying, fishing, and riding in the old Torino with the windows down and the base-ball game on the radio.

The moment I shut my door, the truck rolls forward. He puts the blinker on, even though there is not another car in

159

sight, and pulls onto the highway. A can of Dr. Pepper sits in the cup holder, and he grips the wheel with both hands. They are rough and chapped and tough as canvas.

It is time for me to transform into my new shadow flesh. Hermit, also known as Chad Joseph Miller, had two tattoos I need to get inked onto my body. He is in the earth where he can forever have peace in the outdoors. I buried him in the forest on the wild side of the lake, where the only paths are game trails made by deer.

The earth is not my element and it took me two days to get him buried with his tiny folding shovel. I was covered in dirt, blood, and sweat, but I had no choice.

"You going anywhere in particular?" His voice is loud, and it grates across my nerves like gravel.

"Anywhere downtown will do," I say, loud enough for him to hear me above the wind and road noise blowing through the cab.

My heart skips when I see a black gun holstered on his hip. How did I not notice that before? I am tired and losing my edge. The sense of foreboding comes back, and I glance around for clues about who this man is.

The landscape rolls by in a blur of pine trees that tick past the windows, then open to reveal lakes, meadows, or huge black lava flows. What the hell? My heart pounds against my chest. A golden decal in the shape of a Sheriff's badge is stuck on the corner of his windshield. He is a fucking cop, and I hopped into his truck.

Does he know who I am? I'm sure my face has been plastered all over the news and in the papers. Is he undercover, and I have been caught? I slide my hands beneath my legs so he can't see them tremble—and to prevent me from opening the door to roll out. If I see one single patrol car or flashing light, I will bail.

"You sick?" he asks. "If you need me to pull over, just say so."

My adrenaline pumps until the pressure gets so great it feels as if my eyes will burst. I need to calm myself. He may have no idea who I am. All my hair is shaved off, and I do not look the same.

"I'm fine." Think. Think. "I just need a bite to eat. I'm hypo-glycemic."

He reaches over and pops open the glove box. "There's a Cliff Bar in there. Help yourself."

Four bars sit on the truck's owner's manual and a stack of old yellowing envelopes. "You want one?" I ask.

"Don't mind if I do."

I set one on the seat beside his black holster and gun. The wrappers are old and worn like he has carted them around for years. I spend the rest of the trip taking little bites and forcing myself to chew and swallow past the lump in my throat. We roll into town without seeing a single patrol car or other cops. When he pulls to the curb, I take a deep breath. I am almost there. Keep calm and go slow. Don't blow it now.

I swing the door open, put my leg out, and expect cops to spring out from every corner. Nothing happens. I shut the door behind me, grab my backpack from the truck bed, and raise my hand in a thank you as he rolls away.

I walk, not knowing where the hell I am going, but I need to move. With every step, the tension drains until I start laughing out loud. Holy shit. I wonder if he will ever realize who he had in his truck.

Ink Angels tattoo parlor sits in the middle of a block in a small lime-green building with dark windows. Please let there only be women working here. I want a woman to work on me without any hard-ass dude guarding his territory and staring me down.

My nerves calm. I should not doubt my destiny. Hermit sat on my shore like an offering. Not only his flesh but with a pack of all the earthly items I need to survive—including the cash for me to fully transition into him. And on top of that, a fucking cop drove me into town and didn't recognize me.

The parlor is like a badass barbershop plastered with pictures and sketches of tattoos, but it smells like rubbing alcohol and green soap. Two tatted girls sit at their stations with their legs crossed. One has dark hair in a big bun, and the other has bright ruby-red hair pulled into a tight ponytail.

"You got an appointment?" the dark-haired girl asks.

"No. I'm hiking the PCT and didn't know when I'd be here."

"You think it's a good idea to get a tat while hiking? Are you able to take care of it?

"Yep."

She shrugs and gives me that look only girls can give when they think you are a dumbass. "What do you have in mind?"

I take Hermit's journal from the pack and turn to the sketches I drew. One of the tattoos is a diamond shape with a mountain peak and forest. The other is an armband with a forest, a full moon, and a lone wolf. I rip the pages out and hand them to her.

Her two-tone hair is twisted up into a wild bun. It is almond brown at her scalp and leather black in the bun. She has heavily painted eyes and fake eyelashes that look like caterpillars on her lids.

"You want both today?"

"If you can do it."

"You want them in color?"

"No, just simple black and white."

She studies them, suggests changes, and looks pissed when I tell her I want exactly what is drawn—like my designs are beneath her.

"I can do the diamond tattoo this morning, but I won't have time for both." She looks over to the red-haired girl. "Can you do an armband today?"

"Nope. I'm booked. Jox may have time if she ever gets her ass to work."

We agree to get started, and I drop my pack next to her client chair. She hands me a clipboard with paperwork. I fill it out and show my new ID. She barely looks at Hermit's driver's license, probably just to check and see that I am old enough for a tattoo. The front door flies open, and a heavyset girl, covered in tattoos and wearing a skin-tight stretchy dress, comes in.

"Sorry I'm late. Joel stayed over last night." She drops her bag on the chair at the third station. "When you wake up to a dude with a hard-on, you can't let it go to waste."

Brandy finishes my first tattoo in an hour and a half and passes me off to Jox, who finishes the armband by two o'clock. Once I pay and my tattoos are covered in plastic wrap, I step out to the bright light in search of the Juniper Grove Apartments, just like the little water sprite, Kia, told me.

The apartments are beige with brown trim and arranged in four separate buildings with parking spots running between them. Lodgepole pines, desert scrub, and huge boulders surround the buildings. Ashley, my nymph, lives in one of those apartments. All I need to do is wait for her girls to come home from school—either by bus, on foot, or wait for their momma to leave to pick them up.

I wait in a grassy patch near the apartments with my pack. If you have hiking gear in Rockland, nobody harasses you, and they trip over themselves to help.

An older skinny lady with short bleached blond hair and bangs comes out of her apartment with a brand new jar of Nutella and two bananas for me. She asks me my story, and I give her a few that I read in Hermit's journal. She is all smiles and nods to show her acceptance of me. The bitch better not interfere with me seeing Ashley. When she finally leaves, she glances around to see if any of her neighbors noticed her charity.

In a black-and-white flash, Oreo bounds to the top of a stairwell. He runs down dragging his leash behind. Ashley follows him with the baby in a carrier on her back. She is so tiny it is hard to imagine she can manage the baby without tipping backward. She wears skinny jeans, a pair of slip-ons, and an overly large man's sweatshirt that hides her body, but I know she has tight tits beneath it.

She waits next to the Juniper Grove sign with several other moms and holds a thin plastic grocery bag with something that weighs down the bottom. The big yellow school bus pulls up and blocks my view. When it pulls away, it reveals all four of them—my nymph and her three sprites.

Kia and the middle one climb on top of the boulders with their little pink school bags strapped to their backs. When Ashley calls to them, the middle one jumps off, but Kia carefully climbs down. When Ashley hands the bag to Kia, she fishes out two juice boxes and two white cheese sticks. Ashley helps the younger one put the straw in her juice box, then they all turn down the walkway.

The girls fall in line behind her, like a momma duck and her ducklings—each with distinct plumage in four different shades of blonde: champagne, white, strawberry, and ash.

28

———

ASHLEY

WHEN I PACK CARINA INTO HER CARRIER, OREO FREAKS OUT AND turns circles by the door. I set the carrier on the couch, sit in front of it, and slide my arms into the straps. Carina is too big for her front carrier, and pretty soon, I won't be able to manage her weight on my back. When that happens, I have no idea how I will get a stroller up and down the stairs. Oreo's entire body shakes as he tries to keep still long enough for me to snap the leash to his collar.

I open the door and let him run down the stairs by himself because I'm afraid he will pull too hard and send us all tumbling down to the cement below. He stops at the bottom and shakes with excitement until Carina, and I get to him. I squat down, grab his leash, then head toward the bus stop.

Several other moms are already there. Leesha looks like she's about to pop, but her baby isn't due for another two months. Coreen has her hand on her stomach. Maybe she's pregnant again. Hopefully, she will get a girl this time. Her boys are like two puppy dogs that always tumble around the grass and chase each other through the apartments.

The bus turns the corner and pulls to the curb just as I get to the stop. I look for Kia and Calista's heads in the group of kids that stand up. I know they will be on the bus like they always are, but I get a sense of relief when I see them. You never know nowadays…kids go missing all the time. It's a mom's worse fear.

Eleven kids get off at this stop. The doors fold open, and they exit in a line of bright colors. Coreen's boys jump off the last step. Calista is behind them and does the same thing. As soon as they clear the doors, my girls climb onto a pile of boulders while Carina squeals and bounces in her carrier, excited to have her sisters home. I call them, and they pet Oreo before I hand Kia the bag with their snacks.

Calista pulls the straw from her juice box and holds it up to me. She usually cracks the straw as she jams it in, and then she has trouble drinking through it.

"Remember, no playing at the dog park until you eat your snacks." It is nice to have a dog park close by so I can exercise the girls and Oreo at the same time.

Right now, with all three of my girls happy and healthy, I feel like I've got this. Chris would be proud.

29

———

EMMY

Deanna walks in five minutes before her shift. She's in her fifties with shoulder-length light brown hair and gray streaks. She doesn't wear any makeup and looks her age, but she's pretty. "Is Faye here? I don't see her SUV."

"No, she and Kerry had an appointment at the adoption agency."

"Oh, yeah. Their interview. How was she?" Deanna always arrives with a giant quilted bag.

When she plunks it on the counter, it sounds like there's a giant glass casserole dish on the bottom. I need to get more organized. All I had for lunch was a bag of popcorn and a peanut butter sandwich I brought from home. It didn't even have any jelly on it.

"Faye was nervous. She couldn't focus and paced around the lobby until it was time to go."

"I can imagine." Deanna shakes her head. "Poor thing."

"We had a theft this morning," I tell her. "A family had two bikes stolen from the racks on their SUV."

"Did you call the Sheriff's office?"

"Yes, and Faye sent them the security footage, but it was

dark, and he had a hoody on. He stole the mom's and daughter's bikes. The poor little girl was in tears." I pull the spiral coil off my wrist and put the key in the cash drawer. "Other than that, it's been quiet today."

"The day shift usually is. It's mostly check-ins and checkouts, not the nighttime antics with the crackheads, whores, and the victim's assistance ladies coming with women who got the shit beat out of them by their men."

I pull out the till and set it on the counter. Oh my God. Did she just say that? It's overly blunt. I lift the twenties from the till, count them, and record the amount. She recounts and initials the record. I do the same with the tens, fives, ones, and the change.

Jason pushes his maintenance cart by the lobby window, which reminds me. "I got a report from Izel that the toilet in 119 is clogged."

Instead of sitting in the break room while I wait for Mindy and Izel, I step outside into the sunshine. Tomorrow, I'll bring some cash and get a hamburger. The moment I step out of the lobby, something green and white catches my eye.

Deputy Wright, dressed in his typical tan shirt and khaki green vest and pants, leans against the hood of his squad car. I turn in the opposite direction. A train whistle blows in the distance, and I hear the sound of Mindy's cart rolling across the cement walkway of the second floor.

"Emmy," a deep voice calls behind me.

The wheels on the cart stop, and I look up to see Mindy in her purple scrubs paused between two rooms. She stares across the parking lot at Deputy Wright, then her head lowers, and our eyes meet. I shrug to let her know I did not expect him. I distinctly remember that Faye asked him not to hang around the motel.

"Emmy," he calls again. This time his voice is closer.

I wait for him to come to me. For a cop, he looks like a nice one, but they can't be trusted. I learned that many times growing up.

Once, when I was five, and my dad hit me, the neighbor called the cops. The officer pulled me aside to ask if my dad had hurt me. I was afraid to tell him because it would make my dad even madder. The officer promised to protect me and not tell my dad that I said anything. I told. They took my dad away and called my grandma, who was no better.

Within two days, my dad came to get me, and boy, did I get it. He didn't hit me again, but he took all my toys away and made me eat nothing but tomato soup for a week. He said it was my fault that we didn't have money because he lost his job when I tattled.

I'm grown now, and I know there is only so much the cops can control, but that instinct to keep my mouth shut runs deep.

As Deputy Wright comes near, his leather creaks. Whether it's from his shoes or gun holster, I can't tell. The rumble of train wheels on the tracks gets louder. Deputy Wright is about five foot nine and stocky. He's not overweight, just thick. He looks in his late thirties with dark hair and a clean-shaven face. The giant golden star on his chest has seven prongs with *Sheriff, Canyon County* on an outer circle, *State of Oregon* on an inner circle, and some sort of a crest or scene in the center.

"Can we go somewhere and talk?"

I want to say no because I don't have to unless he has a warrant, but maybe he has some information for me. "I'm not going to the station."

"That's okay. How about there?" He points to a tree on the other side of the parking lot, where there is a bench in the shade, and nobody will hear us.

I agree, and he walks beside me—not in front to lead me like a child and not behind me to force me like a convict.

"You like your new job?" he asks and sticks his thumbs into the armholes of his vest.

Does he do that to assure me he's not going for his gun? "It's fine. I like it here."

"Faye and Kerry are great people."

When we get to the shade, I sit on the bench, and he sits beside me. I didn't expect that and scoot away without thinking until one of my butt cheeks hangs off the edge. He doesn't say anything, but he smiles. The train whistle blows, and the rhythmic power of the wheels rumbles deep inside me.

"I'm here to help you."

"Okay…" I wait for him to continue.

"You said something about Dylan Unger being a serial killer?"

Brian asked me to keep my mouth shut.

"I believe you. Your urine test came back positive for Ketamine."

I knew he drugged me, but the confirmation makes it sink in. Cold shivers spread like ice water through my arms and legs until my entire body trembles and I feel sick.

"We've sent things off for DNA testing, but that may take a while." Deputy Wright sits solid beside me as wheels of the train screech on the tracks. "A girl was murdered in Elk Lake, and she had a clump of her hair torn out."

I knew it. My vision blurs into nothing but tan and green and khaki that melts into the blacktop. He is alive, and I slide off the bench until I am flat on the dirt staring at dozens of brown and white cigarette butts and dirty puffs of popcorn.

Suddenly, a blur of purple runs across the parking lot. "What the hell?"

A strong hand below a tan shirt cuff grabs my arm. "Come on, let's get you to the bench."

"What the fuck, Jessie?" Mindy's arms are out, and she yells.

"Deputy Wright," he says.

"I've known you since you played football with my brothers.

I'll call you whatever the hell I want to call you, especially when you are harassing my friend."

They both help me to the bench.

"I'm fine. I just got dizzy," I say.

Izel comes across the parking lot with a bottle of water, and Deanna stands with the lobby door open.

"I'm fine."

"The hell you're fine," Mindy says. "Why don't you leave her alone and get yourself a warrant or something. You ain't even a detective, so why are you bothering her?"

"Let me help her to the air conditioning," Deputy Wright says.

"I'm okay, really." I stand up and they help me toward the lobby.

By the time Mindy and Izel end their shift, Deanna has me pumped full of Diet Coke and cookies, and I'm thinking straight. I wanted to hang on to the thought that Skid killed himself like everyone thought. Of course it was him. He ripped out her hair to make more flies. I told the detectives from the beginning, but they thought I was full of shit.

The chime on the lobby door rings, and Izel's head pops in. "You ready?"

Mindy already sits in the front seat of her truck, and the engine rumbles. When Izel opens the door, I climb onto the bench seat and scoot to the center. The seat is protected by a woven cover in pale blues, greens, and yellows.

"Thanks for today," I say.

"Of course." Mindy pushes the lighter in. "We've got your back."

I can tell there is a lot more she wants to say, but she holds it in. Maybe she is waiting for Izel to get out or cutting me a break until I feel better.

Mindy lowers the visor and catches her smokes as they drop.

"What are your boys' names?" I ask Izel.

She gives me a huge smile. "Leo and Carlos."

"How old are they?"

"Leo is four, and Carlos is two."

Every day, they wait at the window for her. "They are adorable. Maybe one day I can meet them?"

"Oh yes, just not today," Izel says. My house is a mess. My mom watches them and starts our dinner, but she refuses to do any housework. She says she has done enough housework in her life for five women."

Mindy pulls up to Izel's apartment. The boys must know the sound of the truck because the curtains flutter, and there they are, shirtless and waving with big smiles.

When Izel shuts the door, Mindy taps out a cigarette, puts it in reverse, and pulls away. "Is your boyfriend Brian Cobb?" She asks like she can't wait to grill me.

"You know him?"

"I grew up in Lodell and got the hell out of there as soon as possible." She sticks the cigarette in her mouth.

I want to ask her if she ever dated Brian, but I don't want to know. The lighter pops up. Mindy holds the glowing coil to the end of her cigarette and inhales.

"I also know Skid. Brian, Jake, Skid, and Erin are a few years older than me, so I wasn't in their friend group, but I know them very well. Jake is an ass, and Skid teased us kids and told us he was the Dog Killer. He scared the crap out of us. Dogs did go missing, and several washed up downriver."

I look over at her but can't say a word. She stares straight forward with every muscle in her face tight and a grip on her steering wheel that makes her knuckles turn white.

"Skid is your boogie man…." I say.

She shoots me a dirty look. "Sounds like he's yours too. I don't doubt that Skid is a serial killer. And I know the Ungers will do anything to protect him and their name."

Suddenly, I need to move. I want to run. "Pull over. Pull over."

"What?"

"Pull over. I need out."

She slows the truck, and I reach for the door handle before she can come to a complete stop. She grabs my arm, and I turn to look at her. Her eyes are wide, and her fingers clamp onto my arm.

"Be careful. Brian is practically an Unger. They raised him and will protect him—unless he is against them. Whatever you do, never go up against an Unger." She has an intensity in her eyes that scares me. She lets go of my arm, and when I swing the door open, she says, "The Ungers are scary as shit!"

30

———

HIM

THE MORNING LIGHT IS MUTED AND DULL. I WAKE UP AND SHIVER in the damned sleeping bag. Condensation beads up inside my tent and drips down on me. Some people are meant for the woods, but I am not. In my flesh, I am weak and cold. My beard has come in, but it grows like Spanish moss rather than a thick pelt to keep me warm.

I unzip my tent and poke my head out into the crisp air that smells like sap. Fall is coming. There is no way in hell I am going out there to freeze my ass off, so I piss in the ziplock bag and seal it.

I dig my clothes out of the bottom of my sleeping bag, where I keep them warm with what is left of my body heat. I need to find a warm place for the winter. There are many vacation cabins in the woods. I just need to figure out which ones are stocked and make sure no hunters will come and find me. I wish I was in Rockland with my nymph and her three little sprites, all of us cozy and warm in beds with our naked skin wrapped in comforters.

I am almost out of food. I pop open a can of tuna for breakfast before I pack up my gear. Soon, there will be snow. Once I am free of my flesh, I will not worry about food, warmth, or people. I will be immortal, take who I want, and release who I want.

I walk about a mile to the north and come across a small log cabin. A silver Trailblazer is parked in front with the back hatch open. It is packed with suitcases, a stack of board games, and pillows. I cannot tell if they are coming or going until a man comes out with a five-gallon jug of drinking water and puts it in the back of the SUV.

"Can I shut off the water?" he calls toward the cabin.

"Five more minutes," a woman answers.

He lifts an old wooden rocking chair from the porch and carries it into the cabin, a small one-room structure with an upper window that looks like a loft. He returns with a jug of pink antifreeze and disappears into another building that looks like a full bathroom, not just an outhouse.

I open Hermit's journal and flip past pages and pages of writing. His handwriting is similar to mine, but his cursive *bs* connect at the bottom, and his letters slant more to the left than mine. I'll need to practice.

I get to his last words and flip the page with my map. I plotted out the lakes, the river, and the highway. I put a large *X* at every big cabin and a small *x* at every small one.

This one gets a small *x* with a circle around it. It is perfect for me to winter in. To hibernate. Not too big, not too small, just right.

"I'm going to the river." A young girl calls out when she runs from the open front door. She looks to be about fourteen years old with long golden blond hair. Her legs are long and thin and bare. She is a nymph.

Neither parent answers her, but she keeps going. They do not know she is gone. I close my journal and quietly lift my pack.

The ends of her hair fly up as she hops over broken limbs

and rocks. Her body moves in and out of the sunshine and shadow. I keep back in the trees and measure the distance further and further from the cabin. She heads toward the river —to me in the fluid.

I am a fly fisherman. A hunter of fish. I cast my line and trick my prey to bite. Before they know it, they are caught and stuck on a line they cannot escape. I prefer to catch my nymphs with a line of Ketamine so they do not fight or suffer.

This one reminds me of Erin. Are she and Jake still together? I hope she has realized that Jake is a land hunter. A hunter who seeks his prey and pounces. He takes girls for the pleasure of the hunt—for the win. He may not kill them physically, but he takes what he wants and sets them free, more damaged than when he found them. He is a predator. I am a god. I love and cherish my girls for eternity like nobody else will. I will take this Goldilocks into my waters, where she will be free from hunters like Jake and where she will be mine forever and ever.

When she gets to my bank, she squats down so far that her small breasts press against her knees. Her golden blond hair flows down her back in waves, perfect to tie in my flies, maybe into a Stimulator or a Golden Stone Nymph.

I shift my weight behind a cluster of immature pines and a twig cracks. She turns and stares past me with her pale-colored eyes. Her lips are parted, and she has a gap between her front teeth. She stares through the trees, but our eyes do not lock. She does not see me. She stands frozen and alert like a deer and tips her head to listen. Her intuitions are strong. I can see it on her face, but she is young and does not trust them yet. She turns back to the river and looks upstream.

Where she stands, the water is shallow and bubbles over the rocks. She reaches out to pick up a stick. I will need to take her downstream to the eddy, where it is deep enough for me to hold her under. My heart hurts that I do not have the Ketamine to help her through the initial shock of drowning.

I lower my pack to the ground and stand.

"Jenna..." a deep voice calls.

Damnit! She stands and looks back toward the cabin.

"Jenna..."

I could grab her now and haul her to the eddy, but she may scream, and he would come running.

"I'm by the river," she calls, then bounds off toward her father. "I'm coming."

She tosses the stick into the river, where it catches the flow and bounces over the barely submerged rocks. I go to where she had been. I can almost feel the warmth of her body on the gravel. The stick bounces over the rocks until it enters the eddy, where it circles the calm water and drifts to the center, right where she should have taken her last breath.

31

ASHLEY

ANOTHER BAD THING ABOUT MITCHELL AND STACY LIVING AT MY parents' house, other than the fact that they financially suck Mom and Dad dry, is that they live in the country, so they bring Grace to our neighborhood to trick-or-treat with us.

When I'm slipping Carina into her furry lion costume, Kia ties the back of Calista's Pocahontas dress. Kia is the perfect Cinderella. I twisted her hair up into a bun, and she looks beautiful.

"Can we light our pumpkins so Uncle Mitchell can see them with glowing eyes?"

"Of course." I pull Carina's mane on. She shakes her head and tries to pull it off. That's not going to work. She will need to be a mane-less lion.

We're ready just in time when there is a knock on the door. Oreo and the kids run to it, and Calista reaches for the knob. She turns it and pulls, but the door doesn't budge. The deadbolt is up high, and I keep it latched. One time, I caught Calista pulling a kitchen chair toward the door to reach it. She got a slap on the butt for that one.

"Don't you ever open that door," I remind her. "It could be a stranger."

"It's not. It's Uncle Mitchell."

"How do you know?"

"Uncle Mitchell?" Calista calls into the crack between the door and the casing.

Up high, deep breaths push through the gap. "No, it is the boogie man."

Calista's eyes pop wide open. I look through the peephole to a huge rounded eye, then unbolt the door.

When I swing it open, Mitchell stands there dressed as a pirate. Stacy poses behind him with her hands on her hips in a skanky female pirate costume, with her boobs popping out the top of the bodice. In her pirate heels, she's as tall as Mitchell, and her long brown hair is braided in strips with beads on the ends.

And, of course, Grace struts in, dressed head to toe in a little mermaid costume, complete with a red wig, singing shell necklace, sparkling turquoise crown, and a Flounder the fish trick-or-treat bag. They should have dressed her like Ursula.

"Look at your costumes," Stacy says like she has a sour pickle in her mouth. "Don't you all look so cute."

"Thank you, Aunt Stacy," Kia says.

Stacy turns to Calista. "Are you Annie Oakley?"

Calista's brows furrow. "No, I'm Pocahontas," she says as if Stacy is stupid, which we all know she is.

"Do you like our pumpkins?" Kia asks.

Grace shrugs and says, "They're okay. Ours are a lot bigger."

Kia looks over at me with a wounded expression. I force an encouraging smile. She gives it another try and grabs the bowl of roasted pumpkin seeds that we made last night. "Want some pumpkin seeds?"

Grace looks into the bowl. "No, that's disgusting."

"I'll take some," Mitchell says. "They're my favorite."

Kia's smile returns, and she brings the bowl to Mitchell. After he takes a handful, she swings it to Stacy, who looks into it with pinched lips and says, "No, thank you."

I hand my girls their plastic pumpkin trick-or-treat containers I bought at Walmart, and we head out the door.

The rest of the evening goes no better. At the very first house, when a nice elderly lady drops a candy into Grace's Flounder bag, she says, *That's it?* And...it disintegrates from there. Grace is angry that she can't walk in front of us all and ring every doorbell herself, so she plops her butt down on someone's porch and refuses to move.

Mitchell scoops her up, but she screeches bloody murder, and Stacy yells at him for being barbaric—which is funny because they are both dressed like pirates. The family in the house closes their door and pretends the pirates with their spoiled Little Mermaid are not there. The whole time, the girls and I wait on the sidewalk, freezing our behinds off.

As far as Grace is concerned, Mrs. Simpson's discipline with a belt strategy sounds very appealing.

32

EMMY

THE FIRST TRICK-OR-TREATERS COME BEFORE THE STREET LIGHTS click on. I open the door to two little kids on our step, one in an angel costume and the other dressed like a cowboy. I lower my candy bowl, and they stand there and stare at me like two stunned deer. A light wind flutters the bottom of the angel's dress and the tip of her wings.

"Say trick-or-treat," their dad says behind them and gives me one of those proud dad smiles.

The little boy says it, but the tiny angel is only about two years old. She stands there, bewildered. The boy takes a mini packet of Skittles and a tiny box of Nerds for his sister.

"Say thank you," the dad reminds them.

The boy thanks me, and the dad has to call them off the porch. I close the door and set the bowl on the floor. Brian is missing out on the fun. He can't see the kids or give them candy because he has to work.

Our last Halloween in Lodell was a blast. Brian knew all the kids by name, and they were happy to see us when we opened the door. This year, I am a stranger.

The children laugh and scream and run around the neighborhood in smeared makeup and cheap plastic masks. Another knock comes, and I open it to a huge group of seven kids, from about four years old to one who looks like a middle schooler. There's a witch, a mummy, two Disney princesses, Spiderman, Batman, and a Zombie. Three sets of parents, one with a tiny Pomeranian puppy on a leash, stand at the end of the driveway.

"I love your costumes," I say and hold the bowl out. One by one, they take mini Skittles, Nerds, Laffy Taffy, and Blow Pops.

Spiderman tells me he likes our pumpkins. Mine is a friendly pumpkin with a big smile, but Brian's has jagged teeth and mean eyes. They thank me and start to run next door to the other side of the duplex.

"Nobody lives there," I call out to them, and they all veer off back to their parents.

"Thank you," the mom with the dog calls to me and waves.

Once it is fully dark, the children who come are older, with deep voices, scary costumes, and pillowcases for their candy. The wind picks up and howls and rattles our aluminum-framed windows.

A loud knock comes on the door. I still have about half my candy left. When I bend to pick up the bowl, they knock again. I turn the knob and swing the door open to a single trick-or-treater. He stands on my porch in a scream costume with a full black robe and a white skeleton mask. He is close to six feet tall and doesn't speak. My heart pounds, and I cannot move.

Finally, in a deep voice, he says, "Trick…or…treat."

He doesn't have a bag and slowly extends a black-gloved hand. The bowl falls from my grip, clunks to the ground, and spills the bright packets of candy all over the porch.

His laugh is a terrible and demented man-laugh. I slam the door and bolt it. What the hell am I doing? I should never open the door by myself at night. Skid is out there somewhere, and I can testify against him. For all I know, that is him on the other side of my door.

I turn off the porch light and grab a steak knife and my pepper spray and turn off every single light in the house. He was probably just some dumbass high schooler thinking it's funny to scare the neighbors and get a little bit of candy, but how do I know?

I climb onto our mattress and sit there in complete blackness. Brian nailed a thick blanket over the window so he can sleep in, but it keeps our room dark with no natural light or glow from the streetlights. I sit with the knife in my hand and no sound other than my own heartbeat.

Something loud drops and clatters to the floor on the other side of the duplex. My heart completely stops for a second. Nobody is supposed to be there. It is hard to listen past my heartbeat whooshing in my ears. I don't hear anything more, which is worse. If it were a bunch of teenagers breaking in for a good time or a party, they would be clanging and banging and laughing for a long time. There is nothing. I picture Skid crouched next to the wall as he listens for me to decide when he can break into our window.

It seems like I have listened forever when I hear the front door. It is probably Brian, but what if it is not? I crawl off the mattress, slip into the closet, and slowly slide the door shut. The front door slams, and there is silence. I clasp the knife's handle with the blade out and the pepper spray in my left hand with my finger on the trigger.

I hear footsteps in the hall, then a long sliver of light at the edge of the closet door as the bedroom light is clicked on.

"Emmy?" It's Brian.

A gasp explodes from my mouth, and I start crying. The closet door slides open to a giant square of light and Brian.

"What happened?"

I don't say anything because he will go next door to check

and come back to tell me I imagined it. If Skid was there, would he tell me? Or would he just ask him to go away?

Brian comes, wraps me in his arms, and takes me from the closet. His body is warm, and I smell the sweat and sap in his shirt, but for the first time, it does not comfort me.

33

———

HIM

THE CLOUDS HANG LOW IN THE FOREST AND MUFFLE ALL SOUND in cotton. Any day the snow will dump, and I will freeze my ass off in this tent. It is time to break into Goldilocks' cabin and assess what I need for the winter.

Out of all the cabins in the area, hers is just right—a simple Lincoln Log cabin with a peaked roof and a small covered porch to keep the snow from the front door. The porch makes a hollow thump when I step onto it. The front door is locked, and I've never kicked one in. There could be a hunter or someone snowshoeing close enough to hear the splintering wood, so I wait and listen.

The forest is silent and without wind, except for a bunch of crows that squawk and scream like bratty-ass kids fighting over some scrap of food. I do not hear any humans so I lift my leg and kick the door. It is solid. On my third kick, the door finally gives way, and I fall in, onto my hands and knees— into a cavern of rich brown wood, furniture covered in patchwork quilts, and a black wood stove.

I drop my pack on the rocking chair and push the door shut. I only splintered the casing, which I can fix. Just inside the door and to the right, thick wooden stairs lead up to a loft, not an attic. Beyond the stairs and in the kitchen, a small table sits with one end to a window and only three chairs. Directly ahead is a wood stove on a platform of bricks, a couch, and a coffee table. To the right of the door and below a window is a twin-sized daybed. It must be Goldilocks' bed, and it is just right. That is where I will sleep, all wrapped up in the blankets with her scent.

The breaker for the electricity is in the kitchen. I flip it on and bring the light over the sink to life. Back outside, I turn on the pump for the well and kick in the door to the detached bathroom. It is clean and sparse, with a shower, toilet, and sink. I turn on the pilot light for the hot water and head back into the cabin to assess my supplies.

I find a battery-run radio and turn the knob through the static of the news, talk radio, and rock and roll. I also find propane, outdoor gear, batteries, binoculars, and a portable propane heater that will have to do. I cannot have the smoke of a wood fire draw anyone to my location. A pair of old wooden snowshoes are attached to the wall as decoration, but I can use them if needed.

I lay all of Hermit's things on the table. His dry box contains his passport, driver's license, shot records, and phone charger. I pull out the charger and plug his phone in. I will get my first glimpse of his photos and my new past. When the light of Hermit's phone comes on, I open the photos and scroll through all the landscapes and micro images of flowers, rocks, bugs, and rodents. He has a few with coyotes, bears, and osprey in the distance. The others are of hikers that climb in trees, pose with their packs and trekking poles, or spread out like trash on city streets. Some of them have their thumbs up as they hitchhike to and from towns.

Several photos of Yapper pop up, with her curly dark choco-late hair. One is her preparing a meal, just like she did for me. It is as if I am the one who took the picture because there she is, crouched over her hiking stove in her red bandana. I can still taste the rehydrated chili mac she fed me and the taste of her sweat on my tongue.

Most of the photos of Hermit are selfies with his face plastered in front of a landscape. This is what I need. I zoom in. He has an angled scar between his eyebrows. I zoom in more. It is about a centimeter long, centered above his nose, and angled down at about 135 degrees. The highest end is closer to his right eye and slopes down toward the inner corner of his left.

I draw the line between my eyebrows with his pen and hand mirror. I must walk among the people in my new shadow flesh. My Hermit flesh. The flesh of Chad Joseph Miller. As him, I will find Emmy, and she will be mine like she always should have been.

The tip of Hermit's knife blade presses into my skin and then pierces it. I pull it through the line I drew. Thick bright blood runs along the cut and pools into the tear duct of my eye. It spills over and flows down my nose to the corner of my mouth, where it tastes like a copper penny. I can't wait to be free of the flesh, the blood, and the earth.

34

———

ASHLEY

THE TREES ALONG MY PARENTS' DIRT ROAD STILL HAVE THE LAST few yellow and orange leaves that cling to the branches, but most of them lay on the ground and create a carpet of color all the way up the drive.

I have cupcakes and a broccoli casserole ready to pop in the oven. The casserole is a family favorite my mom taught me how to make when I was in middle school. Now, it is my responsibility to make every Thanksgiving. The girls talked me into cupcakes since they do not like pie. Kia and Calista frosted them, and I bought orange, yellow, and red sprinkles for the top.

A brand new monstrous brown and yellow plastic play structure blocks half the view of the house. The girls silently stare at the two-story playhouse with a twisting tube slide, an open slide, and a swing set with two swings. Mitchell's and my old metal swingset sits off to the side, all cockeyed on a slope.

"It even has a mailbox...." Kia says.

The thing probably cost Mitchell his entire paycheck.

"Can we play on it?" Calista asks and begins frantically trying to unlatch the seatbelt from her booster.

188

"I'm sure you can, but let's be polite and say hi to Grandma and Grandpa first."

The moment I open my door, Oreo bounds out and runs straight for a tree. The girls head straight for the play structure and stand at the white plastic French windows, where they peek inside while I'm taking Carina from her car seat.

"It has a kitchen set and a table," Kia says.

Calista reaches for the door handle, but Kia stops her. "We have to go see grandma and grandpa first."

With Carina on one hip, I grab the casserole and call Kia over to get the cupcakes. The refrigerator is still on the porch with an extension cord through the window. Mom peels potatoes in the kitchen while Dad and Mitchell sit on the couch and yell at the football game on the television.

"There's my baby girl with her baby girls," Dad says.

Calista runs to Grandpa and gives him a quick hug while Kia sets the cupcakes on the coffee table. After the grandpa hugs are done, they climb onto the couch and all over Mitchell. "Can we play on the new swings?"

"Maybe after the tickle monster gets you." Mitchell scoops up a girl in each arm and plops them onto the couch where he was sitting. They laugh and wiggle and kick their feet. When Kia almost kicks Dad, Mitchell scoots them away.

I set the casserole on the counter and give my mom a kiss on the cheek. "Nice play structure."

Without pausing the potato peeler, she shakes her head. "Stacy insisted. She spends Mitchell's money faster than he can make it."

"Speaking of the devil, where is she?"

"Oh, she's finishing up her cooking in the trailer and staying out of my way."

The front door swings open, and Grace steps in dressed in a sparkly princess dress, two sizes too small, complete with a tiara and ballet shoes. Stacy comes in behind her with a baking dish covered in aluminum foil and a plastic grocery sack that hangs from her wrist. Grace crosses her arms and walks to the couch where the girls are in the middle of their tickle attack.

"Oh, Little Miss Sassy Pants, you want some tickles too?" Mitchell puts his arm around Grace, but she stiffens and steps back.

Mitchell wiggles his fingers over Kia and Calista, "Here it comes again."

The girls start laughing before he even touches them.

"Stop it!" Grace yells. "Daddy! Stop!"

Stacy sets the dish down and walks toward the couch with the sack. "Mitchell," she says with a snap in her voice. "Stop making them scream."

Mitchell looks up at her, and for an instant, I see the mischievous gleam in his eye that I am all too familiar with. When we were kids, that gleam meant that I better start running. His expression fades, and Mitchell sits at the end of the couch.

"How about a hug for Aunt Stacy?" Stacy says in a sing-song tone.

The girls sit up but do not get off the couch.

"Grace and I made treat bags for everyone." She hands the grocery sack to Grace.

The girls slide off the couch and give Stacy a hug.

Grace sets the sack down and reaches in. She hands a brown paper lunch sack, cinched at the top with curly orange ribbon, to Calista. Once Calista takes it, Grace reaches in and gives one to Kia. Then brings a third over for Carina. The last one is for her.

"Go ahead and open them," Stacy says.

The girls pull out rainbow-colored slinkies, flowered headbands in autumn colors, and animal masks with a stretch band in the back. Grace has a tiger mask, a panda for Calista, a giraffe for Kia, and a puppy for Carina. They all get plastic unicorns, glow sticks, crayons, and bright-colored twisty straws.

"Thank you, Aunt Stacy," the girls say and give her unsolicited hugs.

"They are from Grace, too," Stacy says.

"Thank you, Grace." Kia moves forward to give her a hug, but Grace steps away.

"Grace," Stacy says. "Why don't you give the girls a tour of your new play structure?"

The girls instantly abandon their goodies and run for the door.

"Thank you," I say to Stacy. "That was very thoughtful."

"You're welcome," Stacy says with a satisfied smile. She holds her arms out to Carina. "Want to come outside with Aunt Stacy?"

Carina puts her head on my shoulder and hides her eyes. I peel her away. "Go to Aunt Stacy, and she will take you on the slide."

Carina lets me hand her to Stacy, and they walk out the door. As soon as the door shuts, Dad turns to Mitchell. "Let's go supervise."

Dad loops his sling over his head, and with his good arm, he positions his paralyzed one into it. They rise off the couch and move toward the door with the football game still going.

"How's dad doing?"

"He gets frustrated. He's a man who has worked his whole life. He was not meant to be idle, and he's driving me crazy." With a pile of newly peeled potatoes on the cutting board and the peels on a newspaper, Mom rinses off her hands and hugs me. "It's so nice to have you and the girls here."

I take the ends of Mom's white-blond hair in my fingers. "Your hair looks beautiful." It used to be silky soft, but as it has turned gray, there is a coarseness to it.

"Thanks," she says. "Stacy bleached it for me."

"The house looks great." It is deep-cleaned and clutter-free.

"Stacy helped me with that too."

"Wow! I'm surprised."

"Dad and I sat down and had a heart-to-heart with the two of them. So far, so good."

"Where's Thistle and Gretchen?"

"Oh…that's a point of contention. They chewed on Grace's new play structure, so we need to keep them in their pens. Don't say anything about it in front of your dad. I don't want to ruin his day."

Mom fills a pot with cold water and drops the peeled potatoes in. "Come upstairs. I have something for you."

I look out the kitchen window. With Dad and Mitchell there, the girls are playing nice, and Stacy is swinging with Carina in her lap. I climb the stairs behind Mom. The third stair creaks, just like it always has. When I used to sneak downstairs in the middle of the night, I always counted my way and took a giant step over that one.

Mom leads me into my old bedroom. It still has my mint green wallpaper with pink roses and a corkboard with the same school pictures and snapshots of my friends and Chris. The fairy lights are still strung over my bed and around the giant poster of the Backstreet Boys.

Mom turns to me with a solemn face. "I'm going to redecorate your and Mitchell's old rooms. It feels like we're stuck in the past, and it is time to move on."

This room represents my childhood and mom wants to erase it.

"I need you to tell me what you want to keep. It will be too hard for you to pack it up, so I will do it for you. Do you want me to box everything?"

I turn my back to her and walk over to the corkboard. I don't want her to see me cry, but my entire body shakes, and the sobs come out in gasps. Mom wraps her arms around me and doesn't say a word—she just holds me. We stand there for what seems like forever, and when I open my eyes, everything on the corkboard is under water. I blink and wipe away the tears. The poem Chris wrote me is still pinned to the board with a red tack.

Every Single Day
I will climb any mountain to see your face.
I will swim any sea to feel your embrace.
When I look at you, it almost makes me faint,
It's so hard to practice restraint.
These are the things that I feel,
And I know that my love for you is real.
I love you so much, it feels like I can fly.
I want to protect you, I will even die.
Whatever our future holds, I cannot say
But I know I want to be with you every single day.

Mom holds me tight, and we tremble together. After a few minutes, I feel the warmth of her breath on my ear. "Maybe facing it head-on will help you put it aside."

35

———

HIM

EVERYONE IS ASLEEP. NOBODY IN LODELL LOCKED THEIR DOORS my whole life, but I bet they do now. Brian's house is dark, and a red rocking chair sits on the porch. I was right. The door is locked. A lightness bubbles up in my chest. They finally respect me. I bet none of them laugh now.

Instead of Emmy's Mazda, Jewell Winkler's old blue mini truck is parked in the drive. It could be a trick. I go to the side front window and place my palms on the glass. The latch has been broken for years. This is one of Jake's rentals, and I doubt he fixed it. He neglects and trashes his things. Why wouldn't he? He never worked for them, just like he never worked to get Erin and does not appreciate her.

The window slides up. I push the curtain aside and climb through onto a couch. Unless Brian and Emmy decided to redecorate, this is no longer where they live. A soft yellow light comes from the partially open bedroom door.

I have been in this house so many times that it feels like mine. I hold my breath and slip through the opening. The bathroom light casts a faint glow across Jewell's dried-up and leathery body. She is naked, with her arms over her head and her tits spread out like fried eggs, sunny side up. Fucking shit! That image will be seared onto my brain forever.

Where have Brian and Emmy gone? I hope his ass is in jail and she is back on the street where she belongs. I take a box of Captain Crunch on my way past the kitchen and out the front door. I leave it open just to mess with Jewell and step out onto the porch.

Two blocks over and lit by nothing but the streetlight and moon, the windows of my house are dark and vacant. I almost expected it to be gone, picked clean, and bulldozed to the ground by my father so he could erase me from my family and my town.

Tomorrow is Thanksgiving, and I have come home. I can almost taste the turkey, cranberry sauce, and my mom's rhubarb pie with whipped cream. Uncle Doc will come with nothing but beer. Jake will bring Erin and expect her to help the women, but she will head straight to the couch to watch the football games with the men. My brother, Emmet, will come from Idaho with whatever girl he is dating. My sisters, Debbie and Susan, will come in from Portland.

Debbie will bring some organic vegetables and tofu to turn into a vegan turkey dinner that tastes like crap, and only she will eat it. After dessert, mom will beg Susan to torture the rest of us by playing her violin. The men will all step outside or head to the river to throw in a line. I wonder if Brian and Emmy will show. Or if they finally cut him off. He turned me in, and family does not do that to family.

The street sits silent and still with nothing but the gurgling of the river and the distant rumble of a train coming toward town. I swing open my gate and step in. Nothing seems disturbed. All my old cars I planned to rebuild still sit in the driveway. My grandpa's old cement deers, which my mom wanted to throw away when he died, still stand by the dried-up pond. The buck only has one side of his antlers from when she tossed it in a pile. The other half is somewhere in my house.

Yellow crime tape hangs from the pillars of my porch, and a sticker is taped across the opening of the door. The goddamned cops better not have taken all my shit. I reach under my porch to the nail beneath the stairs. The key rattles as my fingers sweep past it. The cops are idiots. If they did not find this key, they certainly did not find my stash of Ketamine.

I run the blade of my pocketknife through the sheriff's seal and slip my key into the door. I can't risk turning a light on, so I step in and move through my home by memory, straight down the hall and into my bedroom. In the morning, I will get the Ketamine and my fly-tying tools and materials if they are still here. I crawl beneath the covers and breathe in my familiar and musty sheets.

The next thing I know, the window is lit with morning light, and a truck rumbles by in the street. The town wakes with no idea that I am home. Something is off. Something big. Fuck! Candie, my mannequin, is gone. The spot on my desk where she posed with no arms and bent knees is empty. I dressed her in Amber's bra and Shawna's skanky ho skirt with no underwear and thigh-high stockings, so I could peek at her pussy whenever I wanted.

The fucking cops also took down every vintage Playboy centerfold and left nothing but dark squares on the sun-bleached paneling. Those were from my grandpa's stash, and they are family heirlooms. Of course, they left the movie posters and only took things that make me look bad. They also took my nude Barbie doll collection and my little girl hand puppets. I sit up, afraid to look around. Shit! My entire Nintendo 64 and all the game cartridges are gone. I earned the money to buy that when I was a kid. I helped people with their shitty chores and sold the fish I caught. Fuckers!

I slide open my closet door, get down on my knees, and push

aside all the junk in the back corner. It is dark in the closet, but I feel the edges in the floorboard until they reach the gap of my secret compartment. Please let my stash be there. I get my fingernails into the groove and lift the boards up. I stick my hand in and feel the vials, pills, syringes, and my grandfather's old lighter still there. I scoop everything out and run my thumb over the fly fisherman on the lighter. He stands beside the river with his rod and his line. Everything fades, but the feel of plastic, glass, metal, and the steady thumps of my heartbeat. I am back and have what I need to fulfill my destiny.

36

EMMY

"I'm sick. I can't go." I pull the blanket up and turn over.

"You have to."

"I feel like throwing up." I about had a nervous breakdown when Brian told me we needed to go to the Unger's for Thanksgiving.

Brian puts his hand on my shoulder and turns me toward him. I close my eyes so he can't see that I'm faking it. All I can think of is Mindy and her warning about the Ungers.

"Look at me." Brian puts his warm hand on my cheek.

I'm not totally faking it. I do feel sick about going. I can't do it. I open my eyes. Brian is not mad, but I can tell he won't back down.

"It will be okay. Skid won't be there. I'll bet the sheriff has detectives posted in Lodell to watch for him. Nothing will happen with Rose and Russ's other kids from Portland and Idaho at the house."

I want to tell him what Mindy said, but for some reason, I've kept it in. I also haven't told him about what happened with Deputy Wright. I don't know why.

Maybe I am the one who has created something between us.

Maybe other people are— or perhaps it is a shift in Brian that my body intuitively knows. Whatever it is, there is a fracture between us.

"You went to Thanksgiving there last year."

I give Brian a *you've got to be shitting me look*. "Last year, I didn't know that Skid murdered Amber and the other girls. And he hadn't tried to kill me."

"You still don't know that for sure."

"I had Ketamine in my piss test."

His eyebrows pinch together and he is silent for a moment. "When did you find that out?"

I only shrug.

"Okay…" He puts his hands in the air. "It looks like he's guilty, but there is no way in hell he's going to do anything today."

"It will be horrible. Rose is as scary as shit, and Jake will glare at me the whole time."

Brian takes his hand from my cheek and rubs my shoulder. "Come on, get up and get dressed. It will only be for a few hours, and then we can leave."

"Do I have to?" My whole life has been a series of people who make me do what I don't want. I thought it would be different when I became an adult.

"Yes, we both have to. The Ungers paid for my lawyer and kept me out of jail." Brian slides the blanket off of me. I am naked from the waist down, and he gives my bare ass a tap. "You're lucky we're running late."

"How is that lucky? Making love sounds amazing."

He smiles and shakes his head like he's trying to clear his thoughts. "Plus, Jewell has a few boxes of our things that weren't confiscated by the detectives."

"Why does Jewell have them?" Jewell is the skinny bartender who looks like an old tweaker lady.

"As soon as the sheriff released our house, Jake rented it out to her."

I hate to think of her in our bed. I know it was furnished, and everything belonged to Jake, but that was the bed Brian and I made love in for the very first time.

I get up and pull on a pair of jeans and a sweater and brush my hair into a ponytail. That is all the effort the Ungers are worth. We get into our tan-colored grandpa car and drive to the grocery store for a pre-made chocolate cream pie and a six-pack of Hamm's.

I haven't been to Lodell since the day I followed the sheriff out and finally broke free from the town. It is like I escaped from a Stephen King movie, and here I am, going right back in.

On our way out of Silverdale, we pass by rimrock cliffs on one side of the road with long grasses and brush on the other side. Green and white poles with barbed wire stretched between them divide the road from the scrub.

The mile markers and telephone poles slip past the windows for about half an hour before we come to the turnoff for Lodell and start our descent. The desert transforms into green farmland with black and brown cows and nothing but farms or trashy trailers with beater cars.

Brian turns left at the Lodell sign with a white arrow. I remember that sign. It reassured Amber and me that we were on the right road. We were such idiots. No, I was the idiot because Amber didn't want to come.

"Life is full of things we don't want to do, and you build character by doing them anyway," Brian says.

I stare at him for a moment, surprised that came out of his mouth. "Thanks, DAD...I really don't need a lecture."

"You're acting like a baby. It's only a Thanksgiving dinner."

Now, I'm pissed. "Pull over! I feel sick."

I jump out of the car and squat down with my head between

my legs. I don't throw up, but it feels good to get out of the car. "I'll wait here. Pick me up on your way home."

"Seriously?" He looks annoyed. "Get in the fucking car and pull it together."

I don't move.

I hear his door open and his feet on the gravel. They stop next to me.

"Emmy." His voice is more tender. "I will make sure nothing happens to you, and if it gets bad, we will leave."

The sun glows behind him and turns his body into a silhouette with no features. "Promise?"

"Yes, I promise." He helps me up and into the car. Brian puts his blinker on and pulls back onto the road. "Just hang out with Deb or Susan. They're not fond of their mother either."

We come to the end of the asphalt, where the dirt road drops down into the canyon toward Lodell. This is where Amber and I lost our cell service. She freaked out and said that we were in the middle of freaking Narnia, but it was too late in the day to turn back. It is also the very first place I laid eyes on Brian when the guide truck pulled up, and he asked if we needed any help.

"What about Erin?" I ask. "Is she still around?"

"No. She packed up and moved out before Jake even got out of jail. Nobody has heard a word from her."

"She probably realized he drugged her all those nights he date-raped the other girls."

"You don't know that."

"Seriously? I was there. I saw that she only had a beer or two, and we had to carry her home."

"Emmy! You can't say things like that."

"Can I at least think them?"

"Just don't say them out loud."

"This is a bunch of bullshit."

"Let the investigators take care of it. They will find the evidence. We can't be involved."

"Then why did you blow the whole lid off the day you pulled Skid from the river?"

Brian picks up speed, and it feels like we are driving over a corrugated roof. "I didn't think it through. I didn't realize what a tangled mess this is."

"I know you, Brian. You are a good person. How can you let this happen?" My voice comes out fragmented, broken up by the road.

"I'm not letting anything happen. I blew the lid off, and now the investigators can take over. If we don't back off, we could both end up dead or in jail. Let them do their jobs."

"Pull over, pull over." As soon as the car stops, I jump out and run for the nearest boulder. This time, I do get sick, and when I look up, there it is. The tunnel. The graffiti tunnel with a skull and pitchforks on one side and an owl with giant ringed eyes on the other.

Brian sits in the car with his forehead pressed to the steering wheel. I look up the road we just came down. I could start walking and make him come after me. I could. But what if he doesn't? What if he chooses the Ungers over me? I can't think of anything else to do, so I go around the car and get back in.

Without a word, our car rolls forward, into the mouth of the tunnel, and past the artistically challenged graffiti. Sprayed in red, black, blue, or white is *DEATH. Jason Loves Candie*, and a giant red penis and balls right next to *Becky Sucks Dick*. Becky. I almost forgot about Becky. What a bitch.

We pass the giant brownish-red cliffs layered with crumbly dark rock at the top and we cross back and forth over wooden bridges and follow the creek through the canyon. Just as Brian is about to go under the gigantic steel railroad bridge, he turns to me. "Do you mind if we stop by our...I mean, Jewell's house to get the boxes first?"

I want to say something sarcastic about him finally giving one flying frick about my opinion, but I don't. "Sure."

The land flattens out to rock and desert brush. We drive by the abandoned bare wood shacks and old rail fences with sagging barbed wire of old Lodell. Back there is the old Unger homestead where Skid had Crystal strapped to a mattress.

We pass Bud's Garage, the only business in Old Lodell still in operation and where the road meets the river, we take a left into Lodell where cars line the main street, parked in front of mismatched businesses. Most have a western look, but some are built with cement blocks or brick with giant store windows.

We cruise past Lodell Community Church, Tortilla Flat, Happy Cow Hamburgers, Whiskey Dicks, and Lou's Hardware. Nothing has changed. At least a dozen dogs lie around, under porches or wander loose in the streets. I look around for the three-legged mutt, Lieutenant Dan, but I don't see him.

The same kids run around in groups. They chase each other or play hide-and-seek behind cars and buildings. The entire town is on a loop that replays itself year after year, just like in the movie, *Play It Again Sam*. My heart aches when Brian puts on the blinker and turns down our street. I don't want to see Jewell living in our house like it is hers.

The house has so many memories. It is where I fell in love with Brian and where I grieved Amber. For a year, I rattled around inside and stared at the cracked ceiling and giant nail holes in the walls. Brian pulls up beside Jewell's faded blue mini truck.

Jewell answers the door in a button-up Hawaiian shirt with a cigarette hanging from her mouth. She has thin hair pulled back into a bleached blonde ponytail, and her face is tanned and leathery. "Brian, Emmy! Come on in."

"We can't stay long," Brian says as he steps inside. "We need to be at the Ungers."

"Must be nice to have Thanksgiving up there on their deck or looking out the big glass windows," Jewell says. "I have only been up there when Rose needed me to bring her the bar receipts."

The house smells like baking turkey and cigarettes, and a man I don't recognize sits in a recliner. He has a great big beer belly and doesn't say a word. He sits there with a beer in his hand and stares at a football game on the television. The house is tidy and has the vibe of a Goodwill Store with all sorts of outdated things.

"Your stuff's right there." She points to three reused beer boxes by the door. "Jake told me to throw it out, but I couldn't do that to you."

"I appreciate it." Brian lifts the top box and hands it to me.

I can't get out the door fast enough. We throw the boxes into the back seat of our car and pull away toward the Ungers. Buckskin Mary's, Rimrock Outfitters, and the Whitehorse Inn all look exactly the same as they did the day we left town, but something is off.

"Stop, stop, stop," I say.

Brian hits the brakes so hard that I slam into the dashboard.

"Where's your seatbelt?" he asks.

"Look…" I point to the far side of the hotel, to an empty space with a hole in the ground. "The shoe tree is gone."

"Holy shit," Brian says. "Who would do that?"

I know exactly who did it. It feels like someone popped a cork and released a million tiny bubbles inside me. The detectives believed me, and I bet that all the shoes, including my and Amber's lime green converses, are in evidence and being tested. I want to jump out of the car and run around the hole, but I stay put.

My heart races, and I struggle to keep myself still on the last stretch of dirt road up to the Ungers. When we get to the top of the cliff, two black trucks, Jake's jacked-up silver truck with off-road tires, Rose's blue SUV, and an ugly white Volvo are parked at the front of the house. It is the nicest house in Lodell and is filled with four of the nastiest people.

Brian hands me the pie, and he takes the beer. "Ready?"

"No," I say but follow him in anyway.

Rose and her daughters, Susan and Deb, stand in the kitchen, while the men huddle around the television and scream at the football game. The only woman not in the kitchen is a beautiful blonde with long curly hair wedged between Emmet and Doc. I assume she is Emmet's girlfriend from Idaho, afraid to leave his side. I met Susan and Deb last year but spent most of my time with Erin. They are both from Portland and into everything Zen, herbal, and recyclable—the exact opposite of their mother.

Jake gives us an intentional glare and makes a point of turning away back to the game. This is going to be a long day. I set our store-bought pie, which probably won't be eaten, next to the homemade apple and rhubarb pies. Brian rips open the top of the beer and pulls out two cans. He hands one to me and heads toward the men.

Rose has her hair down and in waves past her bony shoulders. She wears a tight-fitting yoga top with the top third of her boobs exposed. Her daughters are dressed in loose shirts with everything covered, and neither wears any makeup.

"Need any help?" I ask.

Rose hands me a bag of potatoes and a peeler. I stand at the counter and peel while I stare out the window at the entire town below. The cars move through the streets and past the miniature buildings. The people are dots, moving like little black ants. Beyond the town is the river, and on the other side is the Indian reservation with its grassy bank and red bluff.

The potato skin peels away, curls, and falls onto the paper towel as Rose tells stories of Buckskin Marys and the hassles of running both a bar and a hotel. She offers her girls the opportunity to run the hotel, but neither of them seem interested in coming back to Lodell. None of them say a word about Skid or where he is. For all I know, he is here in this house, hiding in a bedroom and waiting for food.

After I peel the potatoes, I step out onto the deck. A cold wind comes up the canyon, and a train rumbles in the distance. It is such a beautiful place with the red and brown rimrock and the deep blue river with long stretches of whitewater. The land is dry and sparse with sage, juniper, and wildflowers.

A tall round table and bar chairs sit at the edge of the balcony, with a pair of binoculars for a centerpiece. I pick them up and press my belly to the rail. I adjust them to my eyes, then roll the focus until the town becomes clear. A red Honda pulls up to Carl's Cabins. The driver's door swings open. An old man in a sweater vest and slacks gets out and walks to the passenger side. He opens it and helps an old woman in a canary blue dress get out.

A hand clamps onto my arm. I scream, and the binoculars drop from my hands and clunk onto the deck. I turn to Rose's face so close to mine that I can see the individual hairs in her nose.

"What the…? You scared the crap out of me."

By the expression on her face, I can tell it is not a joke. Her cheeks are red, and her teeth are bared like a snarling dog. She does not let go and digs her fingers into my arm, almost to the bone.

"Have you kept your mouth shut?" Her breath smells like booze.

My voice is caught in my throat, so I nod my head.

She presses her fingers in further until tears well in my eyes.

"Sometimes fate just grabs ahold of you, and there is nothing you can do," she says, just before I barf all over her feet.

37

HIM

I sift through the mess the Sheriff's department left. They dumped out drawers and bins and scattered my shit all over. They took all my old fly-tying tools and materials, my fly rod and vest, all my mail, the birdcage, several bins of collector toys, and my pink salon chair. What the hell? It would take me a year to figure out all they confiscated. Half my collectables are trashed, cracked, or torn from their boxes. That shit is worth some money. Fuckers!

I want to crash my family Thanksgiving and see the look on their faces, but I know my candy-ass sisters would turn me in. I need my fly-tying tools and materials. It's going to be a long winter and I need to restock.

I wait until after midnight. I have one more stop at the fly shop to take what I need. I am already a fugitive, so why the hell not? I will always be a fugitive in this town. Even if I have Chad Joseph Miller's scar and tattoos, I will never be him in Lodell. I need a new rod and vest, a vise, scissors, bobbin, thread, hackle pliers, whip finisher, stacker...fuck, I need everything. Maybe the shop will have a kit with all the basics, then I can add to it from there.

I slip out my door and pull it shut. My porch creeks, and the scrap of yellow crime scene tape flutters in the breeze. I close my gate behind me. This may be the last time I see my house or town, and my body feels heavy, like it is filled with cement.

A shadow moves and turns up my street. I duck down behind Officer Green's garbage bin and watch. It moves with familiar proud, and cocky steps. It stops. A light flicks near its face, and then the glow of a cigarette. You've got to be shitting me! But what other idiot would be out in the middle of the night at the exact time I am leaving town?

He steps into the light of a streetlamp, and sure as shit, it's him. My heart races, and my breath whooshes in my ears so loud I cannot hear his footsteps. I shrink down and pray that he cannot see me. My entire life, I have cowered from Jake. He always intimidated, mocked, or punched me. He made me look stupid in front of girls, laughed at me, and called me a dumbass.

I take a deep breath. I am no longer the frightened little cousin. I am the river. I rage, and I thunder, or I flow quiet and deep. Just as he is about to pass me, I rise up, and he flinches.

"What the fuck?" Is his immediate response. Then I see that he realizes it is me, and a wash of fear flicks over his face.

Neither of us says anything for a moment that strings out for what feels like an eternity. Jake's fear turns to anger, which is his normal response.

"You dumbass. What are you doing jumping out at me like that?"

I do not cower and do not explain. I stare straight at him and take a step forward. He leans back, and the glimmer of fear returns.

"You sure caused a shitstorm here. What were you thinking to kidnap that girl? We had a good thing going, and you screwed it all up. Thanks a lot." He takes a long draw from his cigarette but cannot hide the tremble in his lip.

"Hello, cousin," is all that I say.

"They arrested me for date rape and kidnapping. And now, I have to go to fucking court. Did you kill those girls? The ones they recovered from the river?"

"Yes."

For the first time in my life, I feel a glimmer of respect from him.

"Where are Brian and Emmy?"

"To hell with Brian." His words come out in a fog of cigarette smoke. "He's a traitor."

"Where is he?"

Jake takes another long draw from his cigarette, which causes the tip to glow a hot and bright orange. He stares at me for a moment, and I can almost see the gears turn in his mind. His eyes narrow, and he blows out the smoke. It would be very convenient for him if Brian disappeared. Very convenient. But I don't want Brian. I want Emmy.

His lip quivers when he exhales. "In Silverdale. In a duplex on the corner of Juniper and Dobbs."

"Is Emmy still with him?"

He nods his head. "And just as much of a bitch as ever."

"You gonna tell anyone you saw me?" I know he won't. Jake is devoted to friends and family. He is also too full of his own arrogance to tattle about anything.

"No, it ain't going to do me any good if you're in jail." He takes another drag and then drops his cigarette onto the sidewalk. "Why'd you do it?"

"Because the river takes who it wants."

His eyebrows pinch together, and I see that he is a coward. I love it. He nods and walks away with his cigarette still burning where he stood. He finally respects me because I am the river, and for the first time in our lives, he sees me for who I am.

38

———

EMMY

It snowed all day. A good foot of it sticks and drapes a white blanket over the cars and hides the dirty black parking lot. Everything looks clean, fresh, and new. Faye brought a huge box of hot chocolate packets for the break room, and I binged on them all day. She also put cinnamon spice air freshener in for the holidays, which is a nice break from the Hawaiian Breeze.

As soon as I go over the till with Deanna, Faye calls me into her office. Several red and green plastic bins sit beside the restroom door, and Faye is in her office chair with piles of mail, all separated and stacked before her. An old cardboard box with several layers of tape sits on the corner of her desk.

"Have a seat." Faye waves her hand toward the chair at the front of her desk.

What have I done wrong now?

A flicker of understanding crosses her face. "It's nothing bad." She lets out a little laugh to reassure me.

I lower myself into the black padded chair.

Faye puts her elbows on the desk and clasps her hands together like she is praying over her bills. "How are you doing?"

"I'm fine," I say.

"You seem more on edge. Is there something I need to be aware of?"

I want to keep my mouth shut, but she has been so supportive—and Mindy and Izel said she looks out for her employees as long as you are honest with her.

"I'm just worried because they have not caught Skid…I mean Dylan Unger."

She nods her head like this is not news to her.

"He may have killed the girl at Elk Lake a couple of months ago."

Her eyebrows pinch together, and she is silent for a moment. "I'm sorry. Is there anything I can do to help you?"

I shake my head.

"Well, that's not why I called you in here." Her voice sounds cheerful. "I know you and Brian have started over here in Silverdale, and I was going through the storage room looking for all my Christmas boxes. I found this box of decorations I haven't used in a couple of years. Would you like to have them?"

"Yes, I would love that. We don't have any Christmas decorations." Her kindness makes me want to cry. She doesn't need to do anything for me.

"Since you always hang out an hour after work to wait for Mindy and Izel, how would you feel about working an additional hour? I'll pay you to do extra things around here."

"Yes, I would love that."

"Great! Want to start now?" A big smile spreads across her face. "I need the lobby decorated for Christmas. Everything is in those bins there."

I give her a smile and haul the bins into the lobby. I'll be paid to decorate? I would have done it for free.

When the door chimes, I'm trying to attach some plastic pine garland to the edge of the front desk, and there's Izel in her puffy black coat.

"Wow! It looks so festive in here. Did you do this, Emmy?"

I nod and look around. I'm halfway done, but it looks amazing with big collectible Christmas gnomes, thick garland, and wreaths. None of that cheap Dollar Store stuff I'm used to. Faye said the tree will be here tomorrow, and I can decorate that too. She has good taste, and I can't wait to see what's in the box she gave me.

I drop the garland back in the bin for tomorrow. "I'll be right out."

Izel steps in and goes to the popcorn machine while I'm dragging the bin into Faye's office. Deanna sits in the recliner with her knitting on her lap as Faye writes checks.

"See you tomorrow," I say, and both women wave goodbye. I scoop up the cardboard box and thank Faye again before leaving.

Izel stands by the door with two red-striped bags of popcorn. "Those for your boys?"

"Yes, I told them I'd bring them something since they put their toys away before bed all week." She steps out and holds the door for me.

Mindy's truck idles, and she scrapes snow from the windshield. "Are we going to be okay?"

Mindy pauses with her scraper, turns toward me, and rolls her eyes. "This is four-wheel drive, and the roads have been deiced and plowed all day."

When Izel opens the door, I set the box on the seat and wiggle it across as I slide in. Once in the center, I lift the box to my lap. Izel gets in, and we wait in the cab with the defrost blowing full and loud as Mindy pushes the wiper blade down and moves to the other side. When she is done, she opens the driver's side door and lets in a blast of cold air.

She dusts the snow from the front of her brown Carhartt coat. "You two cozy in here? Don't strain yourselves by helping me or anything."

"We won't," Izel says in her sweet voice with a tinge of sarcasm.

"I'm sorry," I say. "I'll help next time."

"If there is a next time," Mindy says. "I may just kick both your asses out to walk."

I'm not sure if it is a joke or not, but it doesn't faze Izel, so I let it go. I can't wait until Izel gets out of the truck. Every day, as soon as we drop Izel off, Mindy and I talk about the Ungers and Lodell. I have learned more about Lodell from Mindy over the last three months than I did living there for an entire year.

Mindy wasn't surprised that Rose threatened me at Thanksgiving. She says that Rose does that to everyone, even her own kids. That's why Emmett and her girls moved away as soon as they graduated from High School. Rose and Russ were harsh on their kids, especially Skid, who has always been odd.

Mindy drives slow on the slushy road behind a jacked-up Ford truck that throws up dirty brown road spray. When Mindy puts the wipers on, they smear the dirt more than clear it. She lights a cigarette and lowers her window a crack to let in the cold air. It doesn't do much for the smoke, and it fills the cab.

Mindy hasn't said anything bad about Brian other than the fact that he is practically an Unger. At first, I wondered if she kept things about Brian from me because he is my boyfriend, but I don't think so. I know Brian, and I know he has a good heart.

When we stop at Izel's apartment, Mindy hops out and pours half a water bottle on the front windshield, which causes a wash of brown to slide down. She runs the wipers for a few swipes, and the visibility improves, but there is still a film of brown on the glass.

As soon as she pulls onto the road, I ask, "Do you think Skid became evil because of how his parents treated him?"

Mindy doesn't answer for a minute, but I can tell she is

thinking. "Emmett and his sisters are perfectly normal. If you ask me, they are the only normal Ungers…except for the grandparents. They were nice. The grandmother died in her early sixties, so I didn't know her very well. The grandfather and Skid were very close, so it's not like he didn't have anyone who loved him."

Mindy turns on her blinker, and we turn by the library, which is beautiful. The snow coats the giant pine trees, and the red brick of the building stands out against the white.

"Skid and his grandfather were always in the river, fly fishing together. Growing up, we played by the river, and I always saw them there. In the off-season, or whenever the fishing wasn't good, they spent hours at the family homestead in Old Lodell where his grandfather still lived. They tied flies and sold them at the fly shop."

Could Skid's flies with his victims' hairs be in the bins at Railroad Canyon Fly Shop, mixed in with all the other flies?

Mindy nods her head like something just made sense to her. Her cigarette is down to the butt, and she snubs it out in the ashtray. "If you ask me, Skid went off the deep end when his grandfather died. He was the one who found him dead in the river. I think he had a heart attack. Yes, that's got to be it. Skid was supposed to fish with him that day, but he didn't because some cute girl came to town to go rafting with her family. She said she would get ice cream with him after they got off the river, so he waited for her at Happy Cow Hamburger, but she never showed."

"What happened to her?"

"I don't know. Maybe her parents wouldn't let her, or maybe they left town before she could, but he waited, and when he realized she wasn't coming, he grabbed his rod and ran for their favorite fishing spot by the homestead. That's when he found him."

"Oh God," I say. "That's terrible."

"Are you feeling sorry for Skid Unger?" Mindy asks with a mocking tone in her voice.

"No…I…but I guess I was."

"Yeah, he's nobody to feel sorry for. I know he was the person who killed the town dogs, and now you say that he murdered four girls and almost you."

We drive a block in complete silence with nothing but the sound of the tires on the slushy road and the whoosh of warm air from the vents.

"The only Unger pampered and spoiled is Jake," Mindy says. "He acts like a hard ass, but Doc and Joyce spoiled the shit out of him since he is their only child and heir to everything they have. The only struggle Jake ever had was finding out his mom had cancer."

"She died," I tell Mindy. "I never met her, but she died right before I arrived in Lodell. She had a huge clump of origami paper cranes. They all hung on a string in her office. You know, like the story of the little girl who folded the paper cranes. She thought she could beat cancer if she made a thousand of them."

"Sadako and the Thousand Paper Cranes," Mindy says. "We read that book right about the time Joyce was diagnosed. Our teacher had all of us fold cranes, and she sent them to Joyce. I guess they didn't work."

I had assumed she folded them herself, but maybe they were from the town's children. Joyce's office walls were covered in snapshots of the townspeople, and the river guides, with Jake highlighted as the number one citizen with an age progression of school photos, wrestling photos, football photos, graduation, and many pictures of Rimrock Outfitters. I can't comprehend how someone as loved as Jake can be such an ass. If I had all the opportunities Jake had, I would appreciate it.

Before I know it, Mindy pulls to the curb in front of my duplex. Our talks are like a television series. They happen in segments and always end on a cliffhanger.

"Thanks for the ride." I climb out with my box and swing the door shut with a loud metal creak. "Drive safe."

"Yes, Mom," Mindy says with exasperation. "See you tomorrow."

As she pulls away, I turn toward the door and hug the box. I need to set it on the step so I can rummage in the bottom of my purse for my key. How in the hell is it so hard to find the damned keyring? This happens to me every day. You would think I would learn and put it in the zipper pocket or something. I finally find it, unlock the front door, and grab the box.

The inside of the house is freezing. Brian must have turned off the heat. He complained about the eighty-five-dollar bill he just paid, so it is time for sweats and sweaters in the house. I shut the door, bolt it, and carry the box to the table. I've been dying to see what is in it ever since Faye gave it to me. I lift the flaps to a jumble of pine garland, strings of white lights, clusters of red berries, and all sorts of miniature birds with real feathers.

A draft of cold air comes down the hall and sends shivers through my entire body. Something is not right. That is too much air, and Brian wouldn't leave a window open. I unclip the pepper spray from my belt and step toward the bedrooms. I feel like I'm in a movie, and every little voice in my head screams for me to run away, but where would I run? It's probably nothing, maybe a draft through the vents because the heat is turned off.

There is nothing wrong. You are overreacting. Brian's voice rings in my head. The door to the spare room is closed. We don't use it, and it is empty—except for the miniature toys and a few mismatched little girl socks that were there when we moved in. Once I had shut the door, it was out of sight, out of mind, and I never cleaned it up.

The cold air comes from our bedroom. The door is halfway shut, with a single tennis shoe to keep it from closing all the way. We always leave it wide open and against the wall. I lift my pepper spray to face level and push the door. Please don't let someone be behind it. *What in the hell am I doing?*

It swings all the way to the wall. I don't realize I'm holding my breath until it rushes out. The room is empty, but the blanket over the window drapes down, and the window is open a good two inches. What in the hell? It is fricking cold. As I reach to close the window, I freeze. A smear of dirt is on the edge of the windowsill. I slide it shut and hear it latch.

My heart pumps in my ears. I scan the room. Everything is there, but something isn't right. *Breathe.* The pumping increases, and I feel like I will have another panic attack. *No, no, no. I need to think.* Everything seems off-kilter. Otis, Brian's mom's ashes, the pillow, the dresser. The dresser is angled away from the wall. Not a lot, just a bit. I'm losing my mind. No, there's mud on the windowsill.

I move to the bathroom with my pepper spray. No one's there. Back down the hall, I come to the closed door of the spare room and reach for the knob. It is cold in my hand. I hold up the pepper spray. If anyone is in there, they will be blasted…no question about it. I turn the knob. The room smells musty and empty, with nothing but toys, socks, and dark stains on the carpet.

I let out another breath. The only place left for someone to hide is in the kitchen if they hunker down behind the counter. I step as quietly as I can with my entire body wired and buzzing. I peek around, and there is nothing but the pockmarked linoleum and wooden cabinets. Nobody is here.

I check the sliding glass door. The wooden broom handle is still in the track and keeps it shut. The back yard and trampoline are covered in a blanket of snow. *What the?* Leading straight from the back gate, across the yard, and to our bedroom window is a crisp line of footprints—a single line coming toward the house. But… none that leave.

I run back to our bedroom and look around. Everything is

still shifted as if a spirit came in and shook the room. I reach down for the pillow. I turn it over to a large man-sized foot-print. It falls from my hand, and I run for the door.

I pull it open. Two lines of footprints overlap at the edge of the porch. One set is mine that comes from the curb, up the drive, and to the door. The other are under my prints and head toward the side street, where they disappear at the plowed road.

I go back in for my purse and keys. I have no car, so I run across the street to the neighbor's. I knock on her door and wait.

"Who is it?" A sweet old lady's voice comes from the other side.

"I live across the street. Someone broke into my house, and I need to use your phone."

She is silent for a long time.

"Can you call them for me, then?"

"You want me to call 911?"

"Yes. I mean, no. Can you call Deputy Wright at the Sheriff's office? He knows me."

There is no answer, and I hope she is calling. I didn't grab my coat, and I'm freezing my ass off. Finally, the door creaks open a sliver. She opens her screen and hands an old cordless phone out to me.

"Here's my phone. You can call."

The moment I take it, she pulls the screen shut and slides the little lock.

I sift through my wallet until I find Deputy Wright's card. His personal number is on the back, pressed hard into the paper. I dial it, and I'm shocked when he answers.

"This is Emmy Jenkins. Someone broke into my house. I think it was him."

There is a moment of silence, then he says, "I'll be right there."

"I live at…"

"I know where you live. Are you safe?" It sounds like he is moving, and things slams.

"I'm on my neighbor's porch."

"Stay there."

I turn to give the lady her phone back. The screen door unlatches, and she hands me a folded brown and yellow afghan. "Keep the phone until he gets here, honey."

She is sweet and helpful but does not let me into her house. About fifteen minutes later, Deputy Wright pulls up in his squad car with *Sheriff* and the giant gold badge painted on the side. I set her phone and afghan on the porch and run toward his car. "Deputy Wright…"

I explain to him what happened and we go inside. I walk through my movements and show him the pillowcase, the mud on the sill, the cockeyed dresser, and the prints in the snow.

"Where's Brian?" he asks.

It startles me that he knows Brian's name, but of course he does. He knows our entire case.

Deputy Wright asks me to sit on the couch while he radios the department. After what seems like forever, someone knocks on the door. Deputy Wright opens it to the same detective who interrogated me the day they arrested Skid, Brian, and Jake—the detective with the deep-set eyes who looks like Herman Munster. He is, again, not in a uniform. He wears a blue button-up dress shirt with his badge clipped to his belt, and he has the same black leather portfolio.

"This is Detective Perry," Deputy Wright says.

"I know who he is," I say but do not elaborate.

In reality, I feel like screaming, I told you so. He did not believe me when he interrogated me. He thought I was a crazy woman going on about a serial killer. Now he knows.

I go back over everything I told Deputy Wright. Detective Perry walks through the house and asks me to point out everything that looks disturbed. They ask me to sit on the couch as more people show up, take fingerprints, swarm through with cameras, and come from the bedroom with a big evidence bag that looks the same size as my pillow.

I have no idea what time it is when the front door opens. Brian appears with a Christmas tree in one hand and a look of horror smeared across his dusty face. The moment he sees me, he relaxes and steps in. "What happened?"

Deputy Wright moves forward and blocks Brian from me.

Brian's chest puffs out, and his cheeks turn blood red. "What the fuck? This is my house."

"I know. Everything's okay."

"Really? Sure doesn't look okay to me."

Detective Perry steps from the hall.

"This is Brian Cobb," Deputy Wright says to the detective.

"Can we step outside and talk?" Detective Perry asks.

"It's fucking freezing out there."

"We can sit in my car and turn on the heat."

"You okay, Emmy?" Brian calls past the form of Deputy Wright.

"Yes." I'm not, but what else can I say?

Brian is outside for almost an hour. Everyone has left by the time he comes back in, and it is only Deputy Wright and me. Detective Perry gives the okay for Brian to enter the house, and the two of them leave.

Brian stands with his back to me, and his forehead pressed to the door. The lights of both cars illuminate the windows as they flip a u-turn and drive away. Once they are gone, Brian turns around. I expect him to open his arms, but his eyebrows are pressed together, and he takes deep breaths.

"You called the fucking cops?"

I feel like he has just zapped me with a bolt of electricity, and it buzzes through my body. "What?"

"Never call the cops without talking to me first."

"But...someone broke into the house."

"It's probably just some dumbass teenager looking for a Nintendo or something."

"I think I'm...having another..." I sit up and start gulping in air.

"Put your head between your legs and breathe." Brian comes to me and sets his hand on my back. "It'll be okay."

Once my panic attack goes away, I am drained and feel stiff all over. Brian makes us some Campbell's Chicken Noodle soup with saltine crackers, and we eat in silence. He is still upset, and I bet he thinks I overreacted. Maybe he doesn't, though, and he is afraid that I am right.

After dinner, we leave the dishes and head to bed. Brian finally hugs me and tells me he loves me. I go into the bathroom to brush my teeth, and a scream bursts from my throat. Right by my toothbrush is a tiny, single, hand-tied fly.

39

———

ASHLEY

Carina takes a deep breath and sinks beneath the surface while Kia and Calista towel themselves off. She loves the bath and never wants to get out. I pull the plug and lift Carina from the tub. Her skin is warm. She blinks the water from her eyes and gives me a liquid smile as I wrap her in her Ariel hooded bath towel.

Oreo barks, and a streak of black and white fur races down the hall seconds before the doorbell rings.

"Get your sisters dressed," I tell Kia. I step into the hall, and on my way past the girls' room, I do a quick *one for the money, two for the show,* before I toss Carina onto Kia's bed. Her arms flail out, and she giggles when she lands on the mattress and her bath towel unravels.

The doorbell rings again, and Oreo barks ferociously. I put my eye to the peephole and see a distorted red and white Santa trapped in the bubble of glass. Shit! I cannot deal with this. He comes every year—and I ask him for it to be his last, but he keeps coming.

I know he thinks this is good for the girls, but they do not need what he has to offer. They need their dad, not more toys they will never play with. He says he understands why I don't want him to come, but his own guilt brings him to our door every year. He must figure his guilt is more important than our pain.

He rings the doorbell again and sends Oreo into another fit. I would pretend we're not home, but Mrs. Simpson next door will start pounding on the wall if I don't stop the noise, so I open the door. Oreo freezes at the sight of a Santa and doesn't know what to do, then he sniffs the air and takes a step forward.

"You are the skinniest Santa in the history of Santas," I say to Luke. "You look like shit."

"I know you asked me not to...."

"It's okay," I say and step aside to let him in. "But this is the last time. You need to stop."

His eyes water up, and tears slide into his fake beard. Down the hall, Calista's head peeks out from their bedroom before she bounces out in her green plaid nightgown.

"Santa! Santa!" She looks like she wants to run into his arms, but I can tell she is unsure without Kia by her side. Carina slips out in nothing but her diaper. Her nightgown is around her neck without her arms through the holes as Kia runs behind and tries to stop her.

"Have a seat." I hold my hand toward the couch and position myself to scoop Carina up and get her into her pajamas.

Kia and Calista stop at the end of the hallway and stare at Luke. Kids always seem intrigued about Santa but frightened also. He is a stranger with toys. He is a stranger who wants you to sit on his lap for a toy. All year long, we warn them about talking to strangers. It's a bit screwed up. And this knobby-kneed and emaciated Santa with a pillow in his belly and tears dripping down his cheeks must be terrifying.

I grab Carina and she giggles while I wrestle her arms into her nightgown, but the moment she catches sight of Santa Luke, her eyes pop wide open, and she presses her head against my chest.

I hold my arm out toward Kia and Calista. "Come on, girls, it's okay."

They make a wide circle away from Luke, inch over, and kneel beside Carina and me. Kia cups her hands around my ear and whispers, "That is not Santa."

The moisture from her breath cools my ear when she moves away. "Santa is very busy this time of year, so he is one of Santa's helpers. Remember? That is why there are so many Santas in the stores. They are really elves who are too big for the workshop, so they come and visit children who are especially good."

"I hear you girls have been very good for your momma this year," Luke says.

Kia glances at Calista and looks skeptical. Luke digs into his huge Santa bag and pulls out a beautifully wrapped package with a silver bow. He must have had it professionally done. "This one is for Calista...."

She puts her chin to her chest and shyly looks at the package.

"But it is not Christmas yet," Kia says.

"It's okay, baby," I say. "Momma knows this Santa's helper, and you can each have one gift early."

Kia takes Calista's hand and helps her to Luke. They both stop, barely close enough to take the package. As soon as Calista grabs it, Luke says, "Hang on a moment. Let me find one for you."

He pulls out a tall package shaped exactly like a guitar with a green velvet bow around the neck of it. Kia rises onto her tiptoes and bounces like she cannot control her excitement. She turns toward me with a huge smile and her hand around the neck of the guitar. This is the happiest she has been since she lost her daddy.

They hurry back to my side and sit down with their gifts. Luke takes out a package with red paper and a peppermint-striped ribbon for Carina, but she burrows deeper into my lap.

"Momma will help you," I say. "Let's go together."

I stand with Carina, and we get the package that is almost as big as she is. Kia and Calista sit with their packages before them, not ripping into them like Mitchell and I used to do. Chris and I decided to stretch out our Christmas mornings with the girls. We never had much money, so we all took turns as we unwrapped and enjoyed each gift.

"Babies first," Kia says when Calista digs her fingers into the paper.

"Wait…I have another one." Luke reaches to the bottom of the bag. It better not be something for me. I don't need anything from him. His guilt is more than I can bear. I know it was not completely his fault, but I'm angry that he survived and Chris and Dale did not. He was the one at the wheel. He was the one who decided to keep driving in the smoke of the forest fire instead of stopping the truck. He was the one who got too close to the edge of the service road and rolled them all into the ravine.

"Oh…here it is." Luckily, he brings up a small package in the shape of a dog bone, and I don't have to take anything. "Oreo…"

Oreo snatches the bone and zips behind the couch with it, followed by tiny little ripping sounds.

Kia giggles. "I guess dogs are before babies. Go ahead, Carina. Rip off the paper."

I hold the package for Carina, but she still acts shy. I rip the corner and have her pull it. After that, she gets the idea, and her curiosity takes over.

"A Tickle Me Elmo!" I say.

"It's the new one!" Kia says. "The Tickle Me Elmo Extreme. He rolls around the floor and can stand up by himself."

Carina hugs the box and puts her face to the fur. "We will take it out after Kia and Calista open theirs," I tell her.

Calista rips the paper off and squeals. It is the Wow Wee Alive Tiger Cub that she has been begging me for. I can tell she wants to remove it from the box, but she just hugs it, box and all, to her chest and waits for Kia. Kia's guitar is white with silhouettes of four blue butterflies on the body. She holds it and cries.

Luke's smile drops, and his eyebrows pinch together.

"She loves it," I say. "That's my Kia. When she can't control her excitement, it turns to tears."

She hasn't done this since Chris brought Oreo home three months before the accident. I thought she had lost it forever. A warm tingle starts in my momma heart and spills out of my eyes. I don't want my girls to see me cry. They will not understand, and I don't want to take away their joy.

"I think it is time for ice cream." I shift Carina off my lap and onto the floor. "Maybe Santa can help you get your toys from the boxes."

From the kitchen, I watch Luke with the girls. Maybe this is for them, and I am letting my pain keep my girls from the joy they deserve.

By the time we finish the ice cream, my living room is filled with the hysterical laughter of Elmo and the purrs of Calista's tiger cub. Kia sits on the couch next to Luke, with the guitar across her lap as she learns to plunk out *Twinkle Twinkle Little Star*.

"It's getting late," I say. "Time for bed."

"No...can we please stay up?" Calista whines.

"It's already very late. Take your toys to your room, and you can play with them for fifteen more minutes while Santa and I have a talk."

The smile leaves Luke's face again. His eyebrows turn up in the center and make him look like Eeyore.

"Awwww…do we have to?" Calista says.

"Yes, you have to."

"Can we give Santa a hug?"

"Yes, I think you should. He brought you some very nice gifts."

Calista throws her arms around Luke's neck and about chokes him to death. Kia gives him her typical reserved hug, and Carina puts her head against his knee and then runs off.

"Close your bedroom door. I'll be there in just a little bit."

Once I hear the door shut, I sit on the opposite side of the couch and turn toward Luke. He puts his chin to his chest and won't look at me. He is nothing like the cocky Luke I used to know. He used to slam down shots and ride the mechanical bull at the Buckaroo.

"How is Dale's mom?"

"She's fine. I'm seeing her tomorrow." He presses his palms onto his thighs and runs them over the top of the Santa pants. He still doesn't look at me. "She's got a new man. He seems decent."

"Good job on choosing the gifts. You made my girls very happy."

He nods his head. "Thanks. Carly helped me."

"Are you back together?" I heard they split up a year after the accident. I don't know why and never asked, but I can guess.

"No, but we still love each other."

"You gone back to Woodland Fire yet?"

"No, I'm still working at Discount Tires."

"You should think about it. You were meant to fight fires."

He doesn't answer. He just shakes his head. "I better go."

He sets an envelope down on the coffee table and pushes himself up from the couch.

"What's that?" I ask.

"Just a Christmas card. Don't open it until Christmas morning, please." He is so thin that he looks nothing like the Luke he used to be. Maybe I am part of the reason. Since I can't forgive him, maybe he can't forgive himself. He reaches for the door with his empty sack balled up beneath his arm.

"Luke…"

He turns back to me. "Maybe you should come more often," I say.

The corners of his mouth turn up into a tiny smile. "Really?"

"Yes, but ditch the Santa suit."

His smile widens. "I kind of like it."

"I would rather the girls get to know you as Uncle Luke."

He lets out a breath like he has been holding it forever. "Thank you."

When he closes the door, I get up and latch the deadbolt. I can't cry until I get the girls to sleep so I sit down to compose myself before I face them.

The card sits on the coffee table. I want to rip it open and deal with what is inside without the girls with me. It may just be a card, but he could have put photos of Chris inside that I have never seen before—maybe pictures of when they were in high school or middle school. I take a deep breath and blow it out before I balance the card between two branches of the Christmas tree and go to tuck my girls into bed.

40

———

EMMY

A high-pitched scream vibrates around the bathroom, and I don't realize it is me until Brian rushes in and takes hold of my shoulders. When he notices that I am pointing at a hand-tied fly, a wash of fear comes over his face. It only lasts for an instant before it turns to anger.

"What the fuck?" Brian scoops up the fly.

"You'll get your DNA on it."

Before I can stop him, he wraps it in toilet paper and flushes it down.

"What're you doing? We need to turn that in."

"Emmy! You don't understand. Look at me." He puts his hands on my cheeks and stares into my eyes. "We can't help the detectives."

Tears well up, drip down my face, and into the corners of my mouth.

"You have done enough damage by calling them in the first place."

"They need to find Skid. We're not safe." I take hold of his forearms and pull his hands from my cheeks. "Girls aren't safe."

"They can find him without our help, and they can't do shit to protect us." Brian takes hold of my hand. "You need to trust me."

Mindy's words, *Brian is practically an Unger*, echo in my mind.

"I can protect us more than the Sheriff's department." He squeezes my hand. "Look at me."

I raise my chin and look into his eyes.

"I'm protecting us from more than just Skid."

I still haven't told him what Rose said at Thanksgiving.

"Maybe Jake put the fly here. Did you think of that? Maybe it is to warn us that if we don't keep our mouths shut, he will plant evidence to make it look like I am the one who killed the girls and I am the one who kidnapped Crystal." The tiny bathroom amplifies his voice.

"But Skid had Crystal. He strapped on a mattress to the floor with tie downs."

"WE found her like that, not the sheriff."

"Crystal can testify…."

"How many times do I have to tell you that Crystal was drugged the whole time. She may not remember. We can't rely on her." Brian lets go with one hand and strokes my head. "A good lawyer can create doubt. Don't forget that I am the one who confessed to date rape—not Skid or Jake."

Brian pulls me to him and holds me tight. "Please…we just need to take care of ourselves and let the detectives figure it out. They have Skid's tackle box and the hair. His DNA will be all over it, not mine."

"But I'm home alone while you're at work."

"I'm trying to get another shift. Can you hang out with someone? You could go home with one of the girls you work with, and I'll pick you up when I get off.

I haven't told him that Mindy is from Lodell. There is no

way in hell Mindy will want any of this brought to her doorstep, and I wouldn't do that to Izel either. The image of her sweet little boys' faces in the window flashes in my mind. I can't do anything to harm them. They may already be in danger just because we carpool. Skid could be watching me. Or Jake. Or Rose.

"What about a gun?" Brian asks.

"I've never shot a gun."

"You can learn."

"I don't trust myself with a gun because I act before I think." People have told me that my entire life, and it has gotten me into a lot of trouble. I panic. If I think there is an intruder, I may accidentally shoot Brian or our landlord.

We stand in silence for what seems like forever.

"You ready for bed?" Brian asks. "I need a shower, then I'll join you."

"I'm still wired and don't want to be alone." I pull away from Brian and notice his hair and clothes are still covered in wood dust.

"You can shower with me." He smiles and wiggles his eyebrows up and down. They are also coated with dust, and it is glued to his skin along his hairline and nostrils. I laugh at how silly he looks, but it turns into tears.

I pull on Brian's hand and scoot us closer to the shower. By the time he has the water turned on, I am naked. He runs his dry and coarse hands over my shoulders and down my back as I unbuckle his belt and slide his pants to his ankles. We both look down at his pants in a wad over his boots and start laughing.

Brian sits on the toilet while I loosen the lace of his work boot and try to pull it off his foot. It doesn't budge. I wiggle it and pull. When it finally gives, I fall back on my ass and hit my head on the wall. I look at him with his bare ass on the toilet and laugh again.

Brian stares at me with a slight smile. "I love you, Emmy."

"I love you too." I set his shoe on the floor with a clunk and hold out my hand. "Other foot."

"I better take it from here."

As he strips off each article of clothing, he becomes more and more the Brian I know. The carefree Brian in nothing but his cargo shorts and water shoes. There is no way in hell I want to go back to Lodell, but maybe we can start over on another river where he can guide.

We take a long warm shower. We don't make love, but our soapy hands slide over one another's bodies, and I feel bonded to him again. Nobody knows me like Brian.

Brian turns the water off and reaches around the curtain for a towel. He hands it to me. "I brought a Christmas tree home. I don't know what we're going to decorate it with, but we have a tree."

I almost forgot about the box. "Faye gave me some Christmas decorations. Maybe there are some ornaments." I dry off my body and wrap the towel around my hair.

Once we are in our sweats, Brian gets the tree from the porch. It has two boards nailed in a cross to the trunk so it can stand.

"How do we water it?"

Brian looks at it for a minute like he is weighing our options. "I'll get a stand on the way to work tomorrow."

Brian cuts off the lower branches, so we have room for presents. I don't want to waste them, so I will make a bouquet for the table. I look around. "Where is the vase?"

"What vase?"

"The one Erika brought us flowers in. The blue one."

"Last time I saw it, it was on the table."

It's not there and not in the kitchen. A tingle runs up my spine, but I ignore it and pull the decorations from the box. All the little birds with real feathers have ornament hooks, and two big rolls of red ribbon sit at the bottom of the box. I pull out a string of lights, and Brian plugs them in to make sure they work. The entire string lights up with tiny white bulbs. I watch him wrap the lights around the tree, and an eery feeling washes over me. *Brian is practically an Unger.*

41

———

HIM

THE CABIN IS A SHRINE TO MY NEW SELF. WHILE THE WIND HOWLS and thunder cracks outside, I cocoon inside as I transform and mutate into Chad Joseph Miller from Elkins, Utah, who so conveniently put all his thoughts and history into his journal.

The blue flower vase I took from Emmy and Brian's sits as a centerpiece, filled with a bouquet of crow feathers for wing cases and nymph tails. I wish I was there, like a fly on the wall, when Emmy found the little gift I left for her.

The table is littered with his passport, driver's license, shot records, and dozens of blue-lined notebook paper—all filled with my new cursive that slants to the left. We are almost one.

I take out a size fourteen dry fly hook and clamp it in my vice. Hermit was a Pacific Crest Trail thru-hiker whose girlfriend he had since high school dumped him and left him devastated. Her name is Ashley, just like my nymph. That cannot be a coincidence. I met Ashley, then turned my head, and he was there. They are both part of my destiny.

I slip the end of a thread through my bobbin and wrap the hook's shank that creates a base for the dry fly wings. I am from

Elkins, Utah, and my girlfriend dumped me. I have not seen my dad in five years. My mom remarried and is up to her neck in stepkids, cooking, cleaning, laundry, and yard work.

I choose the perfect brown grizzly hackle feathers, strip off the extra fibers, and bind them to my hook. I miss my missionary work in Ghana, where I distributed mosquito nets and shared the gospel—here I also learned that family and community are essential for survival. In Ghana, the people have "enough" and do not always want "more" like Americans have been programmed to desire from birth. The people are materially poor but spiritually rich. My passport has stamps from Malaysia, Zanzibar, Zambia, Botswana, Namibia, and Ghana.

I lift the hackle feathers, wrap the base so they stand up from the shank like wings, and separate them with a figure eight. I wrap backward toward the curve and tie on some brown and grizzly hackle fibers for the tail. I have come to hike the PCT to find peace and meaning in my life and to find a way to have "enough."

I wrap the bobbin thread with gray dubbing and wind it around the shank to create a thick thorax behind the wings. When I slip the single thick strand of Yapper's hair from the copper wrap, I picture her mouth open in the water with no words coming out. I bind her hair down and wind it all the way from the tail, through the wings, and to the hook eye with evenly spaced wraps.

I finish my fly with a brown grizzly hackle feather and a drop of head cement behind the eye. Trout will always take an Adam's dry fly, for it mimics the whirring wings and frenzied legs of an insect struggling to shed its nymph shuck.

Emmy will be mine. She was a gift from me to Brian, and I will take her back. He may have her for a little longer, but she will be bound to me for eternity.

With the scar between my eyebrows and my two new

tattoos, I am Chad Joseph Miller, aka Hermit, indistinguishable on the surface. But, in my soul and my depth, I am the river, and the river conforms to any shape it needs.

PART 3

42

ASHLEY

The toughest times are the hours between when the girls fall asleep, and I do. Or, like now, while Carina naps and the girls are still at school. Winter days are short in Oregon and give me too many hours alone in the dark. Thank God the days are getting longer, and there are only nine more until Daylight Savings. Everything is easier in the light.

I lost my mailbox key, but I have an extra in my nightstand drawer. It's almost time to get the girls from the bus stop, so I rummage through the snapshots of the girls from last Christmas, the wads of old receipts, and an old birthday card from Grandpa Hudson. I lift the heap of mementos and toss them onto the bed. Everything fans out—and right there, in the middle of everything, is the newspaper article. *THE* newspaper article, with its black letters on dingy paper with torn edges, ripped from the front page away from all the rest of the news that did not matter to me. I lift it from the pile and read the words that describe the worst day of my life.

Two Firefighters Die in Rollover, One Survives

On July 8, a wildland fire truck rolled off a forest service road in the Deschutes National Forest. The visibility was impaired due to heavy smoke from the fire. The driver, Luke Healey, said he completely lost visibility and did not notice the curve in the road.

When Healey realized the passenger-side front tire was no longer in contact with the ground. He tried to steer back, but the momentum caused the truck to tip off the road. The truck rolled more than three times before it stopped against a clump of pines and finally came to rest approximately 150 feet below.

The driver, Luke Healey, was able to climb out through the window, but he could not get the other two men, Dale McCoy and Chris Covington, out due to the amount of damage to the truck. He scrambled up the embankment and radioed for help.

Healey had head trauma and a broken leg. He has no idea how he climbed out of the ravine. Other firefighters and a local ambulance crew arrived around thirty minutes later. Both firefighters had to be extricated using the jaws of life and were evacuated by Life Flight from the incident. Both men were pronounced dead upon arrival at Good Samaritan Hospital in Rockland.

Carina cries from her crib, and Oreo prances into the room. He knows it's time to get the girls. He is extra-hyper like he knows we are going to the dog park today. Maybe it's the weather.

I look back at the heap of paper and cards and *THE* article on my bed and step out to get Carina. My girls are the only reasons I'm able to keep going.

43

HIM

THERE IS NOTHING SO OBVIOUS AS A SCHOOL BUS. IT COMES AT the same time every day, big and yellow and filled with children. It sits in front of the apartments with red lights that flash and cars stop in either direction. Inside, there is movement as children rise and step toward the door.

When the lights stop flashing, and it pulls away, Kia and the middle daughter are the only children there without a mother. Kia takes her sister's hand, and they wait with another mom and her son. Within minutes, Oreo appears on the landing and races down the stairs. With the baby strapped in a carrier on her back and a white trash bag with red plastic straps in her hand, Ashley hurries down behind him.

Ashley wears a pink baseball cap with a long ponytail that hangs out the back. My blood surges, and every nerve in my body tingles at the sight of her tits in a tight pink athletic jacket and her legs in skinny jeans. It is not hard to imagine her body stripped naked with her dark nipples against creamy white skin.

The girls follow their momma to the garbage bin, where she hands the dog leash to Kia, lifts the lid, and dumps the bag into the front right corner. Instead of following the walkway to their stairwell, they go the opposite way through the apartment buildings. As soon as they turn a corner, I step from my cover and follow.

The apartments are all the same except for their balconies. Some are bare, and others have chairs, plants, or toys. I wonder if any of them are Ashley's or if hers is on the other side of the building. One balcony has a little pink table with three chairs and a pink kitchen playset. That has to be it.

Ashley and the girls take a left at the end of the building. Just before they go out of sight, Kia turns her head toward me, and our eyes meet. My heart pounds like I have been caught. She cannot recognize me from the lake. I was clean-shaven then, and my beard is long and scraggly now. I look like a PCT hiker or a mountain man.

They make it out to the other side of the apartments and turn down the sidewalk. I wait beside a cluster of juniper trees behind the apartments and breathe in their scent. We used to collect juniper berries as kids to throw at one another or bring them to old Mr. Morris for his gin. He would give us a dollar for each lunch sack full of hard and dusty-blue berries.

I step out to the sidewalk, and they are gone. Shit! The street is nothing but houses and apartments. I turn the way they went and follow. Two blocks down, there is a gap in the homes with a dog park, gated and filled with grass, boulders, and trees. Oreo is off-leash and chases a ball someone threw while the girls climb on the boulders and sip from little cardboard juice boxes.

Ashley sits on a bench and unclasps the baby carrier. She wriggles it off her shoulders and pulls the baby out. As soon as she sets her on the ground, the baby wobbles toward a woman with a yellow lab puppy.

Something glitters on Ashley's hand as she adjusts her baseball cap. Fuck! She has a wedding ring. I would swear that she is a single mom. Every instinct I have tells me she is raising those girls alone. A rush of heat comes to my cheeks, and my stomach clenches. She is mine, not the possession of an asshole who does not deserve her.

I am about to rage but turn away to get myself under control. I go back the way I came, down the sidewalk to the juniper trees and into the apartments. At the trash bins, I look around. Nobody is near. I lift the lid, reach in, and take the white sack with the red ties in the front right corner.

I will find out who he is.

44

EMMY

Jocelyn said that Erika brought a woman with two kids in last night. They're in room 216, the same room I stayed in. We always put the battered women on the second floor for added safety since it's harder for someone to break in without being seen.

This is my least favorite day of the week because I need to deep clean the popcorn machine. I unplug it the moment I walk in the door so it can cool while Deanna and I go through the till. When Faye arrives, I scoop all the leftover popcorn into a plastic bag, twist the top, and secure it with a plastic wire twist. Faye takes all the extra popcorn to the women's shelter during her lunch break. I unclasp the kettle and remove the pin. It comes free, and I take it to the break room as Faye works in her office with the morning news loop on the television.

The phone rings, but Faye will answer it once she realizes I am not at the desk. It rings four times, and I'm about to run and get it when I hear her pick it up, "Railroad Inn. Be our guest. How may I help you?"

"This is Faye."

It used to take me an hour to clean the damned popcorn

machine, but now I can do it in twenty minutes. I remove the bottom tray and dump the extra kernels into the trash bin.

"What?" Her voice is high-pitched and excited. "Really? You're serious?"

I wipe the tray with the cloth and slide it back in as quietly as possible. Not only so I don't disturb Faye but to listen. I wonder what has happened. I know her husband expected to become a partner at the CPA firm where he works, but it doesn't sound like she is talking to him.

"I can't believe it. Thank you! You have been so wonderful. Thank you!"

Could it be about their adoption? The plastic clunk of a receiver comes from the office, then there is a single moment of silence before, "Emmy! Come here."

I drape the cloth over the rim of the machine and hurry toward Faye. She sits behind her desk, in her big black office chair, with giant eyes and a wide grin. She looks stunned.

"We're getting a baby. They found us a baby." She giggles and talks a million miles a minute. "I mean…We knew there was a possibility of one coming up, but you never know. The mom cannot decide for sure until the baby is born. Oh my gosh. Kerry. I have to call my husband."

She picks up the receiver on her desk phone, and I turn to leave. "No, no, stay." Faye flutters her hand at me.

Faye bounces in her seat with her finger waving over the buttons like she can't remember the number. She finally dials and looks up at me with joy.

"Kerry…" Faye's voice rings through the office. "You'll never guess…yes, everything's okay. Better than okay. Are you sitting down? We have a *baby*."

"Yes, I'm serious!" All the framed photos around her office are of Faye and Kerry, taken all over the world. "A girl. She was born today."

That is one lucky baby. I wonder how my life would be if my

parents had given me up for adoption instead of bringing me home to their dirty house and drugs.

"I don't know. They're going to be in contact and let us know." Faye is literally bouncing in her chair. They have been working on this for so long.

"Oh my gosh, the nursery…do we have everything?"

We could throw her a baby shower. I'll talk to Mindy and Izel. The news flashes on the television.

Faye's excited voice pings around the office. "Ahhhhh! I know! Can you believe it?"

"Okay, I've got to go. I need to get things ready."

"Yes, of course. Okay, I'll see you in twenty minutes." She smacks three kisses into the receiver and hangs up.

Faye jumps from the chair, runs around the desk. She wraps her arms around me and swings me back and forth. She finally steps back. Her eyes sparkle and tears well in them.

"Oh my gosh, Emmy. We have waited so long. I knew we were next in line, and I knew a young woman was going to give her baby up, but we have been here so many times, and something always falls through. This woman is a college girl from a good family who got herself in trouble. Oh my gosh! I can't believe it."

"That is amazing! Congratulations, Faye."

Her eyes pop wide. "I gotta go. Kerry is meeting me at the house. There is so much we need to do."

Faye grabs her jacket and zips out of the office while she rummages in the bottom of her purse for her keys. The door to the lobby chimes, and she is gone. Pain pulses through my jaw, and I realize my teeth are clenched. Life is unfair, and that is not news to me. I am happy for Faye and Kerry. They deserve to have a family.

"A Rockland family is shaken up after discovering an intruder spent the winter in their vacation cabin." I look up at the television. A female news reporter stands next to a man in black-framed glasses with dark hair and a close-trimmed beard. He looks like a typical yuppie rich dad.

"We knew something was off the moment we pulled up. The front door looked like someone had kicked it in and patched the frame back together. It looks like he stayed for a long time."

The camera pans over to a small log cabin with snow still on the roof. The man appears again and leads the camera crew into the cabin. "He left a mess! It looks like a hoarder lives here."

The camera sweeps past a tiny woman and a teenage girl with long blond hair. They both step back and out of view. The camera follows the man past bags and bags of trash and empty propane tanks. He stops in the kitchen and points at the sink and counters piled with dirty dishes and open cans of food. "He left so much food out that the place is filled with mice now."

The man leads them to a twin-sized bed piled with quilts and coats. "He slept in our daughter's bed and left a stack of pornographic magazines on her nightstand. What if he returns while we're here?"

The reporter is back outside with her mic to her mouth and the cabin directly behind her. She looks like a typical reporter, all made up and professional, with highlighted brown hair parted down the center. "Authorities say that the unknown intruder spent the winter in this cabin and burglarized at least nine other ones, possibly as many as thirteen. The intruder rummaged through people's personal belongings. Most of the items taken were food and propane, but he also took higher priced items such as warm clothing, a set of snowshoes, and an antique fly rod."

Hoarder. Open food cans. Fly rod. Skid!

"The Sheriff's department is still looking for the suspect. Please contact the Canyon County Sheriff's office if you have any information or think your cabin was broken into." The reporter gives a highly polished and practiced smile. "Christy Green, KCRK 14, Oregon."

Skid. That's where he was hiding alright. But now he could be anywhere. It's only a matter of time before he kidnaps or kills another woman. Thank God I have a phone now.

The day after Skid broke into our home, Erika brought me an iPhone, used but in good condition. Brian refuses to use it. He thinks whoever is paying for our plan will have full access to every number we call. Like, I give a shit about that. I'm not calling anyone I need to worry about anyway.

45

HIM

I FOUND AN ABANDONED FARMHOUSE BETWEEN ROCKLAND AND Silverdale, halfway to Emmy and halfway to Ashley. The white paint flakes off like dry skin, and several shingles are missing from the roof, but it is dry inside and has a mattress in the front bedroom. There is no electricity or gas, but it has a pump well for my water and a table where I can tie my flies. It is *enough,* just like Hermit was searching for. He should be happy we are here in his name.

A mourning dove coos its ghostly call as I step from my shoes and into the river. The launch is only a twenty-minute walk from my new place, which is just right, close enough to take a nymph but far enough away that the cops will not swarm all over me when someone goes missing. The cool water sends shivers up my legs and wakes me. This is my element. This is where I belong. A train whistle blows down the tracks and makes me homesick for Lodell.

When I went through Ashley's trash, it smelled of diapers, wet coffee grounds, and peaches. There was a purple disposable razor, squeezed children's toothpaste tube, receipts for McDonald's and Dominos Pizza, a chewed-up plastic banana that would go in a children's kitchen set just like the one on the balcony, used tampons rolled up in toilet paper, apple juice boxes with the straws still in them, black and yellow styrofoam trays from fresh meat, junk mail, advertisements, and an empty off-brand cereal bag of Fruity O's.

There were no beer cans, men's razors, aftershave, or deodorant. No condoms or beef jerky wrappers—nothing to suggest a man lives in that apartment. Could he be in the military and out on deployment? Could she be single and only wearing a ring so people don't judge her?

Two orange locomotives with BNSF in large black letters pull a long chain of graffitied boxcars along the other side of the river. The rhythmic thump reverberates through my flesh all the way to my core. The river rises up my ankles, calves, and thighs and seeps into the fabric of my shorts.

I belong in your cool depths, where I can bubble over rocks or rage and froth through the canyons. Why do you forsake me? The last of the train rumbles by, and the wheels screech taking a curve around a bend.

What more do I need to do to fulfill my destiny? Emmy? Did I fail when I released her? Ashley and her girls? You presented them to me, and I have not delivered them. The cold slams against my chest, and I drop to my knees. I extend my arms. Please take me or give me a sign.

"Destiny…" the river calls out. "Come on, you can make it."

No…it is coming from behind. A young woman walks toward me. Her head is down, and she calls to a brown and white puppy that totters beside her. Behind her, a black Jeep sits in the gravel lot. I did not hear her pull in.

I stand and turn toward her. She looks around twenty-five with golden-brown hair pulled up into a loose bun that bobs with every step. She wears a gray zip-up hoodie, jean shorts, and black running shoes.

"Come on, girl, you can make it."

My sign. My destiny. The answer to everything along with a nymph to sacrifice. Everyone loves a puppy. At the dog park, Ashley's baby toddled over to a lady with a puppy. With this little dog, they will come to me.

"Hello." She steps on the back of her shoe and lifts her foot out. As she balances on one leg, she reaches down and slips off her sock. The puppy picks it up and scampers around in a circle. "Put that down, silly."

She scoops the dog into her arms and pries the sock from its mouth. It doesn't look like she has a shirt on beneath her hoodie. Maybe not even a bra.

"Cute puppy." I do not move from the river. "What kind of a dog is she?"

She brings the puppy to her face and lets it lick her lips. "She's a wire fox terrier. I just picked her up. I had to drive all the way to Olympia to get her. My roommate has no idea. I'm going to surprise her."

"Her name is Destiny?"

"Yes." She steps into the water. "Oooh, it's colder than I thought it would be. I can't believe you're standing there soaking wet. I want Destiny to love the river. My old dog used to swim and go kayaking with me."

"You kayak on the Deschutes?"

She giggles and nuzzles the puppy. "Not with the rapids. I kayak on the Cascade Lakes. You know, Sparks, Hosmer, Elk Lake, Devil's Lake, Little Lava, or Cultus."

I look back at her Jeep and notice the off-road rack on the top. She steps in deeper and ambles over the submerged rocks until my water comes to her knees and caresses them.

The river courses and vibrates through my nerves like the pitch of a tuning fork—and the word it says is *YES*.

"I'm Chad," I say.

She gives me a smile, wide and friendly. "Hi Chad, I'm Anabel." Her teeth are perfectly straight and bright-white.

"How old is Destiny?"

"Ten weeks." Anabel bends over and touches Destiny's nose to the water. When she rises, her entire body shivers. "It's too cold for me. How do you stand it?"

"I was born and raised on this river." Shit. I am Chad Joseph Miller from Utah. I need to remember that—but it won't matter with Anabel.

She ambles to the shore with my Destiny in one arm, and the other stretched out to balance herself as she finds her footing on the rocks. Once on dry land, she sets Destiny down and bends over to scoop up her socks. I step toward the shore behind her. She bends over and balances on one leg while she slides the other foot into a sock.

"Need a hand?" I hold out her shoe and extend my arm. She leans an elbow on it and slips her foot into the shoe.

I yank my arm away. As she loses her balance, I snatch her and pull her to the water. She lets out a scream that echoes through the canyon. We are in the water, and her head is below the surface before she can scream for a second time. My arm is still around her waist, and I'm still holding her by the back of her neck below the surface. She kicks and flails, but my blood surges, and I have the power of the river.

Within minutes, she floats still, calm, and rocks with the rhythm of the water. Her hair has come loose, and it ripples in the current, long and free. I wind a clump of it tight around my finger and yank it out. The strands will be perfect for a Royal Wulff or a Golden Stone fly. I wish I could have spared her the surprise and the fear. I should keep my Ketamine on me, for I never know when an offering will come.

I guide her to the shore and pull her beneath the long wisps of willow branches that skim the surface. I unzip her hoody. I was right. She is not wearing a shirt or a bra. Her nipples are erect, and I put my mouth to one. I wish I could take her, but she is already gone. I slip off her hoodie, and it splats when I toss it onto the shore. I unbutton her shorts and slide them off. They catch on her one untied shoe, so I pull it and her shorts off together and toss them beside her hoodie.

I wade out with her and set her free into my waters. She is buoyant and floats with her face, tits, and knees bobbing above the surface. I wish I had a raft to get her further down. Destiny sits on the shore as if she knows to wait for me. I scoop up Anabel's shorts and feel for her keys. They are not in the pockets. Destiny follows me to the pit toilet. When I lift the lid, several fat black flies rise from the bowl in slow motion and swirl up toward the ceiling. I drop her clothes in and kick the lid shut before they hit bottom.

Destiny looks up at me with her head cocked to the side. I lift her up and take her to my new Jeep. The keys are in the cup holder, and a dog kennel sits in the back. Now, I have everything I need to start a new life in the flesh and prove myself worthy. I have a new identity, an excellent vehicle, and some bait.

46

EMMY

THE LOBBY LOOKS LIKE A PINK BOMB EXPLODED INSIDE AGAINST the green walls and red couches. We went all-out for the shower and will meet Faye and Kerry's baby for the first time. They decided to reveal her name to all of us at once, so none of us know.

A giant pink *It's a Girl* banner hangs behind a table with a pink skirt. Pink and white paper lanterns hang from the ceiling, and pink and white latex balloons float around the room with curled ribbons hanging beneath them.

We have plates, bowls, pink and white cupcakes, ham and cheese sliders, turkey pinwheels, mini broccoli quiches, cut veggies, hummus, tater tot casserole, and hamburger empanadas.

A seven-foot tower of Pampers, Huggies, and Luvs sits in the corner. It was Izel's idea to each bring a box of diapers along with our gift. She said she really appreciated that when she had her own boys. The front counter is piled with gifts wrapped in pink, green, and yellow with baby giraffes, bears, ducks, and elephants.

Faye and Kerry are late. We all sit on the couches or folding chairs and wait. Jason and his wife, Amanda, lean against the counter. She has her hand on her belly, already protecting their tiny baby inside. We just found out that she is five months along. You would think that Jason could have said something to one of us, but he didn't. Maybe he did it to protect Faye's feelings.

Finally, Faye's silver SUV pulls in. We all watch from the windows as they fuss with the car seat and baby, huddled in the open car door. When they finally back up, Kerry holds the handle of the car seat carrier. Faye hovers close to the baby with a diaper bag on her shoulder as she arranges a pink blanket and tents it over the handle. They both look exhausted but *pleased as punch*, as Jeanette, my tenth-grade foster mom, used to say.

Jason hurries to the door and holds it open for them. They enter like royalty with their new little princess, with their chins high and big smiles on their lips.

"Oh my gosh, look how beautiful it is in here," Faye says. "I can't believe you did this for us."

I'm sure this is one of many showers they will have. The ladies in Kerry's office will also throw one, and their families will have another. Everyone is so happy for them, especially with all they have been through to get her.

Kerry sets the carrier on the coffee table. We all gather around and strain our necks to see. Kerry puts his arm around Faye's shoulder, and she gets a smile so big it makes my heart feel full of confetti.

"I'd like to introduce you all to…" she reaches for the edge of the blanket. "…our daughter, Maya Delaney Strickland."

Faye pulls the blanket back to a tiny little baby in a pink beanie and terrycloth onesie. She is beautiful with a tiny little nose and lips. Her closed eyes flutter, then open, and she looks around, unfocused, at all the faces. Her eyebrows pinch together like she's trying to figure us out, then she lets out a wail that sounds like a mewing baby cat. Faye jumps to action and unbuckles her from the carrier.

Izel, Deanna, and Jocelyn tense up, ready to help. When Faye lifts Maya, her tiny arms flail out, and she tucks her knees.

"What do you need?" Kerry asks and reaches for the diaper bag.

They're a wreck.

"I think she'll take the binkie," Faye says and lifts the pink binkie that's clipped to her onesie. "You all go ahead and eat while I get her settled.

It takes Faye a good fifteen minutes to get Maya to stop fussing, then Kerry brings her a plate of food. The door chimes, and Herb walks in. As always, his scraggly gray hair sticks out from his head, and he smiles with a mouth full of bright white teeth.

"Wow! What's going on here?" Herb glances around the room and then at Faye. "You got your baby!"

Every surface is filled with food, gifts, or the baby, so I step over to get the newspapers from him. As soon as I take them, he reaches out to shake hands with Kerry. There is nowhere to set them, so I head around the front desk to the office.

I toss the stack onto Faye's desk with a thump. On the front page, there is a picture of a young woman with long brown hair and the headline, **Woman Found Dead in River, Foul Play is Suspected**.

47

ASHLEY

Four boxes of my teenage things are still stacked next to my closet in brown cardboard boxes. I haven't been able to touch them since I brought them home. They are filled with all my girlhood memories. The before memories.

I remember lying in my bed after I found out I was pregnant. Chris and I were scared, and we had to tell our parents. We both decided not to get an abortion and to face it full-on. We could not get rid of something our love created. My childhood ended right there at that moment. At sixteen, I decided to put all my dreams in one basket. I don't regret it for one minute, but I know it wasn't the best situation.

I had planned on going to nursing school, and Chris wanted to become a mechanic. Instead, we had Kia in our senior year while we still lived in our parents' homes. Kia was in every picture of us on graduation day, except the ones of us walking the stage.

I open my closet door, slide my hanging clothes to the middle, and scoot my shoes into a heap. I push the boxes in and slide my clothes back over until all my teenage dreams are out of sight. One day, I will be able to look at them again. Maybe when the girls are grown and teenagers themselves.

It may also be time to forgive Luke and release some of his pain. I go into the kitchen, pull a yellow sticky note from the pad, and search through the junk drawer for something to write with. I pull out a blue and white pen from Rockland Community Bank. In big block letters, I write, *Invite Luke to dinner*.

Oh crap! The clock on the stove says 2:10. It's almost time for the school bus. I throw two juice boxes and cheese sticks into a sack, wake Carina, and change her diaper. While I'm getting her into the carrier, Oreo spins loops by the front door. The dog park has become our routine and something to look forward to every day.

48

———

HIM

I PARK MY JEEP THREE BLOCKS AWAY FROM THE DOG PARK AND climb out with Destiny cradled in my arms. I am clean-shaven and dressed in fresh hand-washed clothes. I look like a clean-cut man from Utah who has moved to Rockland for a better life.

Destiny yipped in her kennel last night until I brought her onto my mattress. She immediately curled into a ball beside me and fell asleep. She is small and fluffy with a white muzzle and brown patches around her eyes. The patch around her right eye is bigger than the left, and black strands of hair stick up around her ears. I woke to puppy breath and a warm tongue licking my face. She is nothing like the feral mutts that roam around Lodell. She is innocent, young, and *my* Destiny.

I am the first person to the dog park. It is small, chain-linked, and tucked between houses and apartments. There are benches, a single picnic table, and a water fountain with a dog spigot near the ground. I set Destiny on the grass. She looks around like she doesn't know what to do. I walk toward a bench, but she stays where I put her and whimpers.

"Come here. You can do it." Has she never been on grass

259

before? What sort of an asshole would breed puppies and not have grass for them?

She lets out a bunch of high-pitched puppy yelps, but I do not go to her. I will not allow her to be weak. Life is dangerous when you are weak. I sit in the grass and call her to me. She finally takes a step and pulls her foot up, unused to the feel.

"Come on, you've got this."

She finally moves toward me and picks up her pace. Her whole body wobbles, and her ears flap in one big fluffy ball of cuteness. She finally makes it to me and climbs into my lap just as some dude shows up with a golden retriever that looks to be about six months old. The moment he shuts the gate and releases the pup from his leash, the pup zooms around. His ears fly, and he zips past us and parkours off the boulders like a maniac.

Destiny looks entranced, and she won't take her eyes off him. When he flies by us, she pokes her head under my arm to watch. He does not slow down for a good ten minutes. When he finally notices us, he comes over.

I hope this dude leaves before Ashley gets here. His pup is so hyper he will scare the girls and keep them close to their mom.

"Is he bothering you?" The dude comes toward us. He has dark hair, a neatly trimmed beard, and a big smile. "Mozzie, come."

Yes, he needs to leave.

"It's her first time at a dog park," I say, "so she's a bit scared."

I lift Destiny, carry her to a bench, and set her at my feet. The pup follows us, but he is gentle and soon loses interest in this scared little lump of fur.

The dude finally calls to his pup, snaps on the leash, and leaves before Ashley arrives. Two school buses drove by, so she should be coming soon. I hope. If she does not come today, I will show up every day until she does.

Little girl voices chime on the breeze just before three blurs of pink appear on the sidewalk. Kia and the middle girl run for the park, and their backpacks bounce up and down with every step. Kia makes it to the gate first and opens it. I set my bait, my Destiny, on the ground at my feet and wait.

The girls drop their backpacks against the chainlink and run to climb on the boulders. Oreo pulls Ashley in by the leash. She latches the gate behind her before she releases him.

Oreo is not as hyper as the pup, but he runs around sniffing for a place to pee. He raises his leg on two bushes and a tree before he notices Destiny and me. As Ashley sits on another bench to take the baby from her carrier, Kia spots us.

She jumps from a boulder and runs toward me. "Can I pet him?"

"It's a her, and yes, you can."

She squats down and plops onto her butt, crosslegged, and reaches toward my puppy. "What's her name?"

"Destiny."

Destiny climbs into Kia's lap. "She's so cute."

Before I know it, the middle girl is here and tries to pull Destiny away from Kia. Kia looks up at me like I am supposed to stop her, but I don't want to do anything wrong, so I shrug.

"Mom…" Kia yells. "Calista is trying to take the puppy."

Calista. That is a beautiful name. Ashely pulls the baby out of the carrier and starts toward us. My bait has worked. Fishing is what I am good at.

Ashley approaches and says, "I'm sorry. Calista, you need to wait your turn."

"Kia already had a turn."

"I just got her," Kia says.

"I'm sorry." Ashley looks over at me with big green anime eyes that send a shockwave through my entire body. "Want me to take them away?"

"No, they're good," I say. "Destiny needs to get used to kids, and I don't have any."

Ashley is tiny, like a bird with hollow bones. She has a worn-out look to her eyes, and her fingernails are bit down to the skin.

"Calista, sit down, and I will time Kia. She has two minutes, then it's your turn."

Calista plops down hard on her ass and crosses her arms.

"You look familiar," Ashley says.

"I just moved to Rockland. I finished hiking the Pacific Crest Trail last September." Calista scoots closer to Kia and Destiny.

She nods her head. "Were you at Little Lava Lake on Memorial Day weekend?"

"Yes, I remember you, too," I say. "Your dog came running toward me dragging his leash."

She gets a big smile. "I'm Ashley."

"Chad," I say, and a loud volley of aggressive barks explode from the back of the park. Oreo stands silent and faces a small, ferocious dog in the back yard of a house.

"Oreo, come," Ashley calls. "Oreo."

The dog doesn't budge.

"Oh, my God! Stupid dog." She looks at me, then down at her girls. Her eyebrows pinch together, and she takes a deep breath.

Before she has a chance to say anything, I stand up. "I'll go get him."

"No, he doesn't know you, and he may snap."

I sit back down. "I'll watch the clock for the girls then. I think she has one more minute."

"Thanks," Ashley says and heads off toward Oreo with the baby on her hip.

Now is my chance. "Destiny likes you."

Kia gives me a smile. "She is so cute."

"Will your daddy be mad that Oreo isn't listening to your mom?"

Kia's smile fades, and she looks down.

"Our daddy is dead," Calista says.

"Calista!" Kia's eyebrows pinch together. "Don't say that."

"But it's true."

"I know," she says, and tears seep from the corner of her eyes, "but you're supposed to say that he *passed on*, not that he is *dead*."

Kia's minute is up, but I don't want her to lose Destiny at this moment. "Thirty more seconds, I say to Calista, then it's your turn."

49

———

EMMY

MAYA HAS CRIED FOR HOURS—OR THAT'S WHAT IT FEELS LIKE. Faye's office has turned into a nursery with a bassinet, changing table, and a brand new white and fluffy rug that she lays her on. Faye walks circles around the office, trying to comfort Maya, who does nothing but cry. She has taken her to the doctor, who told Faye that nothing was physically wrong with Maya—so Faye thinks something is wrong with her.

I slide open the drawer with all the notepads and pens where I buried the newspaper article about the girl. I pull it out, unfold it, and smooth the torn edges on the counter. The woman in the photo has long golden-brown hair and a gorgeous smile.

Woman Found Dead in River, Foul Play is Suspected

ROCKLAND, Oregon—The search for a missing Rockland woman came to a tragic end after a fisherman found her dead on Wednesday, early evening. The Sheriff's department is still looking for answers. It appears twenty-three-year-old Anabel Crosby was the victim of foul play, but there is no suspect information at this time. Anabel was reported missing on Wednesday morning when she never returned from an outing. On Tuesday morning, she told her roommate that she was going to get them a surprise, but she never returned home.

The Sheriff's Department thinks she was killed on Tuesday, shortly after she left her home. She was found in a secluded part of the Deschutes river, where her body probably floated from upstream—possibly from the Juniper Flat boat launch.

The Canyon County Sheriff's Office is taking custody of the remains to figure out exactly how she died. No more information is available at this time.

I know it is Skid. I feel it in my bones. They had him, and they let him escape. Now, two more girls are dead. The one in Elk Lake at the end of the summer, and this one.

Maya's wails tone down to a gasping sob, and I hear a whimper that is not a baby. I fold the article, slip it back in the drawer, and go to the break room for a cup of hot chocolate. I bring it back in one of Faye's favorite coffee cups, the thin one with delicate pink and blue flowers.

I peek my head into the office. Maya continues to cry. Her voice sounds hoarse and scratchy.

"Hey there," I say. "I brought you some hot chocolate."

Faye looks toward me with watery eyes and a glazed look. How long has it been since she had any sleep?

"Do you mind if I give it a try?" I set the hot chocolate on the desk and hold my arms out. "I always comforted the little ones at my different foster homes."

Faye looks uncertain. I don't think she has let anyone hold Maya yet. She looks down at Maya—at her scrunched-up face, all red and pinched beneath her flowery yellow beanie. Faye nods her head, and I take Maya from her arms.

"Why don't you go sit on the couch and rest a bit."

Faye takes the cup of hot chocolate, shuffles out to the lobby, and lowers herself onto the red velvet couch. I put Maya against my shoulder and pat her back. She smells like baby powder and sour milk. I bounce her and walk the room, and after a couple of minutes, she quiets and relaxes in my arms. I peek out to give Faye a smile, but she's already vertical and conked out.

I click on the television and keep walking with Maya. Sometimes the background noise helps babies sleep. The news is on and talking about the upcoming Silverdale rodeo. After a few minutes, I put Maya in her bassinet and keep my hand on her back until I know she will stay asleep. Then I slowly lift my hand and plop down in the office recliner.

The scene changes to a man and a woman who look exhausted. He has short brown hair and a goatee. The woman is blonde with black-rimmed glasses. The banner beneath them says *Parents of woman found in river ask for help from the community*.

"Someone killed our daughter." The man has red-rimmed eyes. His wife stands beside him and shakes. She looks like she will collapse at any moment. "She was a beautiful soul who loved to kayak. She's an artist and just enrolled in business classes so she could eventually start her own shop. If you have any information, please contact the Sheriff's department."

My stomach churns, and a sharp pain rises in my throat. I have information. I know who did it. He was in my bedroom. He left a bootprint on my pillow and left a hand-tied fly in my bathroom.

"Her black Jeep with a rack on the top is still missing. Please keep a look out for it. The license plate is…"

I click the television off. I can't look at those people. I remember the complete helplessness I felt when Amber was missing. I should talk to the Sheriff. I should call the reporters and tell the world about Skid.

Faye sleeps for a good two hours, and when she wakes, Maya is still sound asleep in her bassinet. "I needed that. Thank you."

"Anytime," I say. "She's a beautiful baby."

Faye looks down at her with a proud smile, but it quickly fades. "I'm not good at this. She does nothing but cry."

"She's a baby," I say. "That's what they do."

"You got her calmed right away."

"I think she was exhausted and cried herself out."

"No, she can go on much longer than that." Faye closes her eyes and shakes her head.

Maya sleeps for a good three hours, and Faye seems like a different woman. Before I know it, Mindy pokes her head into the lobby to let me know they are ready to leave. As we pull out of the parking lot, Deputy Wright turns in and looks into the cab of the truck, and our eyes meet. He opens his mouth like he's about to say something as Mindy takes her foot off the clutch, and we lurch onto the highway.

As soon as we drop Izel off, Mindy lights a cigarette and starts rambling. "Did you hear about the girl they found in the river? Do you think it was Skid? I can't believe he came into your house and now this. You should get a gun..."

Her words blur together, along with the greens, yellows, browns, and blues of the houses and trees we pass. I don't want to deal with this anymore. They need to catch his ass and lock him up. The idiots let him go. I wouldn't be surprised if his father orchestrated the entire thing. He was supposed to be next to him in the emergency room. They trusted him because he's the police chief of Lodell and an Unger, and Skid is his son. He should be investigated, but I know he won't be. Men like him get away with anything. They think they're above the law, and they usually are.

"Emmy, Emmy." A hand touches my shoulder, and I turn to see Mindy's face. "You okay?"

I nod and look around. The truck is stopped in front of our

duplex. It is as if we went through a portal. "Oh my God, I completely zoned out."

Dale's maroon and silver work truck is backed up to the other side of the duplex, and two saw horses sit in the drive with wood shavings beneath them.

"You going to be okay?" Mindy asks. "Do you want me to come in for a bit?"

"No, I'll be fine. The landlord is next door."

Mindy puts her hand on my forearm and gives me a sad smile. "Call me if you need anything."

I nod, open the door, and slide out of her truck. The temperatures are warming up, and I catch the scent of pine needles and sage. She pulls away and flips a U-turn as Dale comes out of the other side of the duplex.

"Hey, Emmy! How are things going?" His beard is scraggly gray and dark brown, but I can still see that his dimples sink in with his smile.

"Good. How about you?"

"My guys are about done with this side. You and Brian can switch sides in about a month. It will be all nice and renovated for you."

"Thanks, Dale." I've been waiting for him to tell us we need to find another place, especially after I called the police when Skid broke in.

"Want to see how it's coming?"

I follow him into the door. The setup is the mirror image of our side, like the anti-duplex. Maybe things will be better for us when we move to this side, like a fresh start. It even smells new.

Two men are installing a new kitchen window, one of those white vinyl ones. They both turn and nod at us when we enter. I have seen them many times but don't talk to them. Brian has, but not me.

The new side is fresh and clean, with new floors, a new shower and toilet, and brand-new closet doors. After the tour, I go back to our side, and it seems extra dingy now. I don't feel like eating, but I dump a can of Campbell's Tomato Soup into a saucepan, add a can of water, and turn the burner on. Someone knocks on the door, probably Dale. I set the wooden spoon across the rim of the pan and go to the door.

When I swing it open, I gasp. On the step is Jewell, tall, thin, and leathery, with fine gray hair pulled into a ponytail. She almost looks like a zombie in a tight t-shirt and jeans.

"Hi, Emmy," she says. She has a book of some sort in her hand, and her purse hangs from one shoulder. "Is Brian home?"

"No." My voice barely cracks from my throat.

She looks around me into the duplex. "Nice place you got."

"Thank you." I guess everyone and their mother knows where we live.

"I can tell you're busy," she says and holds the book out to me. It looks like an old laminated blue 1980s journal with wildflowers printed on the cover. "The lady who bought my old house brought me this."

I look down at it but don't touch it. I have no idea why she would bring this to me.

"Claire and Brian lived there until she died."

"Claire?"

"Claire Cobb, Brian's mom. They lived in that house until she died, then Brian went to live with the Ungers."

I don't know what she is telling me or why she holds the book out.

"The people who bought the house are putting in new floors and found this under the boards."

I stare down at it and her thumb with a bruised nail.

"It's Brian's mom's journal. They brought it to me, and I think he should have it."

I take the book. It's heavier in my hand than I had expected. "Thank you."

A hiss and a burning smell comes from behind me.

"My soup!" I say and run for the kitchen. I set the book on the counter and pull the foaming pan from the burner.

"I'm going to head out," Jewell calls from the door. "It was nice seeing you.

The moment she leaves, I run to the door and lock it. I clean up my mess and sit at the table to eat the little soup that is left. The journal sits closed right in front of me. I want to open it and read, but that feels like a violation.

It seems like forever until Brian gets home. When he takes off his ball cap, his hair is sweaty and plastered down. He immediately notices the journal on the table and stops. He cocks his head to the side, stares at it, then turns to look at me. "What's that?"

"Jewell brought it."

"Jewell?" His eyebrows pinch together. "From Lodell?"

"Yes. The lady who bought her old house found it. Jewell said it was your mother's journal."

"I remember it." Brian's eyes turn down, and he looks sad. "I forgot about it until now."

Brian walks over, picks it up, and puts it to his nose. "It used to smell like her perfume."

He takes it to the couch and sits down. "Where did you say Jewell got it?"

"The people who bought her house are putting in new floors. They found it under the floorboards."

He sits there without opening the cover.

"You going to read it?"

He pats the couch right next to him, and I sit down. "It will be easier if we do it together."

I turn on the overhead light and plop down next to him. I put my hand on his leg, so he knows I'm here to support him.

He opens the cover, and the first page is filled with beautiful, loopy cursive writing. October 5, 1983, is written at the top. She started it the day Brian was born.

My son, Brian Joshua Cobb, born on October 5, 1983, is the joy of my life. I am the luckiest woman alive. We may never have a traditional family, but his father and I love him dearly, and he will forever be loved and taken care of.

Brian looks at me with a confused expression. He has always told me that his father was a fly fisherman who came through town, and Brian was conceived without his mom knowing the man's full name. I have seen Brian's birth certificate. It has his mother's full name and *unknown* where the father's name should be. He was born at Rimrock Health Clinic in Lodell, and where it says, *I certify that the child was born alive at the date and hour and place stated,* was *Robert B. Unger, MD.*

We both continue reading.

We have conceived this child in love, and if not for his prominence and circumstances, we would run off together for a full life.

Brian closes the book and stares across the room with pinched eyebrows. He has been lied to. His beloved mother lied to him.

"I remember..." Brian says. "There was a man. I remember a man coming to visit and bringing us gifts. And one morning, I woke up with a bad dream. I ran to my mom's room, and there was a man. I forgot all about it."

Brian continues to stare, and all of a sudden, his face flushes red. He hurls the journal across the room. It hits the wall and clatters to the floor.

"What?"

"Fucking shit! Fucking Doc Unger!"

Brian jumps up, kicks the coffee table over, and stomps across the room. He puts his head to the wall and punches it over and over until he dents the drywall.

"All those fucking years of getting Jake's hand-me-downs and living with Rose and Russ while my own fucking father was right there."

I'm not sure what he's...oh my God. "Are you saying that Doc Unger is your father?"

He throws another fist into the wall and then starts kicking the shit out of it until the drywall crumbles.

I want to run to him and throw my arms around him. He has been lied to by the people he loves. Brian yells and punches, like he is going to tear down the entire apartment. After what seems like forever, he turns around with his back to the wall. He slides down until his ass hits the floor, covers his face with his hands, and sobs.

Brian is not practically an Unger. He *is* an Unger.

50
——

HIM

With a Ketamine-laced hot dog in a Ziplock, I park my Jeep on a side street three blocks from Ashley's apartment and away from any streetlights. This is my eighth time coming in the night. Every time, Oreo comes out on the balcony and stares down at me. Ashley leaves the sliding glass door cracked open for Oreo in the night. It makes sense since she is on the second floor and would not want to leave the girls alone to take the dog out.

I wait until all the apartments are dark, and I cannot hear anything except the crickets and wind in the trees. The slider on Ashley's apartment has the slight glow of a nightlight in the gap where the door and blinds are open for her dog. I click my tongue and wait until Oreo's silhouette walks to the rail. The white on his muzzle and forehead forms an hourglass between the bars. I split the hot dog in half, just in case I miss, and cast my line of Ketamine onto the balcony. The hourglass moves to where it hit. I toss the other half, and he takes that, also.

Within minutes, the legs of Oreo's silhouette fold in, and he flops over. I hurry to the field behind the apartments, where I have stashed an old wooden ladder in a clump of trees. When I return, I push it into the brush beside the lower balcony and take three calming breaths. My heartbeat slows. No lights in any of the apartments click on, and the crickets begin to chirp again.

I climb the ladder, step on the balcony floor, and swing my leg over the rail. I squat down and blend in with the shadows. Oreo is out and does not stir. I step past him and slip into the gap in the sliding door.

Her apartment smells like peaches and baby powder. In the dim glow of the nightlight, I see that it is modern and tidy, with big square pillows on the couch and four chairs around the table. I stop, breathe it all in, and let the atmosphere absorb into my body. I am home. Ashely is in our bed, waiting for me, and our girls are fast asleep.

Down the hall, the first door is open with a blue glow and the faint tinkle of nursery music. I push the door open to the night sky projected on the ceiling and the walls. The stars slowly circle with the music. I stand and watch my girls sleep before I step over to the bed. Carina sleeps in the crib on one side of the room with her arms out and a binkie halfway in her mouth. Kia and Calista lie together on the bottom half of the bunk bed, a double-sized bed with a single on the top.

They float on a pink raft of bedsheets. I slide my hand beneath Calista's head and spread her hair out in a halo. She does not stir. Kia shifts in her sleep, so I wait until her breaths are deep before I spread her hair out over the pillow. I watch my girls, sweet and innocent, under the stars in their slumber.

Down the hall, Ashley sleeps and waits for me to climb into bed with her. I step into the room. She lays on her side with her hair streaming out across the sheets. My pulse races, and I want to take her. Do I take her for eternity in the fluid or as Chad Joseph Miller in the flesh?

51

———

ASHLEY

I WAKE UP WITH A DISCORDANT FEELING, AFTER HAVING THE strangest dream, a dream of a man in my bed who was not Chris. I didn't see his face, but he was there.

I have never dreamt of another man. It has always been Chris. Always. I never even had a crush on a boy until I saw Chris with his friends on my first day of middle school. Even then, he had a tough guy swagger but a tender gleam in his eyes.

I get out of bed and brush my teeth. The uneasy feeling still churns in my body. I pull on my robe, slide my feet into my fluffy pink slippers, and go to the door of the girls' room. The door is shut. I always leave it slightly open. The feeling starts vibrating again, and my cheeks tingle with pinpricks.

I turn the knob and push it open. They are there, asleep in their beds. I don't realize I am holding my breath until it escapes from my mouth. Carina lies on her back with her legs splayed out like a frog and her binkie nipple against her cheek. I pull the blanket over her, and she stirs but falls back to sleep.

I step over to Kia and Calista. Both of them have their hair spread out in sunbursts around their heads. My heart races and a scream rises up my throat. I shut it in with my hand and run

275

from their room. They could not have done it themselves. My mind flashes to the faceless man, the girls' hair, the pink of their room, and the cool air coming in the sliding glass door.

Oreo. Where is Oreo? He's not on his pad or sitting by the front door. The curtains hang still and dark with the morning light in the gap. I step out, and Oreo lifts his head.

"What are you doing out here?" I feel a sense of relief, but it is shallow. Deep down, I know that something is wrong.

52

HIM

THE SUN DIPS BELOW THE HORIZON AND PULLS THE LAST OF ITS glow behind it. I push the bottom of the fence slats, and they lift. Someone has been sneaking in and out of this back yard for a long time. The alley gate has a new padlock, but it does no good. Brian should protect his woman better.

The lights in the houses start clicking on. Destiny, my little ball of fur, is home waiting for me, and my other destiny is here behind these windows. Emmy is the last thread to cut before I move on with my new life. I let her live, and I let Brian have her, but he is unworthy. It is time to bind her to me forever.

The backyard weeds reach high. The thistle will soon poke up through the springs of their trampoline. After tonight, Brian won't give a shit about the yard. The kitchen light clicks on and illuminates the giant rectangle of their sliding glass door. A slat is missing and creates a long column of bright light. I've been half-hard all day planning for tonight, and now I am ready.

Inside, Emmy washes the dishes in a sink full of foam. She wears one of Brian's t-shirts with no pants. As she reaches to rinse a plate, it rises up, and the curve of her bare ass peeks out the bottom.

The plastic syringe taps against the glass vial of Ketamine when I pull them from my pocket. I flick the orange cap, and it flies into the weeds. Shit. I bend over to look for it, but it does not matter. After tonight, I will no longer be me. I will be the Hermit, Chad Joseph Miller.

The needle slides into the hole of the vial. I tip it up in the light, pull the plunger, and watch the liquid slip against the black lines. Not too much. Not too much. Crystal took too much, and I almost lost her before we could have fun.

I unclip the folding knife from my waistband. It is black, ultra-light, and fits my hand perfectly with a textured grip. I hope Emmy does not force me to puncture her with it. Blood is messy. The flesh is disgusting.

I want her death to be beautiful. A ketamine-laced death where I hold her beneath the surface and take her last breath.

Emmy dries her hands on a towel and reaches up toward the window. As she stretches to check the latch, the t-shirt rises halfway up her ass. A red strip of thong is in the crack. My breath fogs the glass, but I see Emmy coming straight toward me through the blur. My heartbeat quickens, and my breath whooshes in my ears. She will see my face in the glass. I step aside, face to face with the dry wood siding. The door rattles when she tests it, then the light clicks off.

In a couple of minutes, the bathroom light glows, and I hear the shower water gurgling in the pipes.

53

EMMY

THE LINOLEUM FEELS COLD ON MY FEET, AND A LONG SLIVER OF my reflection stares back into the glass where we have a missing slat. A shiver runs up my spine and across my shoulders. I check the door, and it rattles against the stick in the track. I reach over to the light switch, turn it off, and look through the glass. It feels like someone is there, but I see nothing but the outline of the fence and trees and the trampoline's black circle lit by the glow of the streetlight.

After I check the front door and all the windows in the living room and spare bedroom, I head to our room. My work clothes lie in a heap by the bathroom door. I think my phone is still in the pocket of my pants. I must remember to charge it as soon as I get out of the shower. It's about dead because I forgot to bring my charger to work.

The rings on the shower curtain scrape against the rod as I push it aside to turn the water on. A warm shower sounds amazing. I've been tense all day. Not only with what's going on with Brian, but Maya cried half the day and only quieted down for me. Faye says I have the magic touch.

I shut the bathroom door to keep the warmth in. Once the

steam from the shower fogs up the mirror, I pull off Brian's t-shirt and drop it onto the floor. It's the one from Rimrock Outfitters that says *Paddle Faster, I Hear Banjos.* Doc gave his golden child, Jake, the outfitters but nothing for Brian. This has got to be hitting him hard.

I step over the rim of the bathtub, pull the curtain closed, and let the warm water run down my scalp and back. Oh my God, it feels so good. Brian and I need to brace ourselves for what's coming. I wonder what will happen when Brian confronts Doc. Or if he will. I have no idea. I squirt some shampoo into my palm.

Something clunks to the floor. It sounds like it comes from the living room. I turn off the shower, still with soap in my hair, and wrap the towel around me. I want to call out, *hello*, but my voice gets stuck in my throat. It could be some workmen in the duplex next door, but it's late. Maybe some kids have broken in.

I stand still with my hand on the doorknob and try to quiet my heartbeat enough to hear. I turn the knob to peek out, and suddenly, the door is ripped from my grasp. I scream. Standing there in the doorway is Skid.

"Hi, Emmy," he says.

A rush of cold chills me to the bone. I take a step back and the cool porcelain of the toilet presses against my legs. I am trapped. Stay calm. "What do you want?"

"You know what I want." He takes a step toward me. A knife blade sticks out from his hand.

"No!" Think, think. "Brian is Doc's son. We just found out. He's your...."

"It's about time." Skid lets out a scornful laugh. "You know how many times I wanted to tell him? But that was before Brian yanked me from my destiny. If he had let the river have me, the two of you could have lived happily ever after in your trashy little house."

No. No. "Brian will be home any minute...."

"No, he won't, you fucking little liar. He doesn't get home until 10:25."

Skid holds the knife toward me and reaches for the towel. I clasp it tight around me, but it comes off with such force I stumble backward. I cross my arms over my breasts.

Skid laughs again. "No need to be shy. I've seen them before. I've sucked them before, and I've fucked you." He holds the knife out again. "Drop your arms. I like to see my nymphs in their flesh before I release them."

I'm frozen and can't move. Even if I could, there's no way in hell I will do what he wants. Before I know it, he reaches out and spins me around with his knife to my throat. He is stronger than I ever imagined, especially for how skinny he is. My knees hit the rim of the toilet.

He puts the tip of the blade beneath my chin. "To think I felt sorry for Brian and let him have you. That was a mistake. He does not deserve you. You are my nymph, and you are meant for the river."

He keeps the blade to my throat and runs his other hand down my back and over my ass. "Mmmm…you are going to be yummy. Don't move now. I have something for you."

A weapon…I need a weapon! My pepper spray is in the kitchen. Shit. I reach for the only thing I can, which is the toilet tank lid. He may cut my throat the moment I move, but I'm dead either way. In one movement, I grab the tank lid and swing around. It makes contact with the side of his head, and he stumbles back.

I push past him and out of the bathroom. I scoop my pants up from the floor and run.

"Bitch," he yells and grabs for my leg.

I trip and fall to my hands and knees. I have a death grip on my pants and run for the hall. He pulls my ankle, and I slide toward him. I kick and feel something crack beneath my heel.

He howls and shoves the bedroom door shut. I scramble for the open closet and crawl in.

He laughs. "Where are you going to go now?"

I pull the phone from my pant pocket. It glows in the dark of the closet. There is one sliver of red battery as I dial 911.

"This doesn't need to be so messy." His words breathe into the crack of the closet door. "You will be immortal. You will be a nymph of the river for eternity."

"911, what is…." Shit! I turn down the volume, set the phone against the wall, and scream at the top of my lungs, "Help! Someone help."

Before I know it, the closet door flies open, and he is on top of me. "Shut up, bitch."

I kick and grab for anything. My fingers close around a shoe, and I swing it. He yanks me out of the closet by a leg, and my head bangs against the doorjamb. He climbs on top of me with his knees pressed into the crook of my arms. It hurts like fucking hell.

I kick my feet, but he has me pinned. "Dylan Unger! Let me go!"

He pauses like he knows I am up to something.

"What did you do?" He looks toward the closet and then back at me. "You're just trying to trick me, you cagey fucking bitch."

Please, God, let my phone still have some life. Skid reaches into his pant pocket and pulls out a syringe. "Hold still, and I will make this beautiful for you."

He's going to drug me, just like he did to Amber and the other girls. To hell with that. I scream and thrash, but he presses his knees harder into my arms. Pain shoots through to the core of my bones.

"Stop!" I yell. "Get the fuck off me. Help!"

He shoves a cloth into my mouth so hard that I taste blood. I suck air in through my nose, but it is not enough, and my head feels light. Please, God, don't let me die like this. Not to him.

"You can make this as painful as you want, but it's all going to end the same."

He lowers the syringe toward my arm. No! No! No! Sirens scream in the distance. Skid stiffens and cocks his head. He hears them, too. I take that moment to twist beneath him and push myself onto my knees. The syringe drops to the floor right by my head, and when he reaches for it, I buck, slip out from beneath him, and run for the door.

"Fucking bitch."

I rip the gag from my mouth and run down the hall. He's right behind me when I grip the doorknob, unlatch the bolt, and burst out the door. I run for the streetlight and scream for help, just as the sirens and flashing blue and red lights come around the corner. I wave my arms until the squad car comes to a stop with me in the headlights. The driver's door flies open.

Deputy Wright jumps out. "Emmy!"

"He's in there. It's Dylan Unger."

His hand goes straight to his gun. "Are you hurt?"

"No. Go get him!"

He opens the back door of his squad car. "Wait in here."

I don't realize I am still naked until I climb in and feel the seat on my bare ass. "You need to get him."

The next thing I know, Deputy Wright hands me a jacket. "Cover yourself."

He turns toward our duplex with his hand on his gun. Another squad car comes around the corner and stops at an angle with its lights flashing. A deputy jumps out.

"Dylan Unger is inside," Deputy Wright says to the other officer.

They both turn toward me. "Is he armed?"

"He has a knife." My heartbeat races and every nerve in my body vibrates. "Go get him!"

More sirens blare in the distance. The other deputy looks at Deputy Wright and back at me. "Stay in the car until law enforcement or a paramedic comes for you."

"He's going to get away!" I say as they slam the car door shut.

The two deputies enter our duplex with their guns drawn. My breath fogs the window while I wait for them to come through the door with Skid in handcuffs. I wipe it clear and see our front door wide open like a mouth with no scream coming out. Please, God, let them catch him.

After a few minutes, both deputies step through the door without him. Deputy Wright says something into his walkie-talkie and then nods toward the side of the house. They split up and head in opposite directions.

My heart drops to the pit of my stomach. He's not in there. Deputy Wright comes around the house and says something into his radio. A moment later, an ambulance comes around the corner with flashing lights but no siren. Our entire duplex is lit in red, blue, and gold. The silhouette of the other deputy comes from the vacant side of the duplex. Fuck! He got away.

When Deputy Wright opens the door of his squad car, a rush of cold air comes in. "He got away?"

"Yes, I'm sorry."

My head spins, and I feel sick. The windows are fogged, and my knees and ribs sting. Someone touches my arm, and I yelp.

"I'm sorry," a paramedic says. He is tall with dark curly hair and a blue shirt. "Can you come out?"

I scoot toward the door.

"I'm going to wrap you in a blanket," he says.

I look down at my bare legs beneath Deputy Wright's jacket. A blanket comes around my shoulders before he pulls at the jacket clasped to my chest, and I release it.

"I've got your arm. Can you slide out?"

My neighbors stand in the street and talk all around me, but I can't register what they say.

"We need to get you some medical attention."

"I'm not hurt," I say, then notice the blood on my knees.

"I'm going to take your arm and help you."

I nod, and we step toward an open door on the side of the ambulance. When I lift my leg to step in, cold air rushes up into the warm blanket. He helps me onto the gurney and straps me in. Just as he reaches for the door, Brian runs up with panic on his face.

"Emmy! Are you alright?" Brian grabs the edge of the door.

"I'm okay," I say. "It was Skid."

Brian freezes, and his face drops.

"We're taking her to Good Samaritan," the paramedic says. "Please let go, sir."

Brian's entire body goes slack and his arms drop to his sides. The paramedic closes the door, and we drive away.

54

———

EMMY

A NURSE WITH SHORT BLACK HAIR STEPS INTO MY ROOM. "BRIAN Cobb is here to see you. Do you want me to let him in?"

My heart hangs by a string. At the mention of Brian's name, it snaps, and tears stream down the sides of my face. "Yes, yes, please."

I have no idea why they moved me to a private hospital room. The emergency room doctor examined me, and the next thing I knew, they wheeled me up here. My injuries are minimal, considering what I went through.

In minutes, Brian rushes in with a pale face and wide eyes. He hasn't showered and is still dirty from work. "Oh my God, Emmy...I'm so sorry. What happened? I'm going beat the shit out of that motherfucker. He better hope the cops get their hands on him before I do."

Brian sits on the edge of my hospital bed and puts his fingers on my cheek. It's like a dam breaks inside, and I sob out loud. The next thing I know, Brian scoots my body and lies beside me. He wraps his arms around my waist and holds me tight against him. The smell of sweat, oil, and pine sap seems strange in this sterile room. I don't know how long we lie there, but soon, my cries stop, and all that's left are a few gasping breaths.

Someone raps three times on the doorframe. "Hello," a male voice calls in. Brian's body stiffens and he sits up.

I open my eyes, and standing there in the doorway, is Detective Perry and another man with a badge on his belt. He wears a button-up shirt and tie, just like Detective Perry, but he is shorter and has a compassionate smile. Brian gets off the bed and goes to one of the padded brown chairs.

"Sorry to bother you," Detective Perry says. "It's crucial that we get a statement as soon as possible. This is Detective Flores, and he's here to help me tonight."

Brian swings his legs off the side of my bed and stands up.

"Are you with the FBI?"

"No, I'm with Canyon County Sheriff's office," Detective Flores says.

Detective Perry steps over to Brian. "Hello, Brian. I'm going to have to ask you to step out of the room for the interview."

Brian leans over me with a hard stare. "You don't need to say anything. You can tell them to leave."

"Why? I am not the suspect. I'm the one who was attacked." Then, it hits me. Brian doesn't want me to say anything about him. Or about the Ungers.

"It's okay," I say. "It will be alright."

"No, it won't." Brian's eyes glare straight through me.

Detective Perry steps closer and lets out a little cough. Brian straightens up, gives me a *keep your mouth shut* look, and leaves. As soon as he clears the door, Detective Flores closes it.

"Do you mind if we have a seat?" Detective Perry points at the two padded chairs.

"Go ahead." Both men lower themselves into the chairs and adjust their ties, so they lay straight along their shirt buttons.

"Detective Perry opens his leather portfolio. We would like to get a statement and ask you some questions."

"Okay," I say. "Will you raise the back of my bed?"

Detective Flores messes with the bed until I am sitting up, and Detective Perry pulls out what looks like the same black tape recorder he used the first time he took my statement. He sets in on the bed table between us and pushes a button. The little black teeth of the cassette start to spin.

"Emmy Renee Jenkins' interview at Good Samaritan Hospital at 12:23 am by Detective Glen Perry and Detective Rolando Flores." The teeth of the cassette spin around and around. "Miss Jenkins is advised that Detective Perry and Detective Flores are conducting an official criminal investigation for the Canyon County Sheriff's office in the state of Oregon."

Detective Perry's deep-set eyes seem darker and deeper than usual.

"Miss Jenkins was further advised that we are requesting her voluntary cooperation and that any information obtained during this official criminal investigation may be referred to the Department of Justice or other appropriate agency."

The tape recorder spins as I wait for my turn to talk.

"Miss Jenkins agreed to cooperate and provide the following recorded statement, which will then be transcribed for her approval and signature."

He pulls a pen from a holder inside the spine of the portfolio. "Can you tell us what happened?"

I want them to know everything so they can put it all together. I tell them about my shower, what happened when I came out of the bathroom, how I tried to get away, my 911 call, and every detail, all the way up until the moment they arrived in my room. When I start in about Amber and the other girls, Detective Perry puts his hand up for me to stop.

"We only need a statement about what happened tonight. We may have a few questions, then we need to take you to the scene for a walkthrough."

"But...it is all related. Don't you want everything? Six women were killed. He is a serial killer."

"We will have you come to the station for a full statement at another time," Detective Perry says in a calm voice like he is my handler. "We have some questions about what happened tonight."

I get it. I don't know what the hell I am talking about. This is their investigation, and they are the experts.

"What about the DNA?" I need them to connect the dots. "The DNA from the hair Dylan took from women he drowned? It was in his tackle box and in his hand-tied flies."

Detective Perry nods. "The results are not back yet. I want to be honest and prepare you. The coroner determined the women's deaths were accidental."

"Even the two new ones?"

"The manner of death in the Elk Lake drowning was determined accidental also," Detective Flores says. "We are waiting for the results for Anabel Crosby."

"Did Anna and Anabel have chunks of hair ripped out?"

Both men have flat expressions. I bet they teach that in detective training—like a poker face, so they don't give anything away. I know I'm right, and they make me feel stupid. No...I can't think like that. Someone believes me. The shoe tree was taken down. "What about the hair?"

Detective Perry takes a deep breath, then blows it out. "His lawyer claims that he took the hair while the girls were alive and someone else killed them."

"His lawyer? He has a lawyer? I thought he escaped and you can't find him. How did he get a lawyer?"

Detective Perry puts his hand up again. "His family's lawyer. Please, I don't want to upset you. We are working on the case and gathering information."

I can smell the Ungers all over this with their money and fricking lawyer. The same lawyer that is defending Brian. A burning sensation rises in my throat. The Ungers are spinning their web and trapping everyone in it.

I thought this would be it. Now that Skid has attacked me, they have to believe me—but I can feel it in my bones that they will always doubt me. I am a troubled girl with a big imagination, and they have to cover their asses because of the Ungers. My stomach churns, and my throat stings. "What about the shoe tree? Have you tried matching the shoes with the missing girls?"

Detective Flores looks over to Detective Perry. He knows nothing about the shoes.

"You took the tree down. Don't you have all the shoes in evidence?"

*Holy shit. They did not take it down. But, who...*My head spins, and I feel sick. The Ungers did it to destroy the evidence. *Oh my God.*

"We have a few questions and need to get photos," Detective Flores says. "Can you please tell us who caused each of your injuries?"

"Dylan Unger. We just went over all that."

"Do you have any injures that were caused by another person?"

"Another person? Haven't I been clear? No..."

"Do you feel safe in your home?"

"No. I was attacked in my home. I have no way to defend myself. What if he comes back?"

Both detectives sit there and nod their heads. I can tell this is not the answer they expected. Detective Flores takes a deep breath and says, "Let me rephrase the question. Do you feel safe in the house with your boyfriend, Brian Cobb?"

They wait for me to answer. Oh shit. "Yes! Brian wouldn't hurt me. He's never laid a finger on me."

"We noticed some large holes in the wall."

My heart pounds a fuzzy beat in my ears. "Brian did that. A lady found his mother's journal in the floorboards of the house

Brian lived in before his mother died. That is how he realized that Doc is his father, and they lied to him all these years." They look at me like I'm rambling and not making sense. "My boyfriend, Brian Cobb, is Dylan Unger's cousin."

This is some news for the detectives—I can tell. Their faces finally crack an emotion, and they look at each other. Both men write on their notepads.

"I don't blame Brian. They deceived him his whole life. I would have punched holes in the wall too."

"Do you know where this journal is?" Detective Perry asks.

Oh shit. Brian is going to be pissed. They will confiscate his mother's journal, and he will know I told them. I close my eyes and feel the warm tears slide down my cheeks. "I'm tired. Can we stop?"

I open my eyes to the blurry image of Detective Flores clicking off the tape recorder. Detective Perry stands up. "We need a woman present while we take pictures of your injuries. I'll be right back."

When he leaves the room, Detective Flores gives me a tender look. "As soon as we get the pictures, the hospital will release you."

"And then what?"

"We need you to walk through the scene and point out where everything happened."

The nurse with short black hair is right behind Detective Perry when he returns. She carefully arranges my hospital gown to give me privacy as they snap pictures of every part of my body, including my neck, ankles, and hands.

As soon as they leave to let me change, I turn to the nurse. "Can you ask my boyfriend, Brian, to come back in?"

"He left the E.R. Maybe you can call him?" She pulls the thin white blanket over me.

I can't call Brian. Our only cell phone is dead in the closet or in an evidence bag somewhere. My entire body shakes.

"Can I help you get dressed?"

"No thanks. You can leave." Shit! I should have kept my mouth shut about the journal. I just ruined everything with Brian. Maybe he is waiting outside the hospital.

Another nurse enters my room. "There's a lady named Erika Wheeler in the lobby. She would like to see you. Can I let her in?"

"Yes," I say. I'm back to the same place I have been all my life when the only person here for me is someone from social services.

55

EMMY

"You sure you want to do this?" Erika opens the front door.

I force a smile and nod. Brian never returned to the hospital for me and he wasn't at our duplex when I walked the detectives through it. They wouldn't release the scene and I had nowhere to go, so Erika brought me to her home—three days ago.

With her always walking around in scuffed shoes and Target clothes, I had no idea she's rich. Erika and her husband own a cattle ranch with a big-ass house. They aren't worried about Skid coming onto their land. They're armed to the teeth and have a house full of four grown farm boys, born and bred to work and hunt.

Erika's husband and boys took me to the duplex after the Sheriff released it, but Brian was gone. He had packed all his shit and abandoned me, just like everyone has my entire life. I don't know why it surprised me. Mr. Wheeler and his boys told me that I could come back to their ranch, so I shoved all my clothes into my old suitcase and hopped back into their truck. Amber's duffle bag, our photo from Shooting the Rapids Photography, and the fly box that I kept up on the closet shelf were missing. I bet they are either somewhere in evidence, or burned to ash in a bonfire in the Ungers' back yard. Now, I have absolutely nothing left of Amber's.

"Ready?" Erika puts her key into the ignition.

She keeps giving me chances to back out. "I'm as ready as I'll ever be."

We've already gone over the pros and cons of talking to the media. Nobody wants me to do this interview—other than the reporter and myself. Erika supports my decision, but she worries about me. Erika usually has a wide big-toothed smile, but I haven't seen it since she walked into my hospital room.

The negative aspects are that it could jeopardize the investigation and create more trauma for me because reporters can be insensitive and aggressive. Anything I give to the media or say to them can be used over and over and could impact family and friends.

At the end of their property, Erika makes a left onto the highway.

The benefits of speaking to the media are that it will bring attention to the case and help future victims cope with the stress of their ordeal. Speaking up can also help bring donations to victim assistance programs. For me, the two most important reasons are that it can save the lives of other women, and I will finally have a voice.

Erika's long brown hair hangs over one shoulder as she silently drives down the highway, past cattle and sheep ranches backed up against the mountains. I don't know what I would do without her.

Since I own nothing and I've already lost Brian, I have nothing to lose but my life—and that is threatened whether I speak to the media or not. My best chance is to make sure Skid gets arrested and locked away for good. I'm tired of being a victim of Skid and of the system. I will not remain quiet and hope other people will do what is right.

We drive past the county jail, courthouse, KFC, McDonald's, and the Railroad Inn. Faye's SUV, Mindy's red truck, and Jason's white Jetta all sit in the parking lot, along with several guest cars and trucks. I can almost smell the popcorn and Hawaiian Breeze.

I have my list of don'ts from Sheriff Briggs and Detective Perry. Don't use the word *serial killer* because it will cause the public to panic, and there is no proof at this time. Don't name Skid since he is only a suspect and is innocent until proven guilty. Don't mention the Ketamine. Don't...whatever I do... don't say anything about the chunks of hair ripped from the victims' heads or that he puts strands of them into his hand-tied flies. That is information they are withholding for investigative reasons.

I get it! They are concerned about their investigation, and their hands are tied about what they can and can't say from a legal perspective—but mine are not. Sheriff Briggs has his own news conference later today. I bet it's so he can clean up anything I say. At least I let him know in advance. Well, Erika did, but I agreed to it.

I will no longer keep my mouth shut. Skid is a killer. Women, and the public, need to be warned. We rise out of the Canyon and toward the Deschutes River.

I worry about Brian and what will happen to him. He still has jail time and registering as a sex offender hanging over his head. That sucks, and it would be horrible, but he will live through it. Women who come across Skid will not.

I am no longer worried about the Ungers coming after Brian. He is an Unger, and they won't hurt him. He is their blood. The Ungers will hurt me, but the more attention I draw to myself, the bigger mess I will make for them. If anything happens to me, the public and all the reporters will descend upon Lodell and the Ungers like Yellowjackets at a picnic.

The sun is high and warms the juniper and sage. We pass

tumbledown shacks and barbed wire fence posts that line the dry land and keep livestock from the road. In the distance, the snow-tipped volcano peaks of the Cascades seem like a fairytale backdrop instead of the hunting grounds of a serial killer. In the last few days, I cried so many tears that I feel as dry as this land of nothing but dirt, rock, and scrub.

Faye worries that reporters will hound everyone at the Railroad Inn. Her number one concern is her motel, employees, and especially Maya. Since there is a waiting period until the adoption is final, it scares her shitless that the agency will take Maya back. I get it, and I hope that they aren't affected.

I understand everyone's concerns, but women are being killed. Their families will suffer forever because of it. It will all be worth it if I can save just one victim. That is much bigger than all the other concerns lumped together and tied with a ribbon.

Erika turns off the highway and onto another dirt road. The tires of Erika's Jeep crunch over the gravel and bring up a tail of dust against the cloudless blue sky. We pass a couple of abandoned old homesteads before we pull into the Juniper Flat boat launch, just upriver from where Anabel Crosby's body was recovered. We chose this spot for impact since this is probably where he killed her.

A single blue and white news van with a satellite dish on the roof and a gray pickup are the only vehicles at the site. The van has *KCRK 14, The News As You Need It* plastered over the entire side, and it is backed up to the river with its doors wide open. Picnic tables and rock fire pits sit helter-skelter along the river.

Erika parks her Jeep, and before she shuts off the engine, she looks over at me. "It's not too late."

"I'm doing it," I say.

She bites her lip and gives me a tight smile.

"I need to." I tuck my hair behind my ears. "How do I look?"

She gives me a little laugh because I have no makeup on, and

I'm wearing a pair of jeans and a t-shirt donated to Sophie's House. "You look as beautiful as you always do. Give 'em hell, sweetie."

We step out of the Jeep and walk to the van. My heart jumps to my throat when I notice a fly fisherman in the river, but he looks nothing like Skid. He casts his fly in beautiful narrow loops while his lady sits on the bank in short shorts and a tank top.

Christy Green steps around the van door and gives us a huge smile. "Emmy?"

I nod. She is as gorgeous as she looks on television. Her hair and makeup are immaculate—and she is appropriately dressed for the location in dark blue trousers, a white shirt, and a light blue jacket with a KCRK 14 patch sewn onto the front of it.

A tall and thin man with a beard and a matching jacket comes from the back of the van with a camera mounted on his shoulder. He hands Christy a microphone. It has a big box around it with KCRK 14 printed on all sides.

"This is Kyle, my cameraman extraordinaire."

He gives me a big smile. "Nice to meet you."

"We are going to shoot over here." Christy hurries me closer to the river, probably to start filming before I change my mind. We stand at the bottom of the gravel launch with the fly fisherman and a giant tan and red basalt bluff behind us. The gravel is littered with bits of broken brown glass, cigarette butts, soda pop tops, and a tangle of fishing line.

Kyle positions the camera on his shoulder and gets comfortable. "Three, two, one, action."

Christy stands up straight, smiles, and waits for two beats. "This is Christy Green with KCRK 14. I am here with Emmy Jenkins, the victim of two assaults by the same perpetrator."

She uses *perpetrator*. She can't name him, but I will.

"Emmy, can you tell us what happened?"

56

———

HIM

A BELL DINGS WHEN I OPEN THE DOOR TO THE FLY SHOP. I HAVE Destiny in one arm and a pickle jar filled with my flies in my hand. I need money, and the thought of men throwing my flies to hunt fish makes my blood rise.

An old Australian shepherd barely raises his eyes when we enter. The shop is lined with rows and rows of display racks and hangers with small plastic packages of fly-tying materials, and the walls are covered with fly rods, waders, fly vests, boots, gloves, and jackets.

I walk straight to an old man behind a glass counter filled with expensive reels. He's wearing an old blue plaid button-up, and a television in the corner is tuned into the news. Two newscasters sit behind a desk on the television and rattle off some sports statistics.

"Cute pup," he says.

"Thanks. Nice shop you have here. You the owner?"

He nods his head. "Bob Peterson."

"I'm Chad." I decide to get right to the point. Many men like to bullshit before they do business, but I've never been good at it. The more I talk, the fewer people seem to like me. "I just moved here from Utah, and I've been fishing my whole life and tying flies since I was ten. I'm looking to sell some of them."

He looks at my jar, and his eyebrows, with overly long gray hairs, pinch together. I expect him to tell me what a dumbshit I am and throw me out the door, but he waits while I twist off the lid and pull a few out. I place a Kaufman's Golden Stone and a Stimulator, both tied with Anabel's hair, on the glass counter.

He bends over to get a good look and nods his head. "Those are nice flies, he says. You've got talent."

I pull more out and place them on the glass as Destiny licks my cheek.

A woman's voice comes from the television. "This is Christy Green with KCRK 14. I am here with Emmy Jenkins, the victim of two assaults by the same perpetrator."

What? Fucking Emmy. There on the television, standing with a reporter at the river where I took Anabel's last breath. Her face is smeared with a smug expression, and her chin is in the air.

"Emmy, can you tell us what happened?" the reporter asks.

The old man turns toward the television.

"There is a serial killer in Canyon County and Cascade Lakes. He is the man who attacked me in my home twice to keep me quiet. He's the same man who was arrested for kidnapping Crystal Rhodes and escaped custody last summer. His name is Dylan Unger. He also goes by the nickname, Skid."

What the fuck? Is that even legal for her to give my name?

"He is twenty-four years old, six feet tall, skinny, and has scraggly light brown hair." Emmy keeps talking. "He killed four women in Lodell over the last two summers. Their names are Amber Ward, Shawna Hall, Kate Harris, and Mandy West."

My head spins, and a wash of heat burns my face. Emmy says, "He is also a suspect in the deaths of Anna Rossi in Elk Lake last September and Anabel Crosby this month in the Deschutes River. In the past, he has drugged women by putting a date-rape drug in their drinks. Do not accept any drinks from strangers and watch your drinks at all times. Please be aware of your surroundings and don't go anywhere alone, especially by any body of water. He has drowned women in the Deschutes River and Cascade Lakes."

My dad is going to sue the shit out of her for dragging my name through the mud. It looks like Emmy is done, but her expression changes, and she stares straight through the television, right into my eyes. "Sometimes fate just grabs ahold of you, and there is nothing you can do but fight until you are free."

Even the reporter looks shocked. "Uh, well, there you have it. The Cascade River Killer is stalking women along the Deschutes and in the Cascade Lakes."

The Cascade River Killer? What the fuck? There is no such thing as the Cascade River in Oregon. If anything, I'm the *Deschutes River Killer*.

My image flashes up on the television, the same photo they used in the newspapers last summer, and the old man looks at me and back to the television.

The practiced voice of the reporter continues: "If you or anyone you know has any information or has been approached by this man, please contact the Canyon County Sheriff's office." Christy wipes the fake concerned expression from her face and smiles. "Christy Green, KCRK 14, the news as you need it."

The old man turns toward me with narrowed eyes. "What did you say your name was?"

My cheeks flush red. When I start to pluck my flies up and drop them back into the jar, he puts his hand on top of mine. It is wrinkled and covered in age spots. "No need to rush away."

I want to yank my hand from beneath his but leave it there. When I don't respond, he says, "I can see you need the money, son. I'll take some, and if they sell, I'll buy more."

"Thanks," I say. "I need to take a piss. You got a restroom?"

"Not a public one." He takes his hand away and reaches beneath the cash register.

"There's one in the park," I say and reach for my jar of flies, but he grabs it with his free hand.

"I'll go through these while you're gone."

Our eyes lock. I hold his stare and smile. "Okay, I'll be right back." I hug Destiny tight and hurry toward the door. I know he grabbed a gun. I pull the brim of my ball cap down over my eyes and step out onto the sidewalk.

I jump into my Jeep, toss Destiny onto the passenger seat, and pull away before he can get my plates. I do not see him in my rearview mirror. The fucker is probably calling the cops.

I will have to lay low in my hideout because of that bitch, and I will have to stay off the radar. Stay hidden. I should never have let her live in the first place. This is the thanks I get. I pull onto the highway and head out of town. I take a deep breath to calm myself and feel Destiny's eyes on me.

"What're you looking at?" I hate dogs, but there's something about Destiny that keeps me from taking her to the river and holding her beneath the surface. Maybe it's the way she's always so quiet and obedient. Maybe it's how she looks at me with those big, innocent eyes, or maybe because she is my Destiny, and I need her.

The sun beats in through the windows, and I grip the steering wheel. I need to come up with a plan and figure out what to do next. I know I can't stay in the tumble-down house forever. I'll need food and water. And what about my nymph and her girls? I made so much progress. Fuck! I should have taken them when I had the chance.

The dirt crunches beneath my tires when I turn onto my road, and a cloud of dust rises behind us. Destiny whines and settles herself into a little brown and white ball on the front seat.

Up ahead, my hideout is swarming with Sheriff trucks and

squad cars. I slow the Jeep and come to a stop. Destiny wakes, senses my unease, and starts to whine. This wasn't supposed to happen. I thought I took all the necessary precautions, but now they've got all my tying gear, and Destiny's kennel is inside. They know I have a dog. I glance into the back seat. My duffle bag is there with Chad's passport, license, and journal. At least they can't link us.

I turn the Jeep back to the highway and turn toward Lodell. It is time to become one with the river, and it will be there where my grandpa died. I can't bring Ashley and her girls with me, but I can bring Destiny, and she will be bound to me forever.

The mile markers between the road and the desert slide past my window, and a red beater truck and an eighteen-wheeler pull up on my ass, but I will not get caught because of a damned speeding ticket. When the road opens up into a passing lane, I pull to the right and let them pass. Behind them is a news van with a giant satellite dish on the top. It passes me also. My lane ends, and I see another news van in my rearview mirror.

At the cutoff to Lodell, the van turns on its blinker and slows. You've got to be kidding me. It turns onto the narrow road, and I follow it. The van behind me also turns and traps me between them. Our caravan follows the familiar road to the gravel turnoff, and we take it all the way to the graffiti tunnel. The first van stops at the entrance, probably assessing whether they can make it through with their satellite dish.

The driver and a young woman with dark flowing hair and red lipstick get out. The driver from the van behind me stops, and his door swings open.

"It looks like you'll clear," he yells past my car. Without waiting for an answer, he walks toward the other driver. Just a foot away from my window, he looks in at me and nods.

I nod back but do not roll my window down, and he keeps walking. The two drivers stand to the side and glance back and forth between the van and the tunnel. Finally, the driver and passenger of the front van get in and inch forward. The other man stands to the side with his thumb up and yells, "You're good. Keep going. Yep, you've got it."

On his way back, he stops at my door and twirls his finger for me to roll my window down. I push the button and lower it.

"Sorry about that," he says.

"No worries." I turn and pick Destiny up. "What's going on?"

"Haven't you heard? There's a serial killer from Lodell."

"What? No, I haven't." Destiny gives a yip and puts her nose out the window. "I'm just here to visit my grandpa. He's been sick."

He pats Destiny's head and gives me a sympathetic smile. "Sorry to hear that. Good luck."

"Thanks," I say. When he turns, I put my Jeep into drive and roll into the tunnel and past the graffiti owl and the skull with pitchforks.

Once through, my Jeep bounces over potholes and beneath the railroad trestle to Old Lodell. The news van keeps going toward town, but I pull off onto the old rutted road to our family homestead. The second van follows the first, both ready to unleash a nightmare for my family. At least everyone will be distracted and not realize I am here until it is too late.

I park behind the old barn and take Destiny from the passenger seat. When I set her down, she picks up a stick and looks at me with deep black eyes. Her entire ass wags with her tail. She follows me into the barn, lit only by the light in the windows and through the slats. I hide the duffle bag in the feeder with the false bottom, where I used to hide my treasures as a child.

Back outside, I take a deep breath of sage-scented air, and a sense of calm washes over me. This is where I belong, and this is where I will become one. Destiny feels it, too, for her instinct takes her toward the river. She leaps over a tiny shrub and lands on the other side with the stick still in her mouth. She will forever be an adorable little puppy.

Destiny leads me right to the rock above Steelhead Rapids, where Grandpa taught me to fish and where I will fulfill my destiny. The cops can search my hideout and seize everything I own, but they can't bind or contain me, for I am the river, and the river is free.

I remove my shoes, unbutton my shorts, and let them fall to the ground. The flesh is weak. The river is eternal. Water gives life and takes life. I slip off my shirt and lift Destiny from the rock. She licks my face, and we step into the water.

The river is the lifeblood of Lodell. I am the lifeblood, born, raised, and embodied. We wade deep, and the cool water sends a shiver up my spine. We will finally be one, no longer the flesh and the fluid, but one single entity finally at peace and free from human restraints.

"What're you doing, Skid?"

Fucking Jake. I don't turn to face him.

"I can't believe you came back after all the shit you caused." His voice is gravelly and dry, like the desert he belongs in. "Go ahead and fucking drown yourself. We'll watch and make sure you do it right this time."

We? I ignore him and hug Destiny's warm body to my flesh.

"He's holding something." A different voice says. Brian? It can't be.

But it is. Brian and Jake stand on the shore with dark brown beer bottles in their hands.

"It's a puppy," Brian says.

"Oh, hell no." Jake sets his beer on the ground and steps into the water.

Brian does the same, and they come toward me like two bulldozers. They power over the rocks and through the current —nothing but flesh and muscle. They stop ten feet from me, and the river bends and flows around them. They are only minor obstructions to the river, and once I am one, they can't stop me.

"What're you doing with the puppy?" Jake asks.

"We just came to cool off." Destiny wriggles in my arms, excited to have company.

Both Jake and Brian look beat to hell with black eyes and swollen lips. Jake has several stitches above his eyebrow. "You two look like shit."

They look at one another and smile. "Just working out a bit of brotherly love."

"He finally figured it out?" I ask, and Brian narrows his eyes.

"Yeah, thanks a lot for keeping that from me," Brian says. "You got yourself a puppy?"

The water seeps up their t-shirts and plasters them to their abs

"Are you the dumb-fuck who drowned the town dogs?" Jake asks.

I shrug and squeeze Destiny tight. She lets out a yelp, and Brian steps toward me.

"What happened to you?" Brian asks. "You're one sick moth-erfucker."

"You two happened to me. You've treated me like shit my whole life, especially you, Jake. You just never knew who I really am."

"We know who you really are." Jake's face is red, and his lip curls away from his teeth. "You haven't changed. You're more fucked up in the head than we thought, but you're still a coward who preys on women and innocent dogs. Let's see how you do against men."

"Give us the puppy," Brian says.

Jake's eyes are on Destiny. "Give us the dog."

"No, she's mine," I say and take a step back. My foot slips off a rock, and pain shoots through my ankle. I lose my balance, and the water envelops us.

Hands are all over me, and Destiny is ripped from my grasp. I struggle to get up, but Jake is on top of me with his hand around my throat. He pulls me above the surface. "You are one sick fuck, and you're going to die."

"Go ahead. Hold me under," I say. "That's what I want."

"Oh no, it's not going to be easy. I'm going to beat the shit out of you, and you're going to suffer for all the fucking pain you've caused those poor families. And for what you did to our town. You made me go to court, you fucker."

I slip away from him, but he is all hands and grabs hold of my arm. Pain shoots through my shoulder, and he pulls me above the surface. Brian is on the shore with Destiny in his arms.

"Jake," Brian yells. "Bring him to shore."

Jake smashes his fist into my face over and over. Pain shoots through my eyes and nose, and I taste my own blood in the water.

Jake screams. I hear him, but they are nothing but animal sounds. Next thing I know, Brian is behind Jake and tries to pull him off of me, but Jake is in a rage, and nothing stops him.

"We need to turn him in," Brian says.

The water around me begins to swirl, almost as if I'm in the center of a whirlpool, with Brian and Jake staring into the void until the water closes in and rises above my head.

That's when I see them along the shore. All my nymphs, with their long, flowing hair—jet black, amber, espresso, strawberry blonde, chocolate, and golden brown. They stare directly at me and slip into the river.

Jake's hand is around my throat, and he pushes me further under. I'm sure that I'm finally going to die. There's a peace inside me. This is where I'm supposed to be. The faces of my nymphs are all around me, but Jake's hand around my throat keeps me from going to them.

Someone is beside me, and I feel a hand squeeze mine. I

want to look but can't move my head. Instead, I blink my eyes and see the rays of light through the water, and my lungs burn. Suddenly, I am free and feel nothing but the current. I turn to see who is beside me. It takes me a few moments to recognize him. He looks tired and sad. "Grandpa?" I whisper.

I am finally free. I am the river.

ACKNOWLEDGMENTS

Nothing in life is done in isolation. This novel would not be possible without all the love, support, instruction, and feedback from the people in my life.

Thanks to my biggest supporters: My children, Brittany Jungenberg, Brennan Romo, and Ryan Romo. Brittany spent countless hours sitting with me in coffee shops from when she was in elementary school until now as a graphic designer. She helps me with my marketing and creates my beautiful cover designs. Brennan and Ryan are always willing to let me bounce ideas off them and help me work through things when I feel stuck. To my newest kids: Chris Jungenberg and Cathy Cogliano—thank you for putting up with my craziness, accepting me into your hearts, and especially for calling me Mom.

To Randy Hopp, thank you for all the love, support, and encouragement and for always believing in me. And for your perseverance-you are the master of that.

My mother, Sandy Folk, has given me more than I can ever repay her for; she led by example and, through her passionate love of literature, instilled in me a passion for writing at a young age.

To my father, John J. Folk II, who left this earth far too early. He always encouraged me to do what I love in life, and I have.

I am also blessed by the rest of my big and loving family and friends. All of you have helped shape who I am and have given me many experiences to draw on for my writing.

I owe a special thanks to my content editors – Ken Scott, Julie Martinez, Colton Donovan, and Danny Bowers – for their invaluable expertise and feedback, which has allowed me to bring this novel into the world with confidence. To my beta reader Diane Peters who is never afraid to express her honest opinions constructively and with encouragement. And last but not least, Mike Magnuson for going above and beyond on the copyedit and helping me to a better ending.

My appreciation goes out to Pacific University's MFA program for providing me with an environment conducive to personal growth and creativity and four of the most knowledgeable and inspiring mentors any writer could wish for—Craig Lesley, Pete Fromm, Ann Hood, and Mary Helen Stefaniak. A special thanks is extended to Craig Lesley for his ongoing friendship throughout this journey. I must also thank Deborah Reed for giving me the opportunity that opened up so many doors.

Last but not least, I want to recognize the individuals who took the time to share their experiences on the Pacific Crest Trail with me—Bee, Sundance, and Totaled—who provided vital information about thru-hiking the PCT.

ABOUT THE AUTHOR

About the Author

Kelly Romo grew up in California but has lived in Oregon for over twenty-five years. She is a retired educator and mother of three. When taking a break from writing, she likes to hike, kayak, fly fish, and camp. Kelly has a Master of Fine Arts in Writing and a Master of Arts in Teaching, both from Pacific University.

Thank you for reading *I AM THE RIVER*. Please visit www.kellyromo.com to join Kelly's VIP Reader Club for advanced reader copies, updates, sneak peeks, exclusive offers, and promos

ALSO BY KELLY ROMO

Thrillers:

Dead Drift (A Whitewater Thriller, Book #1)

Book #3 is in the works

Historical Fiction:

When Sorrow Takes Wing

Whistling Women

www.ingramcontent.com/pod-product-compliance
Lightning Source LLC
Chambersburg PA
CBHW030145310726
48970CB00005B/1596